First Dog
of
Christmas

On the First Day of Christmas

Faith Hogan

HEAD of ZEUS

An Aria Book

First published in the UK in 2022 by Head of Zeus
This paperback edition first published in 2023 by Head of Zeus,
part of Bloomsbury Publishing Plc

9 7 5 3 1 2 4 6 8

A catalogue record for this book is available from
the British Library.

ISBN (PB): 9781803287775
ISBN (E): 9781803287751

Typeset by Divaddict Publishing Solutions

Printed and bound in Great Britain by
CPI Group (UK) Ltd, Croydon CR0 4YY

Head of Zeus
5–8 Hardwick Street
London EC1R 4RG

WWW.HEADOFZEUS.COM

For my family – thank you.

Prologue

The Past

Jade, emerald, lizard, lime, shamrock, seafoam and chartreuse: so many colours, blending and pinging into each other while drumming out their own tattoo from far across the North Sea. It was as if a celestial realm had opened up a window in the sky and with every heartbeat it was tearing up the familiar black, wider and wider, so you could almost believe that very soon, heaven itself would be visible to the naked eye. Liv shook herself out. The last thing she wanted to be thinking about now was heaven, or any kind of paradise that felt no more real than pie in the sky. Or death or dying. She could do that every second of the day if she allowed her mind to wander, even just a fraction from the steady path she'd worn out with wishful thinking. It was really blinkered hopefulness that she knew no oncologist would ever encourage in the face of what was inevitable. It was just a matter of time and not very much of it at that. More nights than she cared to admit now, Liv found herself – in the darkest hours, when sleep raced like a rapid fox just always out of reach – even resorting to prayer.

'Whoever said there were only forty shades of green obviously hadn't seen aurora borealis.' Rachel yawned as she snuggled further beneath the heavy blanket Pete had wrapped around them.

'I don't think they ever meant that there were *only* forty shades.' Liv laughed and rubbed against her twin affectionately. It still shocked her, that feeling that the very fabric of Rachel had changed so much. They had spent a lifetime being identical and suddenly, within the space of months, it seemed that one had wasted away to half the person of the other. Liv gasped. It was a sharp intake of breath at the sadness that had somehow become everything she was now, even if she pretended otherwise. 'God, it's even more beautiful than I ever remember seeing it before.'

'It is the most dramatic display ever; the weather forecaster was banging on about it earlier when I went to visit my nan,' Pete said, taking a handful of crisps and munching thoughtfully. The sky looked as though someone had emptied out a paint box on the other side of the universe and all the most brilliant colours were colliding in heart-stopping splendour. 'I think they've put it on just for you, Rachel.' His voice dipped a little now. Liv was thinking exactly the same thing, even if she wouldn't admit it. Well, not in front of Rachel anyway; it seemed too much like the curtain on the final act drawing closed.

'Well, it's the best present I could have asked for,' she said softly. Her eyes were wide, just like when they were children, her mouth slightly open as her head tilted further and further back. 'The best night ever.'

Pete pulled the huge quilt up closer around the three of

them, tucking it under Rachel's chin, cutting out any chill that might penetrate her fragile body. It was September. Evenings were drawing in cooler, but even if they wouldn't say so, none of them wanted this day to end. For just one night, they could pretend that this would go on forever, for one night only, the sky was clear and aurora borealis was giving them the display of a lifetime, playing out a dramatic backdrop across the sky in the distance.

'It's perfect,' Liv breathed, glancing from Rachel to Pete, but their attention was completely wrapped up in the display before them. They were holding hands, under the blanket, and then as if Rachel knew she knew, she stretched her arm around Liv's shoulders and pulled her closer to them. Liv inhaled the scent of her sister. She wanted to pull down a shutter on this moment and keep them here safe and together forever, but she was a nurse; she knew well enough that you can't do that, no matter how much you love people. There's no stopping the progress of some things. Rachel's cancer diagnosis: its uncontainable march to the inevitable terrible end, was as unstoppable to her as the Northern Lights playing out over their heads.

'It's like emeralds, stringing out across the sky,' Pete said.

'You know what they say about shooting stars.' Rachel's voice was heavy now, dragged down by drugs and weariness. *Every time you see one it's another soul walking into heaven.* 'Always think of me, like this, promise?' She waited a beat, because they knew what she meant. 'Remember when we've been happy, not...' She closed her eyes, falling into a light sleep and for once, Liv was glad because she bit her lip and scrunched her eyes closed tight and willed herself so hard not to cry. She held her breath while her belly burned with unexploded grief and so much love it could only just be contained.

'Okay?' Pete whispered to her and he rummaged beneath the blanket with his free hand and caught hers and it felt like a lifeline, something she could hold on to in the worst of storms, and it would always bring her home.

I

Liv sat in the coffee shop. It was a treat she normally didn't allow herself, but it was her last break of the day and it had been a very long day. In the grip of Christmas holiday madness, everyone was emptying out of the hospital now, patients and staff getting home as quickly as they could make their escape. She could feel the hospital almost growing larger around her, as if it was echoing, looming; the attempt at cheery seasonal spirit falling short when everyone would far prefer to be somewhere else.

For the next three days, it would operate on a skeleton shift. For the most part, unlucky rostered doctors, nurses, porters and catering staff. You could spot a mile off the few who actually volunteered to work Christmas for their own reasons, and they would do their best to pretend that they actually wanted to be here. Not everyone loves Christmas, one of the older nurses had told Liv when she started out, and Liv had shivered, knowing too well that for some, it was the loneliest time of the year.

Of course, Christmas in Ballycove, with her family, her mum and dad and Maya – well, it felt like a million miles away from the sterile, whispery atmosphere of the hospital at this time of year. Yes, it was probably traditional, maybe even boring as far as some people might be concerned: there'd be midnight mass, turkey and Christmas carols; if they had the energy, after dinner, a walk about the farm and maybe a game of charades to finish off the day.

If Liv counted herself as lucky any other day of the year, it was even more pronounced at Christmas. Her mum would have spent the last month preparing for it in her own many small ways: making puddings and Christmas cakes, pretending that she'd made half the amount and giving most of them away to neighbours and friends well in advance of the holidays. Her dad, well, she could imagine him now, making hourly pilgrimages up and down the old stone sheds to check on whichever ewe was about to give birth next. And Maya would be swearing under her breath in the sitting room, trying to decorate the wonkiest Christmas tree her father could manage to find in the small plantation they'd set years earlier.

Maya was Liv's baby sister who, it always seemed to Liv, had been born with far more sense than she needed, probably enough for both of them, not that she'd ever admit that to Maya of course.

Liv loved going home for Christmas. She adored every cheesy tacky tinselly bit of the holiday and even that first Christmas after losing Rachel, her identical twin, although she was achingly sad, somehow she had managed to feel closer to her twin sister than she had expected. Of course, Rachel loved Christmas. The year they found out she was sick, they'd volunteered at a homeless shelter near the training hospital. Liv found herself smiling remembering that time: it turned out that even in death, Rachel could cheer Liv up in spite of herself.

Was it weird that she still felt as if her twin sister might only have stepped out of the room temporarily? It wasn't something you could go telling people. Well, she'd told Pete once, but they were both very drunk and she wasn't sure Pete really counted. He already thought she was a little crazy and anyway, he was Rachel's best friend and in some ways, she figured that the idea might give him the same sort of comfort that it gave her.

She waved across the foyer at old Bill Hickey the porter. He'd worked at the hospital since he left school, never missed a Christmas shift, he told her once. She had a feeling this might be his last year. He still had a spring in his step, but even Bill would have to retire at some point. She wondered if he'd come back as a volunteer or if he would be one of those colleagues who just vanished from the hospital as completely as if they'd been wiped away.

Liv sipped the last of her coffee. It tasted good, strong and sweet just the way she preferred it. She looked at her watch; she wasn't due back on the ward for another five minutes, so she pulled her phone from her bag and began to check through her messages. Her boyfriend Eddie had travelled home to Ballycove already, but there was no word that he had arrived safely. But then, that was Eddie, a man of few words. He'd always been the strong and silent type – Liv adored him, but he could be mildly infuriating when you wanted to know that he'd arrived safe and sound. He was the opposite of Pete who had filled her inbox with funny memes and Christmas jokes, most of which she was ignoring until she finished her shift.

Her mother and her sister had been messaging over and back on the family WhatsApp group all day, everything from checking who was picking up the shopping to trying to figure out what each gift contained under the Christmas tree. Obviously, things were quiet in Maya's office. Liv tapped out a message, letting them know that she was looking forward to finishing up in another few hours. Pete had offered to stay back until the end of her shift and they'd travel home together after she picked up her bags and the family gifts from her flat. She could have sent them home with Eddie, to save the round trip, but she knew Pete wouldn't mind.

It wasn't that she didn't trust Eddie to bring them safely, but with Eddie, you just never knew. Her boyfriend could as easily toss a mountain of wet clothes on top of her lovely wrapping and it would have been a whole load of effort for nothing. That was the problem with being so creatively talented – sometimes it meant that the mundane practicalities didn't really mean as much to him. Poor Eddie, he was so busy the last few weeks, they hardly saw each other. But busy was good, because it meant that his business was making money and if he was going to propose to her this Christmas, they'd need plenty of money for a wedding and then, down the road (hopefully, not too far) they could look at selling her flat and getting a bigger place to start a family.

This thought warmed her.

It had always been her biggest ambition to get married and have children – lots of children. She didn't want to be alone. She wanted a family of her own, a dog, a little house and a husband who'd be her partner until the very end. Just knowing that Eddie had gone to the trouble of making that ring for her, well, it was probably the best Christmas gift he'd ever given her and he didn't even realise it. Even thinking about it made her feel a rush of love for him; he really was the best.

She hadn't told a soul – not even Maya. Well, how could she? It was meant to be a surprise, even for her! She'd found the ring one afternoon in the workshop, quite by accident. It was *her ring*. It was everything she'd ever dreamed of, tiny emeralds shooting across a narrow golden bar. It was a miniature of those shooting stars that had filled the sky the night Rachel had slipped away. If she'd sat down and drawn it for him, she wasn't sure she could make it more perfect.

Automatically, Liv put her hands to her neck, but of course, Rachel's locket had gone missing years ago. It wasn't that it had been expensive, but to her it was completely priceless. It had been their grandmother's, passed to Rachel and then to Liv. It was a strange thing, but she still missed it, still felt its loss, as if with it she'd lost some little connection to Rachel.

She'd dropped a tear when she spotted the ring Eddie had made for her. He'd managed to make the perfect ring, bringing together the future she hoped for and still including Rachel in it even if she wasn't here to share it with her. But that was Eddie – sometimes he made her happy without even thinking about it. Perhaps it came from having a mother who was, Liv thought for a moment, what was the word? Difficult? Exacting? She thought of that old saying: the man who's good to his mother will be good to his wife. Well, that was Eddie all over. He'd spent a lifetime trying to keep his mother happy. In Liv's mind, it meant that one day he'd do the same for her – hadn't he already started by secretly making the perfect engagement ring?

A couple leaving the hospital with two babies in matching navy carry seats bustled by her. Liv loved twins, well, she'd been one herself. But Rachel had died before her twenty-fifth birthday. Cancer – what else. She still talked to her regularly (in her head, not out loud – she wasn't completely nuts!) She even still regularly wrote notes to Rachel in her journal, just to keep her up to speed with how life was going. Sometimes, she felt a striking pressure to live life well enough for both of them.

She sneaked a peek at the baby nearest to her. It was a perfect baby boy with a powder-blue hat falling down about his ears. He was all scrunched-up features and balled-up hands. She imagined being in that woman's shoes right now. Bringing home not one, but two newborn babies. What could be more perfect? Christmas with twins! It sounded like the title of a romcom, but Liv felt it was exactly the sort of happy ending she wanted her own life to turn into. The woman looked tired, completely washed out, but then everything about her changed as she peeked into the carry chair she'd popped up on the seat next to her and Liv was glad. It would be a shame to have two lovely new babies and not be transported to a state of complete and utter bliss at just having them close by.

The alarm on her phone reminded her it was time to get back to A&E. She tidied away the empty paper cup and slipped her phone back in her bag, giving one last glance across at the new mother who seemed to be completely lost in rapturous contentment. Bliss.

*

It felt as if no-one told people on her ward that it was Christmas Eve. When she returned it was ten times busier than when she left.

'You should have called me,' she said to Francine who was putting a lot more effort into making space for incoming patients than any of the innkeepers in Bethlehem two thousand and more years earlier.

'Don't be daft – you deserved your break.' Francine was lovely. She was a very hands-on nursing manager, but she still managed to keep on top of everything else that needed to be done to keep the ward moving at a safe and efficient rate. 'Anyway, this is the least of our worries.' Her expression was weary as she looked along the corridor where a line of trolleys ran with patients waiting to be transferred to examination cubicles that wouldn't be free for a few more hours probably.

'Oh?' Liv knew that already two of the nurses and one of the orderlies had to go home early with the winter vomiting bug. She'd spent over half her dinner break disinfecting the whole ward to try and curb any chance of it being spread to the patients being admitted.

'We have three more nurses due on shift ringing in to say that they are feeling unwell. It sounds as if it's rife.'

'I could call Ashley and Kayla?' They were both great agency nurses. They'd worked right throughout the hospital, but unfortunately Francine couldn't see past their multiple piercings and tattooed wrists.

'No, no, I'm sure we'll manage.' Francine shook her head.

'You know they are saving for a flat. If we don't start giving them hours, they're just going to find work somewhere else, and I know they're both happy to come in at short notice.'

'I've never liked working with couples and…' Francine sighed. 'We'll manage, don't worry.'

'You're the boss,' Liv said and she hoped she hadn't put some sort of hex on the holidays with her thoughts of everything going exactly to plan. She knew too well it only took an icy patch on the motorway to fill up the emergency rooms and put the whole department under pressure. She looked at her watch. Less than two hours to go.

'Good news,' Francine said as she pulled her aside twenty minutes later. 'One of the HR girls managed to contact three nurses for the night shift and none of the remaining rostered staff have called in since.'

'Oh, that is good news. We'll be able to finish as normal so?'

'Well, I'm definitely sending you home as soon as the first one arrives – you've done the work of three nurses today.'

'Thank you.' Liv laughed. She was delighted when Francine packed her out the door before the midnight bells struck, a half hour before her shift was meant to finish.

That was why Liv loved this time of year. It seemed to her that even the most harried people she knew could make time for a chink of something warm in their hearts, just because it was Christmas. She bundled her huge scarf around her neck, still smiling at the feeling of leaving work early. The night-duty nurses had arrived on shift and she almost skipped out of the hospital, having said her goodbyes to everyone for the holiday season.

A hard frost settling on the hospital grounds made the paths slippery, and the green areas sparkled with glittering specks that paled the grass to a minty velvetiness. The huge tree that stood in the centre of the grass was decorated with coloured lights and looked like a beacon for optimism in a place where hope was as valuable a commodity as any other at this time of year. Liv thought of those patients who would not get home to spend Christmas with their families this year. She especially thought of the people in geriatrics, paediatrics and oncology – it was towards those wards the tree seemed to wink the most.

She loved working in A&E, couldn't imagine working in any other department. It was always busy and she was part of a great team, for the most part made up of people she'd worked with for a couple of years now and so, although the transitory nature of it meant that there were no real patients to miss over the holidays, she still felt a small tinge of guilt at heading home to Ballycove for her perfect family Christmas.

Eddie would be there already, no doubt being fussed over by his mum. Bless him, he had the patience of a saint. Liv had rung him earlier in her shift, just as he was leaving the city. He sounded harassed, but then, he'd just wanted to get home, and it was a long drive. Heavy traffic always put him in rotten humour. He worked hard. Liv knew that he'd worked much harder this year than he had let on to her. The secret, of having found that ring – *her ring*, made her smile now. This Christmas, at home in Ballycove, with her family and Eddie was going to be the most special one ever.

She was lost in these happy thoughts as she neared the hospital gates. The main road was always busy and even at this late hour, traffic was thundering past. In the distance, she thought she saw her bus. Having left work half an hour earlier than she expected, she had time to make it home to the flat and save Pete the round trip to pick her up from work first. She could call him on the way and tell him to collect her there instead. If she could make it across in time, she might just be able to catch this one, which would save her a fifteen-minute wait in the freezing night air for the next.

She reached out to press the button to cross at the same time as the man next to her. Their fingers touched the button together. She could feel the weight of his hand press against hers, for just a moment, and she had that crazy feeling you get when you touch metal and get a slight electric shock. When she looked up, she felt her breath catch in her chest because she was looking into the eyes of a man who seemed to be the most familiar stranger she'd ever seen.

'Oh, sorry,' he said. Perhaps he'd felt that powerful surge too. Of course, she knew it was probably just some electrical fault in the traffic lights; surely, there was no other explanation. He pulled his hand away and then stopped, smiled at her as if they'd come to some silent realisation between them at the same time.

'No, I…' she began. His eyes were strikingly blue with heavy brows and lashes, he was tall and broad-shouldered and for a moment, she realised, she was just gazing at him gormlessly. *Good God, woman,* she admonished herself, *what are you like?* So, she looked away, keeping her stare intent on the lights changing before her. But still, she was very aware of him next to her. She sensed that he too was staring hard ahead, forcing himself not to look at her.

At that moment, the lights before Liv changed and she was brought back to the present moment with a rush as the wind at her back heaved forward and she almost lost her footing.

'Okay?' The man had grabbed her elbow to steady her. He smiled at her now and something familiar in the shape of his mouth made her heart lurch. He was taller than her, a good six foot. He was slender too, but when he reached out to her, she could tell there was solidity to him. There was manliness about him that went beyond his five o'clock shadow or the slight nick in his skin just to the left of his chin.

'I'm fine, I just...' She smiled at him and they stopped in the road for a moment, a silence stretching out between them. There was something so familiar about him, but she couldn't put her finger on it. She never forgot a face, but perhaps he was a relative of a patient who'd only passed through the A&E one of those days when she'd been too rushed to take much notice. *That's it,* Liv thought, *I've run into him somewhere before and I'll remember as soon as I'm drifting off to sleep tonight.*

She was about to continue across the road, but the roar of a motorbike at her back stopped her in her tracks. It had come out of nowhere. There was a sickening screech of brakes, and then she felt the man push her out of the way, diving into the path of the oncoming bike himself. She heard the bone-crushing thumping sound of his body as it impacted with the bike. She was on the ground now, looking about dazed to see what had happened behind her, but she knew. The man had saved her life. She was almost afraid to look around to see if it had cost him his.

As the road about her slowly came back into focus, she could just make out the bike. The wheel was still spinning. It had skidded along the road, the biker thrown off with his head and shoulders at an angle that she knew meant his spine could be compromised. Dazed, she began to move towards him, trying to feel for her phone in her bag at the same time. But there was a woman there already, pulling out her phone, jabbing the numbers to get an ambulance out here as quickly as possible.

Liv stumbled backwards, shocked and confused, her eyes finally picking out the crumpled body of the man who'd stood next to her at the traffic lights. He had saved her twice. It seemed as if, for one eternal second, the whole city fell into bottomless silence. Then there was the most pathetic sound she'd ever heard. It was something between a whimper and a cry of pain. It stirred something up in her from deep within her bones. She'd become a nurse to help people, but this was different; this was like the reverberations of a sounding fork struck many lifetimes ago and coming back now to resonate deep in her heart. But, the practical part of her brain knew, the level of noise and pandemonium around her meant that a sound like that would have to be lost on the night air.

Suddenly, it seemed everything was becoming confused – people crowding around, wanting to help – but much too shocked to realise what needed to be done. She heard it again, a soft sound, a familiar and haunting noise. It felt like an echo, catching her breath, making her heart stop in her chest. *Promise*. She looked around. Her eyes gliding over empty expressions, up and down the road and then, on the glistening tarmac, she saw him, surrounded by onlookers. He was stupefied into staring and inactivity. The man who'd stood beside her only moments earlier. The man who'd made her heart flip in her chest as if he'd just turned over a switch that had been too long out of use. Liv began to run, pushing past the people standing about. She fell to the ground beside him, started to check for breath, a pulse, anything that was a vital sign of life.

'Call another ambulance,' she shouted to the people gathered round. 'Now.' She screamed and bent back down over the man. It was so dark and with the people about her cutting out the street lights overhead, she couldn't see if his chest was rising or not. She bent down closer, put her ear next to his mouth and nose. He smelled of musk and lemon and she drew in the scent of him for a moment. *Oh, God. Please don't let him die,* she prayed. She called out again for people to give him space to breathe and then she wasn't sure if she heard or felt it. It was something, a soft noise or a warm breath on her cheek. She looked down at him; he was breathing. She was so close to him now, it felt intimate in a way that she'd never felt in her nursing career before.

And then, she noticed it. A thin trickle of blood was dripping, forming a sinister black pool on the ground beneath his ear.

Oh God. Oh God. No.

The sound of not one, but two sirens nearby pushed

through a deep schism in the crowd around her. A familiar face, she couldn't remember his name, asked people to move back. He was one of the older paramedics. He knew his job well and Liv was relieved it was him and not one of the younger ones playing to an audience.

After carrying out what felt like a million checks, they moved him swiftly and securely to a stretcher and it seemed within minutes they were all racing back up the hospital avenue, speeding to the A&E entrance with their casualty.

His name was Finn O'Connell. Or at least, that's what it said on his driver's licence. It felt wrong, to be going through his personal items, this man who until so recently had been a complete stranger to Liv. And yet, wrong and all as it might be, she wanted to know everything about him. Well, they needed to let his next of kin know that he was here. There could be a wife or children at home waiting for him. There would be family somewhere and friends – Liv had a feeling this man would have good friends. Lots of friends, solid and reliable, and they would worry about him too.

There was no wedding ring though. Liv had checked, surreptitiously, in spite of herself. The blood that had trailed from his ear had stopped now. It dried in a soft line down the side of his head. She wanted to reach out and wipe it away, but of course, she knew that bleeding from the ear, after a fall like Finn O'Connell had just sustained, was not a good sign.

So, instead, she set about trying to help the EMT to fill in the blanks about who he was and what had happened to him.

'Type O bloods,' she said, picking out a donor card. There

were credit cards, a debit card, a couple of cards for franchise coffee shops that looked like he'd never used them. There was cash, notes and coins. A small St Christopher medal, the saint of travellers, or was he yet another decommissioned saint? It didn't matter – she prayed he'd look after Finn O'Connell now. She replaced them all again, her hands shaking so much she almost dropped them as the ambulance reversed and parked in the emergency bay. Liv thought they'd never get him into the hospital fast enough.

'Well, you're not going to be much good to anyone this evening.' The older EMT touched her arm kindly. 'We can leave you home after this, if you'd like. I'll let the matron know that you've had a shock.' But of course, she'd been on her way *off* duty, although she didn't have the words to tell him that at the moment. Finally, just as they'd gotten Finn O'Connell safely unloaded and Liv was carrying the gift that had been tucked into his coat pocket, she heard the midnight bells ring out across the city. Churches dotted all about calling out the fact that it was midnight; finally, it was the first day of Christmas.

*

The sound of her phone, ringing out in her bag pulled her back to the real world. It was Pete, wondering if he could collect her yet. Worst possible timing, as a road traffic guard stood at her elbow waiting to take down her statement. She started to shiver, overloaded with the shock of it all.

'Liv, where are you? Is everything okay?' Pete could hear the commotion around her.

'It's okay, I was just on my way to the bus, but there's been an accident,' Liv said, aware that she was shaking; even the muscles in her face felt as if they were wired to some crazy rhythm beyond her control.

'Oh, dear God. Are you all right?' There was no missing the worry in Pete's voice.

'No, not me, I'm fine, a bit shaken, but fine. It was a motorbike accident, on the road. The place is like a bottle out here. I'm just going back in to the hospital with a man who's been knocked over. He's...' Liv looked down at him now. She couldn't say another word; her breath caught in her chest. *Please, don't die.* It was all she could think.

'So you're sure you're okay?' Pete's words were wound up tight with worry.

'Really, I'm grand. It all just happened so quickly, right before my eyes and...'

'Oh, thank God for that. I mean, that poor guy, but...' He took a deep breath, steadying his voice when he spoke next, so he sounded again like the old reliable friend she'd come to depend on to be strong when she couldn't be. 'Look, just ring me when you want to be collected, yeah?'

'I...' Liv thought for a moment. She was meant to go home tonight, but she looked down at the man lying on the stretcher before her. She couldn't just leave him. He'd saved her life – how could she just get in a car and celebrate Christmas when his life might be hanging in the balance?

But then she thought of Eddie. Eddie, who vowed he'd never get married. It had all been part of the deal – grabbing what she could have when Rachel had lost everything. She was so looking forward to Christmas this year, more than she had since... well in a very long time.

Liv closed her eyes for a second, felt as if the world had somehow closed in on her. She took what felt like a monumental deep breath and said:

'I...'

2

'I should be ready to go in an hour or so.' Liv moved away from the policeman and into the freezing midnight air. She glanced back at the man on the stretcher. She had made her statement, done all she could do for him. He would be in the best of hands; she could make sure of that before she left. But she had to go home, she just had to. She had waited long enough, and God knows, with Eddie, if he'd worked himself up to ask her to marry him, she couldn't jeopardise that in any way. For too long there had been that banter between them. Eddie joking that she'd never tie him down, while she smiled and held on tightly, knowing that under it all, he needed her and loved her as much as she did him. But she'd always hoped that one day they'd get married. She just needed to wait until he was ready, not throw him off course with nagging him about it. That was part of the deal with Eddie, smoothing over everything so he'd get on with things. It was just the way he was.

And at this stage, now that Liv understood that, could plan for it, well, it was endearing. It meant he needed her, probably more than anyone ever had. She took a deep breath, closed her eyes tight. This is for Eddie. 'I just feel very wobbly now –it's probably shock.' It wasn't a lie. Her hands were shaking, her whole body, occasionally taken over by an engulfing tremor, and yet, she felt guilty. Oh, God, the guilt of leaving a complete stranger in the best possible care was making her feel sick to her stomach almost as much as the shock of seeing the accident.

'It's been a shock, but lucky for everyone, you were here when it happened.' The older EMT placed an arm about her shoulder and in a gentle voice added, 'Maybe you should get checked over before you go?'

'No, no, there's no need for that, I'm fine really. I'm just a little shocked. The guy who was run over, well, he pushed me out of the way. I might have been killed but for him,' she said and she was glad to be here to settle him in before she left. It was the very least she could do. She wouldn't leave him until she was sure he was in the best possible hands. Liv would get him moved up the chain so he saw a surgeon straight away, no faffing about with registrars or trainee doctors who were too tired to realise they should have gone home hours ago.

'If you're sure. You just take care of yourself and I'll see you in a few days.'

The whole thing made Liv feel like a fraud. She stood for a moment. Thoughts of the trip home, the holiday season, her impending supposedly surprise engagement all flooded from her mind. Suddenly, the sweet notion that her life finally was slipping into place evaporated, and it was replaced by a heavy sensation that weighed on her irrationally. Instead, she thought of Francine and the doctors and nurses who would have a truly crap Christmas covering everyone's shifts as well as their own.

'There's no point going home and feeling rotten when you can get checked out before you leave.' The EMT winked at her.

'No, no, really I'm fine, just… worried about this patient before I leave.' She shook her head, noticing his slightly lopsided smile.

'Well, just you be sure to make the most of it now.' He took the patient notes she'd been carrying from her. 'Go on now, you've done your bit here. I'll make sure he's well looked after.'

It seemed that she was just in the way after all. She had no business here, not really. She wasn't a relative and nor was she his nurse. It was time to step aside and let Finn O'Connell get the best care he could get.

'I'll try,' she said and then she dug in her bag, fished out her earbuds and turned the music on her phone to full volume. 'The Power of Love' flooded into her ear canals, shocking her with its volume, but blotting out the hospital sounds around her. It was from her Christmas playlist covering the decades. As she walked down the corridor she concentrated on her breathing; perhaps she was having some sort of mini panic attack. She needed to get out of here before they insisted on putting her onto a gurney and checking her over too.

She told herself she was fine; all she had to do was breathe. This anxiety rising up in her was only a reaction to the fright of almost being killed less than an hour earlier. Yes, she told herself, she was suffering from shock. That made more sense than thunderbolts and lightning from a complete stranger – no matter how unnervingly attractive he happened to be.

She raced from the A&E, through the ambulance exit to avoid any of the nursing staff and soon she was out in the freezing night air. The journey back to her flat was oddly depressing. The bus was half full of late-night revellers. Stragglers from the pub bundled up in coats and oncoming hangovers. The rest were like Liv, workers eager to make their way home after long shifts that had emptied them out of any Christmas cheer for a few more hours. The window beside her was wet, condensation from too many journeys seeping down along the cracked rubber at its base. The smell of damp coats and the disregarding faces of the other passengers absorbed in their phones only added to the heaviness that was settling in her stomach. And she couldn't help wondering how Finn O'Connell was doing now.

The EMT was right, she decided as the bus pulled into her stop. She might as well make the very most of the Christmas holidays from here on in. She checked her watch as she made her way into the flat. Almost one o'clock. It would take about twenty minutes for Pete to swing by and collect her. She had packed her bags the night before, so all she really had to do was scoot around to make sure that everything was switched off, the place was secure and they could pull into one of the all-night garages to pick up coffees and sandwiches for the journey home to Ballycove.

Back at the flat, she rang Eddie to distract herself while she waited for Pete. Voicemail. He was probably tucked up in bed now after a night in the pub with a couple of his mates. No doubt he spent the evening sitting at the bar counter in the warm glow of catching up before the open fire in Flannelly's snug, chatting about whatever they talked about when she wasn't there.

It seemed the flat and all of Dublin had fallen into a sleeping silence, oppressive and judging. After a few minutes of sitting there feeling it close in on her, she decided to haul her bags down to the front door and wait for Pete to pick her up there. Never was she as happy to see him pull up against the footpath. She needed to get out of the city, maybe more than she'd realised. Now it felt as if this city couldn't wait to see the back of her for the next few days. As if she would somehow be in the way if she had stayed here, even in her own flat; yes, she badly needed a break away from it all.

'A penny for them,' Pete asked as they drove out through Dublin's deserted streets.

'I think you can afford much more than that if you wanted to know what's on my mind.' She chuckled at him.

'Perhaps, but how do I know they're worth anything more?'

'Cheek.' She nudged him gently, but she had very few, if any, secrets from Pete. 'All right, if you want to know, I'm just thinking about that guy that was involved in the accident before I left...' And then more details about the whole story came spilling out, about the man at the traffic lights and how he'd basically saved her life.

'And you're sure you're all right?' He glanced across at her and there was no missing the worry etched out across his brows. 'I mean, did they check you out? God Almighty, you could have been killed.' She could see him clenching the steering wheel now and too late she realised how much something like this could upset him. He'd taken Rachel's death so badly. Liv could see it for herself: he was never the same again afterwards, as if some little part of him died with his best friend that day in the hospital.

'I'm fine, don't worry. Of course they checked me out, not so much as a bruise on me.' It was a lie, but what did one small fib matter when it came to giving someone peace of mind? Pete had enough to be worrying about – he'd just come out of a relationship that Liv had thought was *The One* for sure.

'I suppose you'll expect doughnuts now.' He raised an eyebrow. It was a joke between them that went back to when they were small kids and she'd managed to wheedle the last doughnut from his mother just because she'd fallen off her bike and scratched her knee. Of course, she'd shared evenly three ways, but Pete had managed to conveniently forget that over the years.

'Too right, I'll need doughnuts *and* éclairs if you make a big deal out of it.'

'You'll ruin my car with crumbs and jam,' he said in a funny voice.

'Oh, shut up, we both know that you're probably going to get a new one as soon as next year's plates are out.' Pete drove a very flash car, too flash really for him, but it was a company car and they insisted on buying the very best for their senior executives. They could banter like this the whole way home, but it was late and Liv was tired after her shift. She closed her eyes and leant her head against the window.

'It'll be nice to get home though, won't it?' Pete said softly.

'It will,' Liv agreed, because there really was nowhere like Ballycove at Christmas time.

'Any big plans this year?' he asked and for a moment, Liv wondered if Eddie had said something about the ring. Probably not – Eddie and Pete weren't that close. Liv was the glue that held them together.

'Nothing special. What about you?'

'Quiet. I'll spend Christmas Day at home, do the washing up before I slump in front of the telly and then spend the next day trying to walk off the effects of my mum's pudding and brandy sauce.' He laughed at this – didn't everyone feel the same way on St Stephen's Day. Wasn't that why the beach was packed with walkers and the village annual five-a-side pulled in even the least sporty bodies around. 'I hear there's big plans at your place...'

'Oh?' Liv tried to keep the surprise from her voice. Eddie *must* have mentioned something. 'Really, I don't know what you're talking about,' she said, but she shot up straighter in the seat, all tiredness falling from her with even the hint of Eddie proposing to her.

'Yeah, I heard you had invited Eddie and Barbara over for Christmas.' He shook his head and made a snorting sound that she knew, if she was honest, she'd probably have shared with him. Everyone in the village knew that Eddie's mother, Barbara, was a complete nightmare. 'Now that really is going the extra mile to spread the Christmas spirit.'

'Ah, come on, Pete, she's not that bad.' Liv was trying hard to think of one good trait the woman could lay claim to, apart from being Eddie's mother.

'You would say that – you never see the bad in anyone.' Pete laughed kindly. It had long been a running joke between them – Liv expected the best from everyone she met and mostly, she figured that was what she got.

'No. Seriously, I know she can be a bit overbearing, but really, she hasn't had an easy life and she might be my mother-in-law one of these days,' Liv said the words quietly, but she could feel Pete's eyes glide towards her. Eddie had never made a secret of the fact that he had no intention of getting married; it was one of those things that sat silently between the two friends, making Liv uncomfortable and Pete roll his eyes and silently seethe. *He should be thanking his jammy stars; he's bloody lucky to get you,* he'd said more than once. Pete couldn't care less if he never got married. What bothered him most was that he knew Liv wanted to settle down, have children and maybe, someday, lots of grandchildren too. *He's too flipping busy being a child himself. You spoil him, you really do.*

'She hasn't exactly made life easy for herself either,' Pete said under his breath.

'Anyway, it's just for a few hours and I'm determined to make it the best Christmas ever,' Liv said and once again she was glad to be making it home – she had a feeling that it was going to be a holiday to remember. She glanced across at Pete. 'Sure you're going to be all right?'

'I told you, I'm fine about me and Anya. I wouldn't have ended things if I wasn't.'

'I know but...' Liv knew no good could come of going over the same old ground. Anya had been fooling around behind Pete's back. It was nothing serious, apparently – well according to Anya – but Pete had ended it on the spot. 'I just thought, you were both, you know…'

'Soul mates?' Pete laughed and shook his head. 'No, I'm afraid not. It'll be awkward for a while, disentangling everything.' He had set Anya up in her own business and she was living in his apartment too. It had all moved very quickly between them, but then, Liv always had that niggling feeling that having a rich boyfriend was as important to Anya as actually being in love with Pete. Pity Liv hadn't said that earlier to Pete, but then, how could she have? She'd been so thrilled to see him finally fall in love with someone. It had seemed no-one could take Rachel's place before this.

'As long as it's just awkward. You'll call me, if you need… anything?'

'Of course.' He glanced across at her now, his smile more of a reassurance than anything he said. Liv was relieved. 'Now, it's after one-thirty in the morning. Why don't you close your eyes for a while and, hopefully, I'll have us back in Ballycove before you know it.'

* * *

'Oh, Pete, I'm so sorry. I can't leave the hospital. I have to stay with him,' Liv said because what else could she do? This guy had saved her life. If anything happened to him when she was stuffing herself with turkey and binge-watching Christmas specials, the guilt would surely kill her.

'There's nothing to feel sorry for. I get it; it's typical of you,' Pete said, 'last woman standing. You'd never desert your post.' Of course, it was what they all expected of her and she knew it wasn't necessarily a good thing for her own happiness. Liv had always been the one to wait up until morning if a sheep had looked like it might be in for a difficult night in labour when she was still at school. And even, on their school trip, she'd been the one to stay behind and sit with the awkward girl who'd broken her leg, just getting into her skis.

'Oh God, I feel awful now. You stayed on especially to give me a lift home.'

'Honestly, Liv, it doesn't matter. I'd prefer to drive on the quieter road anyway.'

'At midnight on Christmas Eve?!' She was laughing, in spite of the fact that her breathing was ragged with shock, and she might just as easily cry.

'Do you want me to come over there? You sound as if… Are you sure you're all right?'

'Ah come on, Pete, I'm in a hospital. I think someone will notice if I need to get looked at.' They both laughed at this, but she had a feeling that she hadn't really assuaged his worry.

'I don't mind staying in Dublin with you, if you feel a little… I mean, going home to an empty flat has to be a bit…' That was typical Pete, only thinking of everyone else.

'Don't be daft, you have to go home and have a proper Christmas—' She stopped, because she was still a little worried about him. It was crap breaking up with your girlfriend just before the holidays. No matter how much he told her not to worry, she couldn't help it. He'd accused Liv of turning into an old mother hen a week ago, so she was reluctant to even mention Anya now. She promised herself she would send him lots of funny texts and memes over Christmas to keep his mind off things.

She'd have to cancel all the plans she'd so carefully made in the run-up to the Christmas holidays. It was unfortunate that her family would be stuck with Barbara, but the Latimers would muddle through – that was just the way they were. Her family would understand that she couldn't just walk away when the guy could have a serious spinal or head injury – it so easily could have been her under the wheel of that motorbike. If she hadn't known what a close shave she'd had at the time, the policeman had been quick to point out how lucky she'd been when he took down her statement. Her family wouldn't want her to do anything less than what she believed was right.

For a moment, Liv thought about all she'd hoped this holiday would hold for her future, but deep down, she knew she'd made the right choice. The engagement ring would have to wait. God knows, she'd waited long enough to settle down already.

Eddie was the only man she'd really dated. He was her first grown-up relationship. Well, she hadn't really dated him at all. Sometimes, she thought Rachel had sent Eddie to her so she hadn't really had a choice. Eddie had just always been there; Eddie, with his slightly too long curly hair that he still tied into a ponytail, which she always thought made him rather arty-looking against his slightly crooked teeth and perfect nose.

If she was honest, she'd hardly noticed him before losing Rahcel and her life had been turned upside down. They'd been at school together and then, one day, walking through the coffee shop in the hospital when she was on a chocolate errand for one of her colleagues, she'd spotted him. He was sitting at a table and he looked as if the world was about to end. For sure, she thought he must be dying, so she went over to him, placed her hand over his and sat down next to him.

It turned out to be nothing more serious than a broken toe and he'd just been thrown out of his flat that afternoon. He hadn't supplied a reason why, nor indeed had she thought to ask – well it seemed a bit obtuse to go opening a conversation around something so awkward. His impending homelessness was down to some disagreement he'd been vague about at the time, but later, she understood, he'd forgotten to pay the rent for a couple of months. That was just typical Eddie. When it came to mundane things like paying bills, he never got round to it. Liv put it down to his artistic temperament – the left side of his brain had never kicked in as much as the right – or was it the other way round? She was never quite sure. She felt it made them perfect for each other: Liv had an abundance of practical humdrum in her life at that point, and Eddie provided the breath of fresh air that she needed.

The day she met him again, he was more concerned that the broken toe meant the end of his five-a-sides. Later, she realised that his football arrangement had more to do with going to the pub afterwards than it did with any kind of sporting achievement. She offered him the spare room in her little flat to tide him over.

And that was it, really. He brought his stuff over to stay for a week or two and never left. One night, after a long shift, because she was too tired to cook, she picked up a Chinese takeaway for them. Eddie opened a bottle of Bacardi that she'd forgotten was in the cupboard and somehow, they ended up in bed together. Against all the odds, it seemed, here they were six years later – he'd never left. It had become comfortable between them, she supposed. They'd fallen into a routine and along the way, they became Liv and Eddie. They'd become a couple.

Eddie was the one she could rely on to take her to the pub if she was depressed. With his cynical take on everything, he could make her laugh by turning her worries inside out with just one mocking comment. He stopped her thinking about what might have been and that in itself was a tiny miracle. And wasn't that enough? She loved Eddie. She wanted to spend the rest of her life with him. She wanted to have a family. With him. Didn't she?

It wasn't a question. Liv was jolted back to the present and this tiny A&E cubicle. They were lucky – at least so far this evening, A&E was ticking over efficiently and when the curtain was pulled across, it felt as if the frenzy of the world beyond could be at least temporarily held at bay. God, he looked as if he had just closed his eyes to sleep, Liv thought; then, she remembered the gift bag that Finn had been carrying earlier. She'd tucked it into her own bag in the craziness and now she pulled it out. She would leave it here, next to him on the locker.

She held it for a moment, examining it. It wouldn't do any harm to just look in the bag, would it? Of course not. She reached in and pulled out a small box. It was perfectly wrapped. A ring perhaps? There was no card. This was going to be hand-delivered, but a small ticket had been attached to the side, in the shape of a blue heart. He had written M. Just a simple M and one small kiss. Whoever Finn was going to see earlier must mean a lot to him. Liv turned the box over in her hand. Could it be an engagement ring? Maybe. She dropped it back into the bag again. No point in thinking about that now. Engagement rings needed to be put firmly to the back of her mind for the next few hours and maybe days.

The buzzing of the heart monitor startled her once more from her thoughts. The bag fell from her hands and she flew to Finn O'Connell's chest, pulling back the covers, checking, though she didn't need to, that the sticky monitors were in place. 'He's going into cardiac arrest. Help, help,' Liv cried out, hoping that someone would hear in the nearby nurses' station. And then, she hadn't time to think, she was taking a deep breath, placing her hands over Finn O'Connell's mouth and blowing in air for all she was worth. Again. Again. It didn't take long before she was surrounded by the EMTs who'd brought him in the ambulance and from somewhere far beyond her panic, she heard a kind but sure voice telling her, 'It's okay, lassie, we have it from here.'

'Come along now.' One of her colleagues was guiding her out of the cubicle, but Liv stood firm. She couldn't leave him. Instead, she watched as the surgeon she'd messaged on the way into ER began to work on Finn O'Connell and all she could do was pray that he would be all right.

3

It was good to be back in Ballycove. The journey home had flown. She and Pete had talked and laughed for most of the few hours it took to cross the country. Liv sank into the sofa next to her sister in the early hours of the morning. Both Maya and her father had sat up to wait for her. There was a lovely ease to sitting there, staring into the dying fire while her father sipped a hot toddy.

Her dad was a big armchair of a man. He was comfortable, solid, a little worn about the edges, but you knew where you were with him. He'd been taller once, but he was still broad, red-faced and there was no missing the vitality of him when you had his full attention. He never missed the daily newspaper, although, these days he caught it on the iPad Maya had talked him into. *Better for the environment,* he chuckled. He'd taken over this farm from his Uncle Mike, turned it over to organically producing award-winning produce; he loved life, pure and simple, from the hedgehogs in the fields to the stars in the skies. He managed to rear his family and, with a little skimping and saving, send them to college for the careers they'd wanted. As far as he was concerned, he'd lived a small, quiet life and Liv absolutely adored him.

It was obvious both her parents had been looking forward to having her home; she should make it her business to come back more often. There was nothing stopping her, not when her shifts ran into each other every few weeks and meant she regularly had four days off in a row. Except Eddie of course; he always seemed to have something lined up for her to do when those little breaks came her way.

Liv looked at her watch. It was too late to call Eddie now. At some point, her phone's battery had died, so there was no way of telling if he'd rung her either; although, knowing Eddie he probably hadn't – time just seemed to slip away from him when he came back to Ballycove. Liv always blamed this on his mother.

No doubt, he was tucked in safe and sound with Barbara clucking maternally about the house, making sure he was warm enough and that his clothes were ready for the following day. Yes. Really. He admitted that when he came home for the weekend, he still brought his laundry, because no-one could iron a shirt like his mother.

In fairness, Liv never really tried. She had enough to be ironing with her own uniform and a million other things to be doing. Secretly, she knew, she might have ironed all his clothes, but he put down the impossible standard of his mother's creases too long ago for her to ever decide to scale that particular barrier with Barbara. Pick your battles, isn't that what they say? And it was much too easy to fall out with Barbara Quirke without actually looking for reasons to. At this point, Eddie's mother had fallen out with half the village and she wasn't a woman to bury the hatchet unless it was squarely in her rival's shoulder blades.

Even the rector in the local Church of Ireland had fallen foul of Barbara when she overlooked the Quirke roses in favour of the slightly brighter, larger flowers two houses down the road. The annual festival of flowers was, apparently, still a marker by which some of the local competitive gardeners set some store. Barbara was a woman of impossibly high standards and she possessed a low threshold for the shortcomings of others. Liv knew that she would have to bite down on any resentment in the years ahead if she meant to stick with Eddie, but if Eddie was anything, first and last, he was Barbara's son and he adored the ground his mother walked on.

She imagined the village off in the distance, silent and sleeping, a fresh layer of snow falling in the darkness, the church bells calling out the hours until they woke in the morning and as she drifted to sleep, she felt a simple contentment, just to be here.

Was it because she had a feeling that Eddie was going to propose to her in the morning? Or was it just being back here, in her single bed, with the silence of the village in the fields far off? It was soothing; a balm to the hectic life of working in the A&E for the rest of the time.

The A&E – she turned it over in her thoughts, stared up at the darkness overhead. Suddenly, it was not guilt that wafted over her as she thought of Finn O'Connell stuck in A&E tonight. She had no reason to feel guilty; she'd done everything she could for him. No, it was something else that niggled at her – something she couldn't quite put a finger on, but it felt as if she was missing something. Something vital and it made her catch her breath.

Like a child on Christmas Eve, it took Liv ages to fall asleep. She ran it over in her mind, a thousand times – how Eddie would propose. She wondered if perhaps Barbara had told him it was time to make an honest woman of Liv – it was the sort of thing she could imagine Eddie's mother saying. Eventually, she began to nod off as the crows shook their feathers in the tall trees that dotted all about her father's farm.

*

At eight o'clock her alarm went off and she silenced it as quickly as she could. She had offered to prepare and cook the turkey; there was stuffing to make and probably a bit of cleaning up to do on the bird before she could pop it in the oven.

'Have you had your breakfast yet?' her father asked after she'd begun in the kitchen. He had already been up and checking the ewes he'd moved closer to the house who were due to lamb at any moment.

'I've just got the turkey started; now, let's have breakfast together.' Liv was delighted to have a little while longer on her own with him before anyone else arrived.

'I've a better idea,' he said taking up Liv's wellingtons from inside the back door and handing them to her. With piping-hot mugs of tea and wedges of her mother's home-made brown bread in their hands, he led her down to the little sheds that sheltered between the house and the huge farm building that he'd constructed further on when she was still a teenager. For some time, that had been his pride and joy, but these days, she had a feeling that the little old sheds, with their wobbly stone, sloping roofs and brightly painted doors suited him much better.

The cold stung Liv's face, the only part of her it could get at, since she was bundled up in one of her father's huge coats, and Maya's gloves and hat that she'd picked up in the porch. Still, it was refreshing, walking along with the crunch of icy gravel beneath her feet and the rasp of the bitter air in her lungs. She looked out across the frosty fields in the distance. The only houses visible from here seemed to meld in with the whiteness of the landscape. The sky was a muted grey and it merely added to the blend of neutrals – the only relief the dark blue Atlantic. It was winter harsh and uninterrupted in its raw splendour.

Mikey Latimer pushed in the first door they came to and the smell of hay and silage caught in Liv's throat, pulling her to a stop as a rush of memories flooded her from years earlier. This had always been the highlight of winter on the farm for her, the newborn lambs. Every other year, there was one that needed a little extra care and Liv had always been in charge of feeding and looking after the stragglers of the bunch. 'Triplets,' he said proudly pointing to a worn-out, ragged-looking sheep and her three tiny lambs.

'Oh, I can't believe it.' They were only just born, probably not much more than an hour old. 'Were you here for it all?' she said a little enviously. 'I wish you'd called me down.'

'What and spoil the dinner – you must be joking?' He laughed. That was her dad all over; he wouldn't want to inconvenience anyone for the world. 'Anyway, Cleopatra and I had it all in hand.'

'Cleopatra?' Liv glanced at the sheep a little dubiously.

'What? Sure, isn't she as entitled to that name as anyone?' He looked a little embarrassed. 'You won't tell your mother, will you? You know, about her name – she might think I've gone a bit soft…'

'Don't worry, it can be our secret,' Liv said and she kissed his ruddy cheek. 'Now, can I get a good look at them?' she asked climbing over the wooden barrier easily and grabbing the smallest of the lambs for a closer look.

'It's lovely to have you back here, Liv,' her dad said later as they trudged back up towards the house. He stopped for a moment next to the gable wall, laid a hand on it and stood silently catching his breath. She knew what he was thinking. They'd been here, years before – it was Rachel's last year with them and they'd stood looking out towards the vast ocean.

'You know, there's a whole lot more out there than just…' His voice petered off, as if what he had to say was too much for him to put into words. But she knew what he meant. In an ideal world, as far as her father was concerned, she'd fall in love with Pete and they'd get married and produce a half dozen grandchildren. Even, after six years, it seemed Eddie Quirke was still not quite good enough for his daughter.

'I know, Dad.' She squeezed his arm affectionately, basking in his love, which felt as if it simmered in the vastness of the moment between them. 'Come on, Dad, I'll make us a nice pot of tea and we can finish our breakfast in peace before they all arrive in on top of us.'

* * *

So far, it was one long night, but it felt as if Liv had stayed in the hospital for a lifetime. Finn O'Connell's heart had finally stabilised and he was breathing independently. Liv had a feeling her prayers (even though, she'd never been particularly religious!) were paying off. Next, they needed to investigate that bleeding from his ear and so they were moving him along for a full CT scan. Liv could only hope that it would show up clear. Regardless of how physically strong he looked, the choice between operating if there was internal bleeding and keeping his heart pumping was one that was too hard to call with any good odds in his favour.

'Any sign of a phone?' Joe, the EMT, asked. The next decisions should be down to his family, which meant they needed to track down his next of kin.

'Hang on.' Liv reached gingerly into Finn's deep coat pocket. Again, the weirdest thing, to think she had been standing next to him – gazing into his eyes... yes, she could admit it, gazing at him only a few hours earlier and now, here she was rifling through his belongings. 'I have it,' she said, slipping the phone out easily. It was one of those finger recognition ones. She touched his finger to it. Bingo. She tapped in ICE, hoping there would be a contact number there that would make this easier. Nothing. 'Damn,' she said.

'Okay, love,' the older EMT said. 'We're on the move.' He began to unclamp the bed so they could transfer him to radiology.

'There's no emergency contact,' she said, but they weren't listening to her. Instead, she was shepherded out of their way while they got on with bringing Finn O'Connell in to get him seen to as quickly as they could.

'Try the last call he's made or received,' the younger of the men called to her.

'Of course,' she said. The last call was to a woman called Estelle – not M, so? She thought of that expensively wrapped little box and dialled the number for Estelle.

'Hey, Finn.' The voice was young on the other side, probably twenties, breathy and obviously happy to hear from this phone.

'Hello, Estelle?'

'Yes, sorry, who is this? I thought…'

'No. It's okay.' Actually, it wasn't, but it's what you said, wasn't it? 'My name is Liv Latimer. I'm ringing you on Finn's phone. He's been in an accident and I'm trying to track down his next of kin. Can you tell me if…'

'Finn. Oh no, is he all right? Where is he? When did it happen? How…' There was the usual, understandable barrage of questions, the inability to wait for answers – it wasn't the first time Liv had to make a call like this.

'It's okay. He's here at St Columbanus's hospital. He's in the very best of hands. I was next to him when it happened. I'm a nurse here in A&E. I was just coming off duty when…'

'Oh, thank God. But how is he? Is he going to be all right?'

'It's too early to say; he's just going down for a scan now,' Liv said, keeping the details light. She could tell Estelle the rest when she arrived to be with him. 'He really is in the best of hands. Are you his wife?'

'Huh? No. I mean, we're not…' Estelle stopped for a moment. 'That is, we're…'

'Are you his next of kin?' Liv had to ask directly, because for all she knew, this woman might be his cleaner… or his mistress. She eyed the bag that she'd dropped down on the floor next to Finn

O'Connell's gurney. He'd spent a lot of money, probably, on a gift for M. And Estelle was certainly not an M!

'I'm on my way now,' Estelle was saying on the other end of the line. 'Don't worry; I'll let everyone know who needs to. Just take care of him for me.' And then, she ended the call and Liv was left staring at her phone, not quite sure what to do next.

'Oh. Thank God, Liv, you're here.' Francine looked like she'd aged about a decade in the little over an hour since she'd seen her last. 'How are you? Have you been checked out? Are you…?'

'I'm fine, really, not even a scratch,' Liv said although her legs still felt wobbly and she could feel nerves jangling on ends that she'd never noticed before, but that was just shock – nothing compared to what had happened to Finn. Even beyond herself though, there was no missing the fact that the Emergency Department had filled up considerably since she'd left; there was no mistaking the fact that her colleagues were under pressure. 'Anyway, I'm here now, I might as well stay on if you need an extra pair of hands.' She would have to change back into her uniform; it was definitely all hands on deck for the rest of the night. 'I was there when it happened. The motorcyclist?' She looked towards one of the junior doctors who'd just popped his head through the curtains.

'It's cuts and bruises mostly; he'll be aching for a few weeks, at worst a couple of cracked ribs,' the doctor said, then he looked towards the empty space where Finn O'Connell had just been moved from.

'He's just gone for a scan,' and when she looked at her watch, she realised at least at this time of the morning, there wasn't too much hanging about – it was too early for day appointments and too late for drunks to clog the place up. All they could do now was hope for the best.

*

It was less than an hour later when a nurse called Maxine told Liv there was a girl looking for her at the desk, but it seemed as if time had been fractured in some strange way, as if she was somehow working outside the normal confines – it was shock, she was pretty sure about that.

'Liv?' the girl asked. She was no more than twenty-four, strikingly pretty, red hair, cherub lips and skin that looked as if it was made of porcelain – she was five eleven if she was an inch, willowy, more than thin. A model?

'Hi,' Liv said and smiled at the girl. 'Estelle?' She realised this could only be Estelle – because she would absolutely remember meeting this girl otherwise.

'Yes. I'm Estelle. I'm here to see Finn,' she said and there was no mistaking the worry that hung about her.

'He's…' Liv checked her watch again. 'At the moment, he's down at radiology, but he should be back up at any minute.' She bit her lip, God, she hoped he was all right. She hadn't mentioned his cardiac event on the phone, feeling she'd imparted enough bad news for one conversation. 'They're doing a CT scan.' She saw the girl's eyes widen. 'Don't worry, that's normal. He was struck by a motorbike.' She didn't need to know all the details – the sickening thud, saving Liv and the fact that he was thrown so far into the road. She didn't need to hear about the blood at his ear and the fact that the CT scan was all about checking to see if there was a brain aneurysm. Liv shivered. The last time she'd prayed so hard for anyone was… Rachel. 'We just have to make sure that there's no internal bleeding. It's not painful and he'll be transferred back up to A&E then, hopefully.'

'Hopefully?'

'Yes.' Hopefully he wouldn't need surgery and there was no point mentioning intensive care just yet. With a little luck, Finn O'Connell would have gotten off as lightly as the motorcyclist, although, deep down, Liv knew that he probably wasn't going to be as lucky.

'So, where do I go?' the girl asked and Liv wondered if she was even twenty-four – she sounded about twelve now; she reached out and put her arm around the girl's shoulder.

'It's okay. It's a bit of a shock, I know. You can wait here – this is where he'll be coming back to after his tests are finished. You'll be able to sit with him for a little while before we know what's happening next.'

'What's happening next?' The girl was on the verge of tears.

'Don't worry. You know as much I do, for now. Sit here and try not to worry too much, okay?'

Bunkum. Of course she was going to worry. Wasn't Liv herself in a bad way, and she didn't even know the man, however drawn she'd felt to him.

4

'It's the phone, for you, Liv.' Her mother, still in her dressing gown, handed the phone over, rolling her eyes as she did, so there could be no mistaking who was on the other end of the line. Barbara Quirke. Her mother never actually said it, but Eddie's mother was like salt in an open wound. They didn't get on, but Yvonne would never admit to the fact. Or at least, not once it became obvious that Eddie was going to be a regular feature in their future lives.

The most recent skirmish involved Imran, a yoga instructor that her mother adored. Barbara had managed to scupper his Mindfulness classes in the local community centre. It was exactly the sort of thing she did, and probably how she'd managed to step on just about every toe in the village over the years. The weekly classes had been popular with everyone, from the mother and baby club to the local retirement group. It was all going so well, until one evening when Barbara had arrived for her 'chat and crochet circle' (or 'the knit and knife coven' as Maya called it) and spotted Imran rolling up his mats.

Hard to know if she's an old-fashioned killjoy, or just an out-and-out racist, Liv's father had said. Liv worried it might be a bit of both, but she'd never admit this. Soon, Barbara was on a mission to shut down the yoga classes and by piling on the pressure with the committee about health and safety, eventually Imran had to move the class to the next village over.

'I was just telling your mother – I'm sure you already know, Eddie will have mentioned it – but I seem to have developed an allergy to gluten now.' Barbara paused for a moment, waiting for this news to settle on Liv. 'It's shocking how these things just creep up on you. One moment, I had the constitution of an ox and the next, well, I suppose, I'm a lot more fragile than I was...' Barbara's voice quivered pathetically as she let the words hang in the air between them.

'No. He never said a word about it.' To which of course, Maya would say, *Well, wasn't that just typical of Eddie?*

'Oh, dear boy, I'm sure he's been so worried about me, but what with how busy he's been in the run-up to Christmas... He probably doesn't get a chance to talk to you properly these days anyway.'

'So, you're coeliac now?' Liv was mentally checking through every part of the lunch she'd finished preparing. She looked at the clock. They were due in less than half an hour. If Barbara had a decent bone in her body, she'd have let them know a few days ago.

'Oh, those labels – poof for all that. I simply can't have any gluten; it makes me terribly unwell and I'll be in absolute agony for days on end if I so much as look at the stuff.'

'It's a pity Eddie didn't mention it.'

'I'm sure he did.' As usual, Barbara jumped immediately to her son's defence. 'It's hardly his fault if you're so taken up with everything else that you don't listen to him properly.'

'Never mind, hardly the end of the world. I'll just make sure that everything is gluten-free for you, okay?' Liv managed not to sound as if she was speaking through gritted teeth.

'Fine.' Barbara sniffed, perhaps hoping that it would take a little more work than just mentally ticking off every item that had already been prepared, cooked and was just being browned off in the oven.

When Liv put down the phone, she took a deep breath. Eddie and Barbara were due at two o'clock, which she knew meant closer to three, if she factored in Eddie's tardiness. They would be here for roughly three hours – leaving again at six, hopefully. If they hadn't left by then, her dad would probably insist on them all trotting down to the lambing shed, which would be enough to make Eddie want to get home as quickly as possible. Eddie didn't entertain anything vaguely agricultural and he'd appreciate the sight of a birthing yew even less. Yes, Liv was fairly certain that by the time her father wanted to sit in front of the evening news, they'd have the place to themselves again. There was no doubt that a discussion of sheep tick and an invitation to pet the lambs would be enough to send Barbara scuttling back to her own tidy if a little shabby semi on the far end of the village.

Liv felt vaguely guilty for counting down the time until Barbara Quirke left before she had even arrived, but then she could easily convince herself she was only doing it out of consideration for her own family. Anyway it would all be worth it when Eddie dropped down on one knee and... She felt that familiar rush of prickliness creep over her, a mixture of excitement and something else she couldn't quite put a finger on, but it had to be all good – after all, it was all she'd ever wanted, wasn't it?

'Okay,' her mother said examining a list of foods on Google. 'The only thing that I can see here that might be a problem is the gravy, stuffing and the pudding.'

'It will be fine. She can steer clear of the stuffing and we'll give her stewed apple and cream for dessert,' Maya said. She had already checked the deep freeze in one of the sheds and pulled out a container that she'd filled with apples stewed in sugar, ginger and cloves at the beginning of autumn when the trees around the farm were weighed down with far too much fruit to get through in apple tarts. Maya had even less time for Barbara than her mother, but because Maya was a solicitor, Barbara tended to look at her with a certain amount of grudging respect. Probably, she would much prefer if Eddie had fallen in with the solicitor in the family than the nurse, but the truth was, Maya wouldn't have looked twice at Eddie. She was happily single until she met someone amazing – Liv figured; she was waiting for the movie-star version of their father.

By the time Eddie and his mother arrived, the Latimers were all suitably braced for Barbara. They'd dressed up in their finest; Liv's mother had bought a dark green velvet dress for the occasion, which showed off her still-great curvy figure perfectly. Maya looked elegantly expensive in palazzo pants and a silk blouse and Mikey had donned the Christmas jumper, complete with a flashing-nosed Rudolph that Liv had given him earlier just for fun. Liv had brought down a simple cream woollen dress she'd bought at the local mills a year earlier when she and Eddie had been invited to a rather posh party one of the consultants was throwing for New Year's Eve. For now, of course, it was covered over with one of her mother's aprons, but she quickly tugged that off to welcome Eddie and Barbara.

They sat for a while with pre-dinner drinks in the sitting room, making small talk about what was happening in the village, with Eddie, Maya and Liv taking it in turns to give an update on how things were with them. It was too early for her mother to pull out her seat at the piano – Barbara would need a lot more sherry in her before she'd be rattling out the Christmas carols. Liv wondered what she'd be like if she ever truly let herself go.

'I think I smell turkey?' her father said jovially after half an hour.

'I'll just check on it.' Liv looked across at Eddie meaningfully. He'd already had two glasses of brandy and her mother was about to pour another for him. Thanks to Yvonne's heavy hand with the brandy bottle, he wasn't in much of a condition to take a broad non-verbal hint. 'Will you give me a hand, Eddie?'

'Sure,' he said, taking his glass with him.

'Hey,' Liv said once they were alone in the kitchen. 'I got you this…' She pulled out the slim envelope she'd been waiting to hand to him; honestly, she wasn't sure how she hadn't already blabbed about it to him a hundred times over.

Pete had helped her get two VIP box tickets to a premier game with his favourite team. It was near what promised to be the high point of the team's decade, if they continued to play as well as they'd been playing. Or at least that was what Pete had said and she believed him; Liv had next to no interest in soccer.

'What is it?' For the first time since he arrived, Eddie left down his glass; he looked at the envelope a little dubiously.

'It's a summons? What do you think it is? It's your Christmas gift from me.' She leant in to give him a kiss, but he was so intent on opening it, she just about skimmed past those enviable cheekbones. His hair smelled of minty shampoo and she imagined him, jumping into the shower before he left – he smelled and looked good. Better than he had done for the last few weeks, when all he seemed to do was go to work and stay there far too long each day. He'd looked tired, he'd been irritable, but he told her often enough that was just the price of trying to keep his bespoke jewellery-making business afloat. The last few months were his busiest season. Hopefully, this January, they'd be able to put some money aside – they'd need it if they were going to have any decent-size wedding.

'Bloody brilliant.' He looked at her, his eyes shining and bright. Honestly, sometimes, she could see that enthusiastic eight-year-old he'd been in school. He was still standing right there in front of her and when that happened, it made her feel a little... guilty? Yes, she could admit to herself, sometimes, that she had settled for Eddie – they had fallen into a relationship after Rachel died and she used to wonder if she'd just been trying to fill the huge emptiness left by her sister, rather than falling in love with him. 'How on earth did you manage to get these?'

'Pete.' It was all she needed to say. Actually, the mention of his name made her feel a little guilty too. He'd rung her twice already today and between all the preparations for dinner, all she'd managed was to send him a quick text hoping he was having a lovely day. Pete had been Rachel's best friend forever. He missed her as much as any of them, and Liv knew that he'd promised to look after her, but she really should be looking after him too.

'Ah.' He shook his head. 'Good old Pete.' Eddie made a face and Liv wasn't sure exactly what was behind it, but she was sure he loved the gift, which was really all that mattered to her at this point.

'What?' she asked now as he shook his head.

'Ah, just Pete, you know,' and he said it a little scathingly. Pete and Eddie were very different. Eddie was an artist, whereas Pete was a numbers man. He worked in insurance and his company provided cover for every big game and concert from the Aviva in Dublin to Wembley Stadium in London. 'Good old Peter,' he said sardonically and Liv had a feeling that the brandy was hitting an empty stomach and giving his words a harshness that was out of character in Eddie's usually passive nature.

There was a rivalry between them that had been there since school; Eddie hid it well, mostly, until he'd had a drink too many. It had started on the football pitch where Eddie was just that little bit faster, that little bit more brutal, whereas Pete, as a kid, just wasn't sporty. Pete had always been a tangle of arms, legs and geeky glasses. But people change and it seemed that as the years wore on life had evened out the score. Now Pete had a fantastic job with so many perks – he owned a luxury apartment in one of the most sought-after city addresses, and until recently he had a girlfriend who, to Liv's mind at least, made Kendall Jenner look like an old crone.

'You can thank him yourself next time we run into him.' She bent towards him for another kiss, and this time, he held her in his arms and looked into her eyes for just a moment before kissing her forehead softly and pulling her into him for a hug. That was Eddie – he was a great hugger. Liv loved when he pulled her close like this. It felt as if he was shielding her from any harm that might decide to come knocking on their door.

'So, this dinner?' he said looking round and topping up his glass from the open bottle of red wine her mother had left on the big old kitchen table.

'Ahem?' she said, holding her hands out.

'Oh, yes.' He smiled at her. 'Your gift? It's in the car – do you want me to get it now?' he asked.

'If you think it's the right time?' Liv could hear everyone moving about in the sitting room. Her father was shepherding them into the old parlour that they'd set up as a dining room with her grandmother's long mahogany table at its centre and mismatched chairs that her mother had picked up from auction rooms and charity shops over the years before she'd lovingly restored the lot.

'I don't mind...' he said, although she could tell by his body language that he was only reluctantly making for the door. It was hardly the most romantic spot to ask her to marry him.

'No, we'll leave it until later,' she said, reaching out to his arm. At this stage, with her father in the hallway and a dinner to pop on the table, it would all feel a bit rushed. Liv didn't want to be proposed to in a hurry, as if it could be slipped in between courses. It needed to be more special than that. The anticipation of finally getting that beautiful ring on her finger might just kill her over lunch, but it would be worth it. She was going to be Mrs Quirke, hopefully by the end of the coming year, and then they could start on having a family and really settling into life as she'd always imagined it.

She dipped the ladle into her home-made French onion soup for starters. She would have to avoid the croutons for Barbara – but otherwise it tasted great.

It was perfect; everything was going to be just wonderful, wasn't it? Just as soon as they got this dinner over with and she and Eddie could be alone together, he would sweep her off her feet – wouldn't he?

* * *

It had been a very long night. For everyone.

Finn O'Connell was transferred to ICU. Thankfully, as yet there was no sign of any internal bleeding; however, he was still unconscious.

'Peggy?' Liv said when she saw one of the nurses replacing her. For a second Liv did a double take.

'Yes, it seems ye can't survive without me after all.' The old nurse shook her head. She'd only retired two weeks earlier, but thanks to some HR glitch, she was still on the system. She'd never wanted to retire. 'I was meant to go to my sister's, but…'

'It's so lovely to see you.' Liv bit her lip; it had been such a truly emotional few hours since the accident, she wasn't sure if she was ready to laugh or cry at the sight of her.

'Ach, you know I'd come in – even the best of custard and Christmas pudding couldn't keep me at home if I'm needed here,' Peggy said picking up a clipboard, eager to get back on her rounds.

Out in the main corridors, the hospital had that forced cheeriness of Christmas Day that always made Liv feel a little sad. She'd only worked a handful of holidays, the first when she'd been training and Rachel had also stayed in Dublin helping out with one of Dublin's busiest homeless shelters. That had been one of her happiest Christmases, even though they hadn't actually celebrated it properly until two days later. She had been working on the maternity wards and Rachel had been waiting outside for her after she'd finished. She could remember them walking back to their flat as if it were yesterday. Sometimes, it seemed those days together were only a whisper away. They were young and it felt as if nothing could ever touch them – of course, they hadn't figured on a tumour growing silently, behind Rachel's quick blue eyes.

This morning, the tinsel and Christmas trees couldn't quite penetrate her sadness. She knew that everyone who worked in the hospital did everything they could to make the place as cheery as possible, but there was no covering over the fact that they would all much prefer to be at home, surrounded by family and friends, celebrating near a warm fire or at least sitting in their own favourite armchair.

It reminded her of a text she'd received from Pete. It had arrived on her phone late last night. She pulled it out now; it was a meme making fun of her for having to work over Christmas Day. She texted back, tried to think of something snappy, but could only manage a quote from the Carry On movies – any mention of sore misgiving never failed to raise a smile between them. It was their thing. They'd watched every Carry On movie they could get their hands on while they'd sat with Rachel. They'd lapped up anything that would make them laugh, anything that would take their mind off things; so now, when there was nothing else to say, they often threw random quotes at each other.

And then, that familiar ping back from Pete: instructing her how to treat any and all misgivings she might have. Liv smiled because, suddenly, the hospital didn't seem to be quite so depressing all around her. She raced up the three flights to ICU. It was eerily quiet up here. There was no tinny sound of piped-in Christmas music on repeat; everything here was hushed. It almost felt as if she'd stepped into a parallel universe, empty of another living soul beyond herself and her squeaking footsteps along the disinfected corridors.

She pushed through the double doors into the waiting area near the ward and looked in through the glass rectangles. Directly across, she could see Finn. He was still unconscious. Beside his bed, Estelle sat watching him.

Liv managed to catch the eye of one of the nurses making her way back to the nursing station in the centre of the ward. She knew the woman by sight, had seen her often in the canteen on her break.

'Hi,' she whispered when the nurse opened the door a chink. What was it with ICU? She always found herself whispering here, as if to respect that sacred space people were being suspended in: somewhere between fully alive and lingering on the brink of some vast footstep that would take them away forever. 'I'm just checking up on Finn O'Connell – I'm from A&E.' She watched as the nurse curled her mouth slightly. Accident and Emergency were very much considered the poor, uncouth relations when it came to a choice between there and ICU. 'I brought him in last night; I was there when he had his accident.'

'I see,' the nurse said looking back at him. 'Well, he's remained stable. We're still waiting for the consultant to do his rounds this morning. His vitals are good and there's been no signs of any internal damage so far, but he's still in a coma, I'm afraid,' she said gently, as if breaking news to a relative rather than a colleague.

'Well, that's good so, I suppose,' Liv said, trying hard to get another glimpse of him over the nurse's shoulder. 'Has Estelle been here all night?' she asked.

'She hasn't left his side, just sitting there. I don't think she closed her eyes once.' The nurse's tone had softened.

'And she's…'

'His wife.' The other woman gave her a hard stare now. 'You know that only next of kin are allowed to visit ICU,' she said sharply.

'Of course.' Liv found her tone dropping even lower. 'And there have been no other visitors?' She was thinking of M. The note attached to the gift he'd been carrying when the accident happened. For some reason, unclear even to Liv, she'd stashed the gift in her own locker, hoping for a chance to meet the mysterious M and pass it on, without upsetting Estelle. As the night had worn on, she'd become more convinced that the gift was for a lover; he was probably having an affair. He was, she confirmed again with one more glance, a very attractive man. 'It's a long time to be sitting there,' she said as the ICU nurse began to close out the door so she could return to her duties.

Liv set off for the coffee shop on the ground floor. Everything was closed up today, but the concession owner had left the coffee machine outside the shutters and on a nearby table a selection of pastries and sandwiches with best-by dates probably better ignored as the day wore on. Still, it was a thoughtful festive gesture. Staff needed coffee breaks to keep going; today more than any other it was a vital service. She made two cups of strong coffee and slipped milk, sugar and a couple of small pastries in her bag. She had a feeling that Estelle probably wasn't a chocolate woman, not with that figure, but Liv needed sugar this morning like usually she needed air. The journey back to the flat alone would be enough to test a saint, what with only skeleton bus services and the icy roads.

This time when she arrived outside the ward, she managed to catch Estelle's eye. She held up the coffee cup and motioned her to come out and join her.

'God, that's good,' Estelle said after taking her first sip of hot black coffee.

'Actually, it's not really, but with the night you've spent here, anything probably would taste good.'

'I couldn't sleep.' Estelle blew across the surface of her cup. As Liv had expected, she'd turned down the offer of food, even the one protein bar that Liv found at the bottom of her bag.

'No.' Liv knew that feeling well, sitting there all night long, with a knot in your stomach, waiting for something to happen. It was a completely different sort of exhaustion to actually working the night through.

'I was just so worried. I mean, even today, they can't tell me how he is or what's going to happen to him.' A large tear formed at the corner of her eye. 'Sorry,' she said, as she managed to blow her nose elegantly, like a cute kitten compared to the blubbering wreck Liv would have been if she'd been in the same boat. 'You're really very good, bringing coffee up to me. I…'

'Stop. It's the very least I could do,' Liv said sipping her own milky sweet coffee. 'Actually, if you want to go home and tidy yourself up, grab a couple of hours' sleep, I don't mind staying with him.' The words were out before Liv realised it. But, it was funny, the tiredness she'd felt on finishing her shift had all but evaporated now sitting here with Estelle.

'Oh, I couldn't do that; it's too much to ask…'

'Is there no-one else who can come here and sit with him?'

'Not really. His parents are on a Christmas cruise. It's his mum's birthday tomorrow and last I heard they were walking around Mexico City. I rang them of course, last night, but…'

'Shouldn't you go downstairs and check to see if they've rung back?' Liv suggested, realising Estelle would have had to keep her phone off anywhere near this ward. 'I'm sure they'll be worried sick when they hear he's been in an accident.' She looked at this girl. She was indeed very striking, but very young too, much too young to be married to Finn O'Connell. She hardly looked twenty-two now that her make-up of the previous night had worn away and he was, according to his driver's licence, the same age as Liv – thirty-six years old.

'I suppose,' she said, standing now and glancing through the narrow window at the bed opposite.

'Go on,' Liv said taking the empty paper cup from her and walking her towards the stairs. When she turned back, she saw the nurse she'd spoken to earlier was on her way home after her shift. She looked like the type of woman who would go home to an organised house, probably with teenagers and husband already having dinner cooked and on the table for when she arrived. 'Happy Christmas,' Liv said as she passed her. Liv watched as she left and then pushed the door through to the ward.

She padded across the floor to Finn O'Connell's bedside and sat in the seat so recently vacated by Estelle, picking up the notes that had been left there by the last nurse who'd done obs. Liv couldn't help flicking through them. There was nothing more to add – he was stable, hopefully healing beneath the coma that shut him off from the rest of the world for now. She drank in his features, so weirdly familiar although they'd hardly really met at all; she'd thought of those few words between them, many times over the course of the last few hours.

It was strange – sitting here, watching him sleeping. It was almost intimate in a way she'd never really imagined it could be. Of course, she'd sat in chairs like this often with Rachel. There had been many times when her sister had been so emptied out by her treatment that she slipped off and away from her for hours on end and Liv would just sit there, waiting for her to come back to her, somehow always believing that she'd never completely leave her in spite of what the doctors were intent on telling them.

It felt like that now. As if she was waiting for someone who meant far more to her than a stranger she'd hardly met. She wasn't sure how long she was sitting there when Estelle tapped her shoulder. They walked outside for a moment. Their shoes pinched the floor with loud rubbery squeaks in spite of their attempt to be as silent as they could. This ward was filled with too many signs telling them to be quiet and reminding them only one visitor was allowed to each patient.

'They're coming back,' Estelle said when they were standing in the hallway. 'His parents; they've booked a flight out of Miami. It's a bit of a nightmare as you can imagine, what with Christmas and everything. And to make things even more complicated, they're out in the middle of the ocean at the moment, but they dock in Miami tomorrow morning and then they'll fly back immediately.'

'Well, that's good news,' Liv said, feeling an unexpected rush of relief almost overwhelming her. Weirdly, it was that same feeling she got when she returned to Ballycove; she felt it now, as if she was nearing home after a very long time away. Home. God, she hadn't even called her parents to wish them a happy Christmas yet. She'd do it as soon as she got down to the ground floor. 'Are you really sure there's nothing I can do?' she said, gathering up their discarded cups to dispose of on her way.

'No. I think I'll hang about here for a while longer and maybe later I'll go home and clean myself up a bit,' Estelle said. 'Thanks, you know, for the coffee and everything...'

'Oh, don't mention it. Really.' She looked at the girl again, so young, so fragile. 'Look, I'm working again tonight,' Liv said, having just offered to pick up another shift before she left A&E – well, in for a penny, in for a pound. It seemed she couldn't just walk away now; although she knew the department would survive without her, something was pulling her back. 'I'll come in a little earlier and sit with him if you're not here, if you'd like...'

'Would you? That's so kind of you,' Estelle said softly and then she was gone, back to her seat by his side, and Liv watched a little enviously as she placed her hand over his and whispered something to him that no-one else was meant to hear. And then,

Liv thought of M – and everything about the scene before her was somehow turned inside out. She shook her head, walking towards the stairwell. Perhaps she was lucky; at least her life was straightforward, wasn't it?

*

Her dad wouldn't say it, but she knew he was disappointed she wouldn't be home for Christmas dinner. 'Ara, sure – isn't it all part of the vocation?' he said when she called. 'You just mind yourself and don't be killing yourself. I know that you'll come back to us as soon as you can.' And she imagined him, standing over a shed full of newborn lambs, her favourite part of living on a farm. 'We can have our own Christmas when you do come home.'

'It'll be a bit strange, the three of you there with Eddie and Barbara. I'm really sorry for having organised it and now…'

'Oh, don't be worrying yourself. Isn't it only penance for the next world? Won't we be shoo-ins for sainthood if we can get through it all without you?' he said, laughing.

Liv tried ringing Eddie next. Still no answer and she began to wonder if he was mad at her for staying on in Dublin. He was so different to Pete. Last night, she'd had to convince Pete not to stay in Dublin with her. Eventually, he drove home and texted her earlier with a photograph of Ballycove church with a white dusting of snow around the steeple. Damn it anyway, Eddie never really understood what it was like; she really didn't have a choice – well perhaps she did. She wasn't sure she could fathom exactly why she'd stayed, except some part of her felt she needed to take care of Finn O'Connell, which of course she knew was silly. He'd be well looked after even if he turned out to be the devil incarnate.

She rolled her eyes. She should be at home getting proposed to, brewing up plans for an autumn wedding, admiring that sparkling ring on her finger. Well, she couldn't think about that now, it would only edge her deeper into loneliness for what she was missing out on in Ballycove. Perhaps, Eddie would propose in the New Year instead – that could be every bit as romantic, she told herself. In a strange way, that felt like a lifetime away now.

5

Christmas dinner was a nightmare. Never in all her years had Liv or indeed any of her family endured a meal like it. Barbara Quirke was quite simply the limit. It started with the seating arrangements – not that there were any, beyond everyone grabbing a chair. The only exception to that being her father, who had taken his place at one end of the table, next to where Rachel had always sat. He had a slightly taller chair than the rest, which helped in making it easier for him to stand up again. Barbara, obviously sensing that he'd managed to bag the best possible spot, complained bitterly, endlessly, until he swapped with her. Her chair was too soft, too straight, too low; she was sitting in a draught; she was too close to the fire – it didn't stop until she'd managed to discommode everyone around the table, so right up until dessert, they were still playing a form of disgruntled musical chairs.

When her father tried to make their annual toast to Rachel, Barbara had talked over him, and only Eddie could have knocked back the glass of port they always poured for her, even though he swore he hadn't seen it. Before they'd even pulled their crackers, her mother was flushed and her father had the look of a rabbit in the headlights of an epic strain of myxomatosis.

And then there was lunch – the soup was too oniony; her potatoes were lumpy; she was quite sure that there was gluten in the ham; oh, how she missed the bread stuffing; and finally, no, she couldn't possibly look at dessert. 'Women of a certain age,' she'd said, and looked pointedly at Yvonne, 'need to have a little self-restraint or they are in danger of really letting themselves go.'

And all the while, Eddie seemed to be totally oblivious. Years of listening, or perhaps learning not to listen, had made him completely immune to his mother's insufferable whining. He just sat there, bless him, complimenting Yvonne on the food and Mikey on the wine. Unfortunately, he'd ended up sitting next to her mother and that meant his glass was never empty and so probably without even realising it, he was steadily making his way through whichever bottle was within easy reach. He made no offer to help with clearing away dishes or refilling anyone else's glass. Instead, he became drunker as lunch went on and by dessert he was grinning like a fool with hardly two words to say for himself, leaving the pleasantries to everyone else around him.

By the end of the main course, when he belched loudly, Liv wasn't sure if she wanted to strangle him, Barbara or her own mother for making him drunk – even if she hadn't meant to. Measures were never Yvonne's strong point. Somehow, Liv managed to keep calm and found herself talking too much to cover over his obvious bad manners, but inside, she was ripping. How could he not realise that he was becoming drunker with each sip of wine he was knocking back? How dare he turn up here without so much as a token for her parents and then sit there as if his place at their table was his due?

'So, then, Eddie,' her mother said, trying to jolly things along and take the focus away from Barbara's complaining about the new doctor in the village. 'I hear you've been really busy this year in the run-up to Christmas?'

'Yeah, well…' he managed before draining his wine glass.

'I expect it sets you up for the cold month of January,' her father chimed in, obviously delighted to be moving away from the bitching session Barbara wanted to embark on about recent changes to the village surgery.

'Have you made anything exciting this year?' Maya asked, when Eddie said nothing for a while. A year earlier, he'd made a pendant for a C-list celebrity who was more famous now for her plastic surgery than any other notable career credits. His mother had obviously hoped that it would catapult him into making the next crown jewels and she'd told the whole village about it. 'Any royal engagement rings? Earrings for Michelle Obama? A toe ring for Madonna?' She was laughing now, but that was Maya – full of *joie de vivre* after a single glass of mulled wine.

'No famous people this year, but he's made some beautiful pieces,' Liv said, thinking of the ring that was sitting out in his car waiting to be slipped onto her finger later.

'I'm sure you have,' her mother said warmly. 'You really are quite brilliant.' She fingered the tiny brooch that Liv had commissioned for her a few years earlier. It was only made from silver and synthetic diamonds, but she loved it as much as if it was a priceless gem.

'Of course, it's very hard to make a living at it.' Barbara turned towards Liv's father. 'I mean, he's talented and hardworking, but if people with money don't want to buy jewels, or if they don't know enough but to settle for something off the shelf, then...' She'd been pouring money into her son's business for years. It was Barbara who set Eddie up in the workshop. She'd bought and paid for it from the lump sum she'd received in her pension when she'd retired from her job a few years earlier. Although Eddie never admitted it, Liv suspected that, even now, Barbara was making regular payments into his account. A mother's love – eh? There was no doubt, Barbara adored Eddie – so much so that Liv sometimes wondered how she'd cope when they got married and she'd have to share him with a wife.

She shrugged off the notion. She could handle Barbara Quirke. All she had to do was smile and show up occasionally and let the caustic comments wash off her back. She would learn to be a swan, perhaps, gliding effortlessly through their relationship, while paddling furiously beneath the water to keep up. 'I always think if only he had the right contacts...' She looked towards Liv and her nose wrinkled in automatic disdain. 'But well, poor Liv – the only girls she knows are all nursing and, let's face it, they can hardly afford to keep body and soul together these days, never mind know what good quality jewellery was from cheap tat.' She delivered this gem without a qualm.

'Some would say that having a calling to help others is a far better quality in a partner than having a calling to help yourself,' Liv's mother mumbled, but she kept her voice low when she caught the silent warning in Liv's glance.

'Oh, some of my friends have already commissioned pieces from Eddie – isn't that right Eddie?' Liv said. He was useless, really, up against his mother.

'Yes, but they'll be mainly silver, won't they? I'm sure you'll be lucky to get a cubic zirconia between them,' Barbara said and looked pointedly across at Yvonne's brooch, which she was so fond of.

'Anyone for coffee?' Maya asked a little too loudly to halt the conversation there. And so began the clearing away of dessert dishes and the making of coffee in the huge pot her mother took out only when they had a full house. It was a special treat – they'd bought it on a camping holiday in France years earlier – even then, it had been rustic. It was too large for one, and when it sat on the stove, brewing slowly, even Liv's father couldn't refuse a cup of heavy dark coffee. Liv and Maya began scraping off plates and loading them into their mother's dishwasher while they waited for it to brew. 'Honestly, I don't know how you put up with that woman,' Maya said under her breath. 'And as for…' She stopped. Liv already knew that Eddie would never be good enough for her in Maya's eyes.

By five, they had exhausted all attempts at small talk. It felt as if the day never really got going, in spite of all the hard work put in, and Liv knew she wasn't alone in breathing a sigh of relief when Barbara asked Eddie to find her coat so they could make their way home.

Eddie stumbled out of the parlour and fumbled with the coat stand. He was so drunk at this point, he could barely walk straight and hit off the walls on either side of the narrow hall. He returned to the parlour looking obscenely triumphant, his mother's coat bundled over his arm as he narrowly avoided smashing into a standard lamp in the corner of the room.

'Thanks for… you know…' Eddie patted his pocket where he'd placed his gift with almost reverential care. 'It's great and…' He hiccupped. 'Sorry about…' He looked at her with an expression that said it all.

'Yes?'

'Well, Mum and everything. I know she can be hard going, but really her heart is in the right place and being invited here today meant more to her than she'd ever let on.' He smiled then and in just that moment, Liv remembered why she loved him.

'I know; I get it. She's her own worst enemy. It's fine, really, Eddie. I just hope you both had a nice time.'

'We did.' He leant towards her so she could just about catch his familiar aftershave beneath the smell of wine and brandy. He put a hand up to her face, moving a stray strand of hair from her cheek. 'It was just grand.'

'Eddie,' Barbara called from the car. 'Are you coming? It's freezing out here. Do you really want me to catch pneumonia on top of everything else?'

'Yes, Mum.' Eddie rolled his eyes and they both began to laugh, and in that moment, Liv had a feeling that the afternoon wasn't a complete disaster.

'We'll make up for it,' Liv said, putting her arms around his neck and hugging him close before he pulled away to the sounds of his mother's calls from outside.

'Well then, be seeing you tomorrow, I suppose,' Eddie mumbled as he fell into the passenger seat of his mother's car. 'Flannelly's around three, if you're up for it?'

He didn't even kiss her goodbye. That was Eddie, she supposed, not a man of the grand gesture when there was an audience, or at least, so she'd thought until she'd spotted her gorgeous ring.

'You've definitely got your gift?' Liv checked hoping that he wouldn't lose it on the way.

'Yep.' He patted the inside pocket of his jacket. 'Thanks for that,' he said and then she watched as he was chauffeur-driven home by his unfortunately still-sober mother.

Strangely, she realised, rather than feeling disappointed that Eddie hadn't proposed to her on Christmas Day, in some unfathomable way, she actually felt relieved. She told herself it was just that the time hadn't been right – it should feel more special, more intimate, more for just them. It felt as if a weight had been lifted off the house when Liv went back inside. Her mother had made a fresh pot of coffee and she was topping each of their cups up with Baileys and fresh cream. 'Leave those for now, love,' she said, steering Liv away from the sink. 'You've done enough for one day. Let's all dive into them later.'

'Your mother's right – you've done Trojan work since you came back down from Dublin. Time to sit for a while and enjoy the day.' Her father looked about ten years younger now that Barbara Quirke had left.

'Eddie certainly knows how to put away the booze, doesn't he?' Maya said later when they walked down to check on the lambs.

'You know very well that was as much Mum's fault as it was Eddie's; every time he turned sideways she was topping up his glass.' Liv stopped. 'And you know he's always a bit out of his depth when he comes here.'

'Actually, I thought he was a bit distracted,' Maya said softly.

'You could be right. He's not normally so quiet; I don't know what was up with him today.' The more Liv thought about it, the more she realised she'd never seen him as wrapped up in himself before. It was as if he'd tied himself up in knots over some worry too big to share; he seemed to be a million miles away even though he was just across the table from her.

'I'm glad to hear it.' Maya linked her arm in Liv's. 'It's enough to be putting up with his awful mother – I'm not sure anyone but you could possibly sign up to a future with all that complaining and not happily throttle her after the first week.'

'Ah, she's not that bad.' Liv stopped, because in spite of the disaster of dinner, she couldn't help but feel that bubble of excitement well up inside her again. 'If I tell you something, Maya, will you promise to keep it to yourself?'

'Of course.' Maya was the best at keeping secrets; even the KGB couldn't get information out of her if she promised to keep it under her hat.

'I think Eddie is going to propose to me this week,' she said, hardly able to keep the excitement out of her voice.

'Really? Well that's…' Maya stopped to look at her sister, suddenly serious. 'If that's what is going to make you happy, it's brilliant news.'

'Come on, at least pretend to be happy for me,' Liv said, even though, deep down, she hadn't expected much elation from Maya. She let out a high-pitched laugh that sounded nervous and odd even to her own ears.

'Of course I am, sis. It's great news. I'm probably just a little *Quirked* out!'

'Yes, well okay, I'll admit Barbara Quirke can be hard going – maybe it was just nerves today? You know, being surrounded by Latimers?'

'Maybe,' Maya said and then she pulled her sister close and hugged her hard. 'Oh, Liv, I'm delighted for you, really, if Eddie is who you've set your heart on, I'll be over the moon for you.'

'It's not that he's said anything as such,' Liv admitted.

'Oh?'

'No.' She shook her head. 'It's just that I found the ring…'

'The ring?'

'It's beautiful, with emeralds shaped like shooting stars. It's everything I could have wished for and more. Oh, Maya, it's like he has just known all along and…'

'Oh, Liv, emeralds and shooting stars?' Maya knew exactly what those things meant to her. Shooting stars had been her and Rachel's thing. Out here, in the darkness, it seemed that shooting stars marked some of the biggest moments of their lives together. Sometimes, Liv thought about that last time they'd been sitting out here late one summer evening. Rachel had finished every treatment she could possibly have and they knew it was only a matter of time. They'd bundled her up and lit a fire at the back of the house and they sat outside until the sky had grown black, like soft felt dotted with a million stars and then, as if performing a heavenly fireworks display for both of them, stars began to shoot across the sky. There were six in total. She'd thought about it so many times over the years. And sometimes, when she closed her eyes, she could feel her sister's thin hand in hers, the hope that was still in her eyes to the very end. It was a crushing blow when she'd died, but somehow, every time Liv thought about that night it gave her a feeling of peace.

'You see, he's not as self-absorbed as you've always assumed.' Liv was smiling; her happiness was a mixture of the memory of Rachel and the growing certainty of knowing that Eddie was finally going to propose.

'Ah, that's so lovely; perhaps I've misjudged him all this time,' she said.

'Honestly, Maya,' Liv said now, standing back, holding her sister's hands and looking into her eyes steadily. 'He's really much nicer than you think. Don't judge him on today's performance. When we're in Dublin we're quite content without his mother breathing down our necks. Sometimes, I think we're like an old married couple already.' She laughed at this because it was true: they'd slid into a routine years ago and a wedding would simply be making it official.

* * *

When Liv eventually arrived home, after waiting what seemed an age in the freezing cold for an empty bus, she pushed through the flat, flopped into bed and fell into a deep sleep that lasted until after six o'clock that evening. When she woke, darkness painted her bedroom window; the silence felt as if she might be the only person still left in Dublin, never mind on her own in her little flat. Hunger woke her in the end and she padded back through to the kitchen, noticing for the first time that Eddie had left the place looking like a tip again. Honestly, Liv could never get over the fact that anyone could just discard clothes and leave them where they landed. She gathered them up and plopped them into the laundry basket. She might as well put on a wash.

Suddenly, it never felt less like Christmas Day and Liv felt a trembling sadness descend on her. Here she was washing Eddie's socks when she should have been swept off her feet in a romantic proposal and wearing the ring that meant so much more to her than maybe even Eddie could possibly know. She took a deep breath. She was being silly; she was just tired and overwrought after the accident and the long shift; and seeing the flat like this, well, it felt a little like the final straw in her exhaustion.

After she made beans on toast and a pot of tea she sat down with her iPad at the little kitchen counter and called her mother on Zoom. 'Hi, Mum. Is the party over already?'

'No, not at all,' her mother said – she was in the big old farmhouse kitchen and it looked as if she was waiting for the kettle to boil. 'Our guests have gone home, but we're all settling down to a lovely cup of tea and then Maya and your dad are going to go and take a look at the lambs.'

'Hi, sis.' Maya stuck her head in over her mother's shoulder. She looked beautiful as usual, relaxed and happy and, for a terrible moment, Liv felt as if she might cry because she missed being at home with them so much. 'Thank goodness you've finished for the day. Can you come home now?'

'Nope, I'm afraid not. I've never seen the hospital busier, I can't just go and abandon them.'

'Gosh, I don't know how you do it, honestly,' Maya said. True enough – Maya almost fainted at the sight of blood.

'Well, I couldn't be a solicitor if you paid me, so there you go.' That was also true – Liv didn't have enough fight in her to win an argument with the cat, never mind represent someone else in a courtroom. 'How was Barbara?' For some reason, asking about Eddie was like admitting that he hadn't picked up the phone to so much as wish her a happy Christmas.

'The usual,' Maya said about to go off on a long reel about Eddie's mother's current list of complaints.

'Ah now, she was very well behaved.' Her mother cut her off, but Liv noticed the sharp dig she gave Maya with her elbow. 'And as for Eddie, I think he had a grand old time. There's peace in him; he just helps himself and you don't have to worry about him,' her mother said kindly.

'Yes, show him the drinks cabinet and he really knows how to help himself.' Maya rolled her eyes.

'So, that's enough about down here. What's going on there now?' Her mother peered closer to her phone.

'Oh, I just came home to eat and sleep. I'm exhausted; honestly, I could sleep for Ireland.' Liv shrugged. No point telling them that she had beans on toast for her Christmas dinner since she'd hardly the energy to open the fridge door after tidying up the mess Eddie left in his wake.

'And will Eddie not go back and keep you company?' her father asked from somewhere beyond the camera.

'Ah no, Dad, there's no point. I'm only coming home to sleep. He's better off down there spending Christmas with his mother.' It would be a lonely time for Barbara if her only son didn't show up for the holidays. 'And anyway, with a bit of luck, I'll be down in

Ballycove in a day or two and then we can have our own, low-key Christmas. How does that sound?'

'As long as we're not inviting that awful Barbara Quirke again,' her father mumbled, but he was too close to the camera for Liv to miss it.

'So now, we'll be sending you on pictures of the lambs,' her mother said loudly and darted a reprimanding glance towards where Liv assumed her father was standing. 'So you can help us think up names for them, okay?'

'Lovely.'

Liv shivered when she ended the call and pulled her dressing gown tight about her. The flat was cold, although she'd turned the heat on when she came home from the hospital; Liv had a feeling that it had more to do with the emptiness of the place than with the actual temperature. It had felt like this after Rachel died. An emptiness that she couldn't sweep or dust or scrub out of the fabric of the place. Of course, she knew then it was coming from deep within her own heart, but now, today, was it just because she felt so lonely knowing that Christmas was going on for her family in Ballycove without her?

She turned the heating up to full blast. She hadn't put on a real fire here in years, not since Eddie had moved in probably. Funny, but it was the open fireplace that had been the clincher on her and Rachel buying the place at the time. There were other flats in much more modern buildings at a much lower cost, but when they had thought about sitting before the open fire on long lazy weekends, there really hadn't been much of a choice.

She closed her eyes now, a stream of memories flowing past her. Each of them running into the other. She remembered when they had received a generous legacy in their Great Aunt Sabina's will. It was enough to put a really good down payment on this flat. It felt as if they had trawled through endless rounds of estate agents, looked at every apartment in the city and then finally, Rachel had found this place. A small robin's nest at the top of an Edwardian baroque house, not on one of the more sought-after squares, but the area was nice enough – a side street that fed easily on either end into busy traffic. The city was walking distance one way, the route to the motorway easily driven the other. It had been her home for more than ten years; tiny, filled with memories and over the last couple of years, accommodating Eddie and his growing collection of ridiculous trainers and hair products.

It was funny, but even now, Eddie still felt like a guest. He'd never think of fixing a leaking tap or going to IKEA with her to pick out a flat-pack they could assemble together. It was very much her flat as far as Eddie was concerned. He was still a visitor. If no longer sleeping on her couch, neither was he making any contribution towards the mortgage in paying rent. She had a feeling he wouldn't be very handy with DIY jobs, not even at home with Barbara. The Quirkes were the sort of people who got a man in to do the work – whether that be a plumber, a painter or someone to clean their windows – not that they had that many to clean.

It didn't do her any good to go comparing. The Quirkes and the Latimers were very different families; there was nothing wrong with that. Liv took out her phone. She called Eddie's number and this time, to her relief, he answered.

'Gosh,' she said jokingly, 'I thought you were ghosting me.'

'Humph, if anyone was avoiding anyone, I would have thought

it was the other way round.' He sounded grumpy, maybe a little drunk from the day at her parents' house.

'Happy Christmas, Eddie.' Time to start again. 'Did you get my gift for you?' She'd left it at the farmhouse the last time she was home, to make sure he didn't manage to come across it accidentally when he was cleaning the flat – although, deep down and looking about the place now, she had a feeling that nothing was less likely.

'Um, yeah, Maya handed it to me,' he said neutrally.

'And?' She thought he'd be over the moon. It had cost her an absolute packet and not an inconsiderable amount of planning and twisting of arms on Pete's part.

'Oh sure, thanks. It's great, yeah,' he said, and then she wondered if he was doing something on his phone while she was talking to him. 'Sorry,' he said.

'Sorry?'

'Well, your gift. I have it here, in the car…'

'In the car?' Liv repeated. Surely he hadn't left a ring worth a couple of thousand euros sitting up on the dashboard of his car?

'Yeah, well, it's just – if I'd known that you'd be still there…' he said.

'Perhaps it's for luck.' She couldn't imagine anything less romantic than opening it up here alone over the remains of her beans on toast Christmas Day lunch and being on the receiving end of a hurried, half-baked proposal from Eddie who sounded as if he was too steamed to actually remember any of it the following day.

'It's teatime, Eddie?' Barbara Quirke had a long habit of trying to cut off their conversations if she could.

'Well, I'd better be going. Mum's soaps are starting on the TV here, so you know…' He managed to sound slightly put out that she'd rung him.

'Okay, I just really rang to wish you a happy Christmas, see how you got on for the day.'

'Eddie.' Barbara sounded irritated in the background.

'Yeah, it was grand. The dinner was good. Your mum knows how to keep the glasses filled; sure, what more do you want on Christmas Day?' he said. 'Better be going now.' And then she was left holding her phone with only the silence of his abrupt call ending for company.

6

'So Pete has finally seen through his arm candy?' Maya asked as she tugged a huge scarf about her neck. She'd let the dogs off. All three ran excitedly in circles around the car, waiting for the sisters to wrap up against the cutting north-westerly wind. Once on the beach, they could take off and run for miles before turning back to repeat the same lap again and again until finally wearing themselves out. It was a perfect day for it. This stretch of beach was empty. The tide was out and although the temperatures were low, there was no breeze; the air had an icy stillness to it that quietened the usual roar of the waves.

'Well, apparently, she's been fooling around behind his back, so...' Liv said. It wasn't a secret, well not from Maya at any rate.

'Does he know who she was seeing?'

'I don't know. I mean, I don't think he does. From the way he spoke about it, I'm not sure there was anyone serious. It was just a fling, but...'

'Who needs that in their life? Right?'

'Absolutely.' It was the one thing Liv couldn't imagine

having to put up with, but she was lucky with Eddie that way; all he ever did was go to work or meet up with his mates. 'It'll be awkward though, what with the business and her living in his apartment and everything.'

'I'm sure Pete will extricate himself from it fairly quickly.' Maya smiled.

'What?'

'Well, they weren't exactly a match made in heaven.' Maya shook her head. 'I was just surprised that he'd made that sort of commitment with her to begin with. Everyone knows he'd drop her in a second if you needed so much as a fresh cup of tea.' She stopped then.

'Ah, don't say that.' Pete was one of her best friends; she couldn't bear it if that friendship was somehow standing in the way of his happiness.

'Don't beat yourself up about it, sis. He deserves much better…' Maya stopped now, lowered her voice; she'd never been one to gossip. 'And Anya… well, Anya will probably always drift from one man to the next. Anya will always make sure she's taken care of.'

'Ugh.' Liv shivered, although she was too wrapped up to feel the cold. 'Do you really think she's like that?'

'Well, when you told me I wasn't exactly surprised.' Maya didn't appear to take any pleasure in admitting it.

'I'm sure you're wrong. I'm sure she's just fallen for someone else. That's love, isn't it? Maybe Pete wasn't the one for her, but maybe she's met someone else who is.'

'You really refuse to see anything but the good in anyone, don't you?' Maya said almost with pity in her eyes.

'No, not at all. Well, maybe. I thought Pete was utterly

crazy about her.' Liv thought about them together. Actually, although she hated to admit it, in the beginning, she'd almost been a little jealous of the way he seemed to adore every syllable that slipped from those perfectly pouting lips. By comparison, she and Eddie felt like old socks: they went together, sure, but there was never any great sparkle about them. Certainly, there had never been that adoring puppy phase where he'd looked at her as if she was the best thing since ripe bananas. 'It just seems like such a shame; I can't imagine why she'd want to go seeing someone behind his back.'

'He's too bloody nice, that's why. Now stop thinking about it. Pete would never want to spoil your holiday with feeling sorry for him – you should know that better than anyone.' Maya shook her head and of course, Liv knew – as usual – her sister was spot on.

'You're right, of course you're right,' Liv said. She'd call him later – before she met up with Eddie in Flannelly's; maybe she'd talk him into coming out to the pub with them too.

The beach was lovely. Here the fresh morning snow iced along the edge of the village but didn't manage to slip onto the sand. The two sisters walked at a smart pace, and it felt good to breathe in the fresh sea air, cold and biting against her face, but reviving too after the day before when Liv felt as if she'd eaten too much and spent her day waiting for it to start, which it eventually did only after she watched Barbara Quirke's car drive out the farm gates.

'Is it just me or does the notion of having to go into Flannelly's pub on such a lovely day just seem all wrong?'

Liv said as they turned back after walking to the end of the beach.

'No, I wouldn't fancy it either,' Maya said, and of course, Liv knew that her sister would spend the rest of the evening reading one of the hardback books she'd stockpiled for the Christmas break next to her favourite chair in the cosy sitting room at home.

'I sort of envy you being able to just suit yourself today,' Liv said a little regretfully.

'You could do the same. I mean, you hardly ever get home these days and who do you want to meet up with in Flannelly's anyway? It's just going to be Eddie's cronies and, let's face it, not much ever changes with any of them.'

'Hmm.' The problem was, if she left it too late, Eddie would be settled in with his buddies and there'd be no leaving until closing time. At least, if she got down before dinner, she'd be able to talk him into some food and there was a very slim chance she might get him to go for a walk around the village with her too. In her mind's eye, she imagined him down on bended knee in the village square when all was silent, beneath the huge Christmas tree – by the looks of the sky at the moment, they might even have fresh snowfall.

'Liv.' Maya was biting her lower lip in that way she always had when they were younger and she was trying hard to keep a secret from her older sister. And it dawned on Liv that there had been a reason Maya was so adamant on them fitting in this time alone together today. She had something she needed to tell her.

'What?' Liv had a feeling that whatever Maya was going to say, she wouldn't like it. 'Is it Eddie?' She could do without

Maya trying to prod and poke at the news that he was finally going to propose to her.

'No.' Maya looked out towards the sea; it seemed as clean and sparkling today as Liv had ever seen it. 'It's Dad.' She shook her head. 'Look they don't want to worry you, but it didn't seem fair. He wanted you to have a nice Christmas without anything hanging over you, but I know that it makes a difference. I know you'd never forgive me if anything happened…'

'Oh, God.' Liv felt her chest constrict. 'You're scaring me, Maya; just say it, whatever it is.'

'You know he's been on cholesterol and blood pressure tablets?'

'Yeah, but I thought everything was under control?'

'We all did, but two weeks ago, he woke with a terrible pain in his chest – of course, being Dad, he didn't tell anyone. He just drove himself to the doctor and she – you know Lucy Nolan took over at the surgery last year?' Maya nodded her approval, because old Dr O'Shea would have probably given him a packet of indigestion tablets and sent him on his way. Lucy Nolan was a different breed. They were lucky to have her, even if the likes of Barbara Quirke wanted to dream up things to moan about. If Barbara won the lottery, she would still moan, even if the winning ticket was a gift. 'Anyway, she packed him off to hospital straight away and they confirmed that he wasn't having a heart attack, at least, but he's been booked in for an angiogram as soon as the Christmas break is over.'

'I can't believe it. He seems so…' Liv shook her head. Perhaps if she could be cross with her parents for keeping it from her it might quell the terror she felt at the thought of anything happening to either of them. But it was no good. How could she be cross with them, when all they wanted was to have a happy Christmas with her? After all, she knew, they worried about her as much as they worried about anything. Since Rachel died, they never really stopped worrying about her – it was unnecessary. She had managed to get her life back together again. It wasn't the same, but she knew she was lucky.

She needed to say something. Maya was waiting for her to say something; anything. 'Thank you, for telling me. I mean it – you're right, at least this gives me the chance to choose where I'm going to spend my time this Christmas and it's definitely not going to be sitting in Flannelly's pub nursing an orange juice and listening to the same stories I heard last year.' She put her arm around Maya. It wasn't fair; her sister had carried this worry about with her for the last two weeks. Liv decided she would share the load, whatever that meant in supporting her family going forward. She was only sorry now that she'd invited the Quirkes to the farmhouse the previous day. What a waste of a perfectly good Christmas Day now that this news reminded her how precious each one was for them as a family.

*

It seemed to Liv that everything about Ballycove was just a little more Christmassy this year. Of course, it was the snow. It was such a treat to have it still on the ground as they walked back through the village on the way home. The square was beautifully decorated, with golden lights hanging on the bare branches of every tree and the huge fir tree at the centre decked out in its seasonal finest. As they walked the narrow country road to the farm, Liv heard the hunt horn being sounded somewhere across the fields, so they fastened the dogs' leads on their collars; the last thing the local hunt needed was three working sheepdogs joining their beagles.

It was probably her favourite day of the year – St Stephen's Day, or Boxing Day. It was the one day when, if she wasn't at work, there was absolutely no pressure. She and Maya normally went for a very long walk and then, when they returned to the farmhouse, it was leftovers from the previous day for dinner, which her dad always said were nicer on the second day and Liv quietly agreed with him. Then, they'd settle down in the sitting room, her dad snoring before the TV, her mother knitting or channel-hopping and Maya and Liv snuggled up with a book each for the night.

She rang Pete as soon as they got back to the farmhouse and he was his usual chipper self.

'Everything is fine,' he said breezily. It was typical Pete – he wouldn't want to make a fuss or have a drama all about him. It occurred to Liv that his personality was the complete opposite of Barbara Quirke's. As long as she'd known him, he'd never been the one in need of any sort of help or support. He'd given freely over the years, whether it was taking turns with her at Rachel's bedside or hauling heavy furniture up the three flights of stairs to her flat or picking her up from town because her shopping bags were heavy and it started to rain.

'Are you sure you're all right?' Liv asked, double, triple checking, but then, she realised, perhaps it was different for men; after all, Pete didn't have a biological clock ticking inside him so loudly he felt as if he was counting down the final minutes to an atomic bomb. For Pete it was just a relationship that didn't work out; if the shoe was on the other foot, for Liv it would be the end of the world, or at least that's what she thought it would be, so she cleared the awful idea from her mind quickly.

'Sure, everything is fine. It had run its course; it was time to move on for both of us, obviously. It's just a little depressing that Anya would do something like that behind my back, but I think it says more about her and, really, why I was having doubts about her to begin with.'

'I'm just glad that you're okay, but if there's anything I can do, you just need to let me know, okay?' Liv said, and she knew she had to stop worrying about him.

'Sure,' he said. 'We'll meet up for coffee when you get back?' he said but she had a feeling that he was only pacifying her; otherwise, he knew only too well.

She put the phone down, thinking she'd far prefer to go for coffee with Pete than have to show up at Flannelly's pub. She thought about it now and it was bloody miserable. She actually dreaded the journey down, the too-loud music and the smell of all-day drinking, and for what? To make sure that Eddie got home in one piece. She'd much prefer to be at home in her snuggly pyjamas and padding off to bed when it suited her. She was glad that she'd decided against going earlier now.

It was nine-thirty when the call came.

'Liv, where are you?' It was Eddie. To be fair, she'd have thought he'd be completely hammered by now, and she didn't want to be proposed to when he was too drunk to ask properly. It was funny, but hearing about her father had pushed her priorities around. Now being proposed to came a distinct second after spending time with her dad. She'd sent Eddie a couple of texts over the course of the evening to make up for not going to the pub, but he hadn't replied. It would have been too noisy in the bar to hear the notifications probably.

'Didn't you get my messages?' she asked.

'But I thought you were going to turn up later?' He sounded disappointed. Well, she supposed, at least it was nice that he missed her. 'And it's nearly closing time now,' he said.

'I know. Hang on, I'll drive down and you can buy me a glass of lemonade before they call time.' She looked across at her parents, both snoozing contentedly. She shivered at the idea of having to leave the cosy sitting room and head out into the freezing air. God, she'd love to snuggle up here for the night, but this might be the moment – she couldn't not turn up if Eddie was going to propose to her in the snow, could she? 'It'll take me a few minutes.' It took ten minutes to shrug out of her pyjamas and brush a little blusher on her cheeks and then she was driving her dad's jeep into the village. The snow really had begun to pack up now. A car would be useless at getting out onto the main road, which had a steep hill; it was sheer enough to send her backwards if the roads were any way icy.

Eddie was waiting at the front door of the pub when she arrived. No lemonade so, it looked as if she'd missed closing time. For a moment, she thought there was something different about him, something unfamiliar, as if she'd missed a step and somehow the universe had let her off on the wrong stop. He dropped the remains of his cigarette to the ground and mashed it into a dirty black mark on the snow.

'I've been waiting for you.' He gave her that lopsided grin that made her heart flip over with love for him. 'What happened to you?' he asked as he hopped into the jeep next to her. 'It's bloody freezing. What took you so long?'

'Nothing, I just got held up.' There was no point telling Eddie about the angiogram – he'd probably tell her she was worrying over nothing and would have forgotten it by the morning. She drove towards his mother's house, pulling up at the gate and switching off the engine, presuming he was going to ask her in – had he planned on proposing to her today? She checked the rear-view mirror; maybe he'd ask her now, or in his mother's house? Did she want to be proposed to in Barbara Quirke's gingham kitchen or faded, but still strangely overwhelming chintz sitting room surrounded by china figurines?

'Right, well, the big match is on tomorrow, usual time, so I suppose, I'll see you then,' he said getting out of the car and obviously completely oblivious to her racing thoughts.

'Hey.' She leant over for a goodnight kiss.

'Hey, yourself,' he said kissing her while he stood on the footpath at the open jeep window. Even here, outside his mother's front door, he could elicit desire in her with a drunken kiss. Perhaps, it was because they couldn't just fall into bed together, but still, it was nice. 'I've got to dash. I've been standing out there in the freezing cold; if I don't get to the toilet quick, it's not going to be good…' he said pushing open the front gate of his mother's house and disappearing inside before she had a chance to say goodnight.

Driving back to the farm, Liv was overcome by that familiar loneliness that had the ability to smash into her as if it was just holding out behind the next invisible corner. It had been like this for the last decade: startling moments of desolate wretchedness, creeping up on her and pushing tears into her eyes from somewhere deep within her. She missed Rachel so much. How on earth could she call her life completely sorted when it still felt as if there was this gaping wound right in the middle of it?

* * *

It was a lie. Of course it was a lie. Well, it was a fib, at any rate. Liv wasn't okay. She was lonely and miserable here in Dublin on her own. On Christmas night, when she should have been dreaming of her wedding to Eddie, she'd slept badly, tossing and turning, thinking about the accident and Finn O'Connell lying in ICU and the impossibly beautiful Estelle and the fact that she'd felt such a strong connection to him just before it had happened. She was meant to be getting engaged for heaven's sake – what on earth was wrong with her? Like most things that hit you when you're overtired at three o'clock in the morning, it was all out of proportion.

There was no such thing as love at first sight. Look at her and Eddie. They'd known each other for years and there hadn't been any fireworks, just a gentle easing in, a rubbing along to the point that they arrived where they were now. So, Liv had tried to focus on that instead. She listed off the reasons that she had to consider herself lucky. She thought about that beautiful ring, imagining it on her finger and then knowing that even though Eddie would have picked up the emeralds at cost, it still would have taken a lot of work and effort to fashion it out properly. She smiled in the darkness, seeing it in her mind's eye. It was delicate and intricate and cold when she slipped it on her finger, but it fitted perfectly and it touched her beyond belief that he'd somehow managed to get her size right, although she'd never had a piece of jewellery for that finger to measure it against.

It was no good. In the end, she got out of bed. It was officially St Stephen's Day and at five o'clock in the morning, she'd already spent an hour pacing about the flat. She looked at the pile of hardbacks she'd bought and wrapped for Maya for the holidays. She could open one – Maya certainly wouldn't mind – but she knew she couldn't settle to reading. She couldn't settle into anything, because she should be at home in Ballycove, with her family. And then, she realised that there was only one other place she could go that would maybe make her feel a little better.

Outside the morning was cold and dark. Soft flakes of snow drifted across the city streets. She'd pulled on her hiking boots, folded her uniform into a large shopper and headed out into the deserted streets. It was funny, but somehow, out here, she felt less lonely. The roads were completely empty, all of the buildings closed up, flats in darkness and even the green man on the traffic lights, it seemed, had turned in for the night.

The hospital, however, was not deserted. Liv felt that familiar blast of warm air cascade down on her as she walked through the main doors. She wasn't on shift for another two hours, although, probably, they wouldn't turn her away if she arrived early. Instead of walking towards A&E she made her way up the stairs and padded along the endless, noiseless corridors until she came to the intensive care unit. At the nurses' station she spotted a nurse she remembered from a training event earlier in the year: Morgan. She waved at him and he buzzed her through.

'Hey,' he said glancing at his watch and then taking in her casual clothes. 'For a minute I thought it was later than I realised and you were coming on shift.' He looked disappointed. It was a long night here, with constant obs and form-filling. These patients would not be pressing buzzers for help with their reading lights, nor would they need to be transferred for x-rays or to other wards.

'No. I'm just looking in on Finn.'

'Is he a friend of yours?' Morgan asked, obviously a little more relaxed about the visiting rules than some of his colleagues.

'Yes,' she said. It was a white lie as much to save Morgan getting into trouble as it was to make things easier for herself. 'Any change?'

'He hasn't come round yet, if that's what you're hoping for, but he's stable and his vitals are definitely stronger. You can take a look at his chart; I'm just finished filling it in for the night.' He handed it to her and she brought it across to Finn's bedside.

Liv sat there in the broken silence of the ward for the next hour, somehow content. All Finn O'Connell had to do was open his eyes, and although she knew that was a big order, she had a feeling that he was strong – his obs confirmed that much. Liv closed her eyes, remembered standing opposite him at the traffic lights before the accident. He was tall and broad, but it was more than that. There was a sort of vitality to him that struck her and that was it, wasn't it? He seemed to be so very much alive compared to every other grey face around them.

Then again, if he had Estelle to go home to (and perhaps a

lover called M on the side), maybe there was a very good reason for him looking like he had lots to live for, she reminded herself. She smiled then, because, she supposed, he was probably what her mother would have called a lovable rogue. Perhaps he was a girl-in-every-port sort of guy. He was certainly good-looking enough to get away with it.

Maybe the other reason she liked sitting here with him was because if she closed her eyes, she could almost pretend that the clock had turned back the years and she was still sitting next to Rachel. She felt a small tear escape her, but it didn't matter here, there was no-one to see. She reached out, her eyes still closed, imagining Rachel lying there, and she took Finn's hand in hers. Although it was big and strong, at the same time, it felt so very vulnerable. She felt a small smile draw up her lips, in spite of her tears. She had been so happy sitting next to Rachel, even though her sister was dying. When she left her side, God knows, she cried bucketloads, but every second she had next to her had been so precious.

'Hey,' the voice was hoarse, pulling her back from her dream. 'Hey,' he said again.

'Huh?' Her eyes flew open. 'Oh, my God.' She was staring at Finn O'Connell, not her darling twin sister and he was smiling at her, as if he'd just woken from a very pleasant dream. 'You're awake,' and then she realised she'd been holding his hand – he must think she was a complete idiot. 'I'm so sorry, let me get the nurse.' She pulled back from him, leaving his hand lying empty on the bed cover.

'Wait…' he whispered. 'What happened? How did I…' He cleared his throat a little. 'Where am I?' he asked, obviously too diplomatic to ask what on earth a complete stranger was doing sitting by his bed, mauling his hand and smiling like a demented pigeon with her eyes closed.

'You're okay.' She thought she might explode with embarrassment. 'You were in an accident. I was standing next to you, just outside the hospital, and then the ambulance brought you in and you've been…' She stopped, knowing she shouldn't say too much in case the doctors suspected any memory damage. 'Hang on, I'll just get Morgan.'

'Morgan?' he said hoarsely, as if the name should mean something.

'Sorry, Morgan is your nurse,' she said, standing now, flustered in a way that she shouldn't be if this was just a patient on her rounds. 'You're really doing fine; I've taken a look at your chart. You've been unconscious since it happened, so it was just a waiting game. I'm sure they'll be throwing you out of here before you know it.' She managed to smile then, because it was impossible not to. Seeing him awake was not only the most cheery thing that had happened to her all Christmas, it was probably the only jolly thing to have happened.

She would need to start her shift in A&E by the time Morgan had called a doctor to examine Finn and had checked his vitals once more.

'You look good,' Morgan said appraisingly.

'Well, perhaps I can thank this one for getting me in here.'

'Liv.' She supplied her name; it was the least she could do after all. 'Anyway, I'd better get to work. I have Estelle's phone number, if you'd like me to ring her and let her know that you're awake,' she said backing away from the bed.

'Estelle?' He said the name as if it amused him. 'Ah no, it's fine. There's no rush.' And then he looked at her and, for a moment, it seemed there was something more to say, but then he smiled and shook his head as if thinking better of it.

'Well, I'm glad you're awake, at least.' She managed to break the standstill in the end. 'I really am… Good luck, so, I suppose.' His eyes were beginning to close now and she knew he would probably drift in and out of sleep for a little while yet.

'Liv,' he said as she was backing away from his bedside, a small amused smile drawing up his lips.

'Yes?' she said a little too eagerly, really not wanting to go, just yet.

'I'll see you later, so…' He was drowsy again, drifting back to sleep, but that smile flickering about his face in a way that seemed almost like a flame dying on a candle made Liv think her heart would break if he didn't make it out of here, even if it was to go back to the beautiful Estelle or the mysterious M.

7

Early morning, snow drifting in across the hills, and Liv was standing in the barn with her dad, large mugs of tea in their hands with the unmistakable glow of happiness in her belly. Eight more lambs born overnight. They were here when her father checked on them at five o'clock in the morning.

'I think it could be a bumper year.' Her father smiled in that absent way she remembered from her childhood as if his thoughts were already running back to previous seasons and he was savouring every memory.

'How have you been, Dad, really?' she asked him while they leant over the gate admiring the newborns.

'Ah, sure I've been grand, just grand. Who could complain when I'm blessed to be among all my favourite girls for Christmas.' He nodded towards the sheep, but she knew he meant her mother and his two daughters.

'Are you?'

'Of course,' he said sipping his tea. So, she decided two could play at that game and she looked across the pen, trying not to let her worry about him show across the furrows in her brow. 'Why do you ask?'

'No reason.'

'Do I look as if I'm not well?' he was watching her now. The world of medicine, beyond the birthing of lambs and calves had never held any great interest for her father.

'Of course you look well; as a matter of fact, you've never looked better.' But the thing was, now that she knew about his recent heart scare, she was beginning to notice things. There was nothing big, but it was little things that she hadn't spotted before. He'd shrunk, his eyes had lightened and there was no denying the fact that when he walked, it was more slowly than before.

'Well, that's good so.' He sounded relieved. No harm in that. Liv knew believing you were well was half the secret to being healthy. 'Sure, who has time to be anything but healthy with lambs on the way and the cottage to ready for another writer?'

'Oh?' Liv knew he was talking about the little house that her parents had inherited from her mother's aunt. It was perched high above the sea on the way into Ballycove and her father rented it out each year to tourists. 'Another writer?'

'Aye, well you know the last one, Dan, he only hit the bestsellers list and now it seems we're inundated with would-be authors knocking down the door to spend a week or two writing their masterpieces with a curlew's view of the Atlantic.' Dan had arrived in the worst of weather, written a hugely successful book and last Liv heard he was getting married to Lucy, the local GP.

'But you haven't let the cottage out for Christmas, have you?'

'Of course, the fella as good as begged me for it.' Her father shook his head.

'Well, that seems like a lot to take on, especially in the middle of lambing season. When does he arrive?'

'First thing tomorrow, but he'll be no bother. Everything is already organised. Your mother has the place spick and span with a few provisions in the fridge and I dropped down enough turf and firelighters to keep him warm for a month if he fancies staying any longer.'

'Well, in that case, I'll go down and meet him; let him in and show him about the cottage.' Not that she was sure there was a lot of showing about, but the water was finicky at the best of times and it was the least she could do to help out. 'Will you come along to the match, later?' she asked. It was an annual event, current players on the Ballycove Gaelic team took on anyone from previous teams who was brave enough and hopefully fit enough to tog out and turn up for the game. It was always fun and takings on the gate went to a local good cause each year.

'Ah, I think I'll give it a miss this year. It won't be the same indoors.' He looked out through the small pane of glass that served as the only window in the shed. The snow was falling thick and fast outside now.

*

He was right. The local community hall had been cleared out and the usual game of Gaelic had to be played as soccer this year, with five-a-side teams turning out for three shorter sessions. Maya had come along since her firm was sponsoring the game. Eddie had been sent off for fouling another player in the first fifteen minutes, which probably suited him because he was already well out of puff. It was unlikely he'd have made it to the end anyway.

'I swear, all of those young fellas are working out,' he panted.

'Go on, that makes you sound as if you're as old as the church clock.' Maya shoved him in the ribs.

'Well, I'm not, but I hardly have the time or the money to join a fancy gym when I'm trying to keep body and soul together in the city.' He huffed and Liv wished he hadn't because it was always a sore point with Maya, the fact that on the one hand everyone heard how successful he was, while on the other he never seemed to have enough money to pay his bills. Maya never called him a freeloader, but that was because she didn't want to upset Liv.

'Oh, there's Anya,' Liv said spotting the willowy blonde standing at the door across from them.

'Hmm, wonder what she's doing here?' Maya said, because there was none of her old gang about. They were much more likely to be recovering from yesterday's hunt. 'She looks a bit lost; I don't ever remember any of her old cronies turning up for the charity match before...' She looked at Eddie who might have some idea of who'd be togging out for the day.

'How would I bloody know?' he grunted before flopping back on the bench.

'Hey,' Liv said when Anya came over and stood next to them. She had no intention of falling out with anyone

– Ballycove was much too small for that. Even though Pete was her friend, maybe her best friend, apart from Maya, it didn't do any harm to say hello.

'Hey, I wasn't sure if I'd be welcome here today.' There was something far more fragile about her than Liv had ever noticed before.

'Public event, everyone's welcome,' Maya said, and she pushed over to make room for her along the bench seat.

'Hullo,' Eddie said through gritted teeth; he had inherited his mother's sense of awkwardness around situations that needed defusing rather than further aggravation.

'Hi, Eddie, have you finished playing already?' Anya asked, which was nice, because Eddie was hardly the star player of the day.

'Yeah, well, they brought out some of us more experienced players to get things going; otherwise some of those yobs would just hand the game over to the youngsters.' He straightened up, managing to look embarrassed and pleased all at once.

'Sorry I missed that,' Anya said kindly. 'I just thought I'd take a look-in, you know. There's not a lot else happening in the village today.' Her eyes were pinned on Eddie – well, he didn't look anything like his usual self, doubled over and trying to catch his breath after his spurt in the soccer game.

'We're all going to Flannelly's afterwards, if you fancy coming along,' Eddie volunteered before sauntering off to sit on the sidelines in the hope of being brought on to play again.

'Were you out with the hunt yesterday?' Maya asked, keeping her eyes on the game at the same time.

'No. I gave it a miss – not really in the form this Christmas, you know?' Anya smiled a little apprehensively then: 'Actually, I thought I'd go cabin crazy if I didn't meet anyone I knew here today.'

'It's Ballycove; you're always going to meet people you know,' Liv said, although Anya hadn't really lived here since primary school. After that she'd been sent to boarding school so most of her friends were spread across the county and probably the country. Her family had been really well off, well, until the whole country crashed and they lost everything so suddenly, Anya had to go out and work for a living, probably not something she'd ever planned on.

'You know what I mean.' Anya lowered her voice.

'Yes, I'm sorry about you and Pete,' Liv said. They were sitting next to each other now Eddie had moved. 'None of us were expecting that; you seemed to be so perfect together.'

'Really, it's probably been over between us for a while. I just didn't want to admit it, I suppose; we've so much tied up together…'

'The coffee shop?'

'Yeah, and the apartment…' Anya said, talking about Pete's super-plush apartment that overlooked Dublin Bay.

'Gosh, yes, where will you stay when you go back?' Liv asked and almost regretted it immediately.

'I'm really not sure,' Anya said and there was an uncomfortable moment when Liv wondered if she should offer her couch, but unlike with Eddie, Anya couldn't stay forever and she was fairly sure she wouldn't want her to. They really weren't that close; actually, today was the first time Anya had ever really sought her out. They were chalk and cheese – nothing in common beyond Pete, and now that thread too had been ravelled away.

'I'm sure something will work out and in the meantime, can't you always stay over with some of your friends?' Maya cut in and Liv was grateful to her sister for deflecting the conversation from that awkward unasked question.

For the first time, in Liv's memory at least, the retired players won the match. It was up to Maya to present the prizes and there was lots of joking and cheering and, in the end, they'd all trooped to the pub and tucked into sausage rolls and sandwiches put on by the sponsors.

'So Pete's keeping a low profile?' Anya asked Liv as they waited by the bar.

'Yeah, he's staying with his family; I think he's set on a quiet Christmas this year.'

'So, you've spoken to him?'

'Of course, I speak to him all the time – you know that.'

'And he didn't say anything about…' Anya stopped.

'You know Pete, loyal to the end; of course he didn't say anything. We've been friends a long time and I've never heard him say a bad word about anyone,' Liv said softly, because regardless of what had happened between them, Ballycove was too small to go falling out with people – Barbara Quirke had done enough of that for everyone.

Later, when Eddie joined them, Liv asked if he'd checked in on Pete, just to say hello, make sure all was well; after all, if he did need to talk to someone, maybe he'd prefer to talk to a bloke rather than to Liv.

'Eh?' He looked at her blankly between popping cocktail sausages into his mouth. 'Course I didn't call into him. What would I do that for? Don't we always run into him in the pub?'

'Yes, but things are different this year. He might need a mate to check in, you know; have a chat, man to man, just let him know that people are thinking of him.'

'Come on, Liv, what do you think we are – Brokeback Mountain buddies?'

'No, of course not, but I mean, what if I broke things off with you and no-one bothered to check if you were all right? You're his friend.'

'Well, that's not likely to happen is it?' He shook his head and for a moment, she wondered, which bit wasn't likely to happen, because going on the amount of quality time they'd spent together over the holidays, she had to admit, even though he had made her the perfect engagement ring, it felt as if he wouldn't be one bit gutted if she broke off their relationship in the morning. 'I mean, if any of us is more likely to move on, it's not going to be you, is it?' He made a face. She hoped it was a badly made joke.

'Okay, very funny,' she said, because of course, he always played this card. He'd said from the very beginning that there was no tying Eddie Quirke down – and even though they were like an old married couple that he'd never walk up the aisle. Well, it looked like she knew different now. 'Oh, Eddie, you're impossible,' she said leaning over and kissing him. She really did love him, even if he drove her mad sometimes with all his teasing.

'What?' he said, feigning complete innocence.

'I think I'll go home now,' Maya said. She'd been drinking white lemonade all evening, keeping a clear head for the following day. She'd told Liv she planned to go into the office and sort out some files that were hanging on since before the holidays. 'Mind if I leave you here?' She touched Liv's arm.

'No, not at all. Take the jeep. You'll walk me home in a little while, won't you, Eddie?'

'Huh? Yeah, sure, I suppose so...' he said looking around. The walk would do them both good; it would give them a chance to be alone together for the first time since they got back to Ballycove.

By teatime, most of the players and supporters had emptied out of the bar. It was dark outside and Anya had drifted away when someone had offered her a lift home.

'Come on,' Liv said, taking Eddie's hand. 'You can walk me home and come back down and meet your buddies later.'

'Fine,' he said. Eddie liked to pace himself for big drinking occasions like today. They walked back towards the village square and she was right, it was absolutely perfect. Thick fresh snow had fallen and piled up in corners. The lights from the trees seemed to sparkle extra brightly and the night sky had cleared over to a silky black so the moon seemed to hang far closer to the ground than ever before.

'Haven't you forgotten something?' she asked. Over their heads a sprinkling of stars glittered high up in the heavens, but all of them were still, fixed determinedly in place. There was not a movement between them. Was it foolish to be hoping for a sign from Rachel? That would just make things perfect – a shooting star to let her know she approved.

'What?' he said, a little irritated.

'My Christmas gift?' She smiled at him. 'Don't pretend

you've forgotten, Eddie Quirke, because I know that you're not the sort of bloke who forgets things like that.'

'Damn.' He shook his head. 'It's still in the car. Do you really want to go back and get it now?'

'It's only down the road to your mother's house. Come on, you can't leave me in suspense any longer.' And so they tracked through pristine white streets. The snow had stopped falling, which was probably just as well, or she had a feeling that Eddie might have refused to walk back to his mother's house with her. He could be a bit of a grumpy boots, but Liv was too happy to let that bother her. She loved him; he was her old grumpy boots and once they got married and had a family, she was quite sure, everything would be very different.

*

'It's...' She was almost speechless when she looked at the gift he handed her. Her heart sank. She wondered if he couldn't actually hear it plop to the pit of her stomach and she had to fight hard to hold back the tears of disappointment. 'It's great.'

It wasn't. It was a huge coffee table book about gemstones from some small African country that Liv had never heard of.

'I just thought, y'know, it'd look good in the flat.' He was obviously completely oblivious to her disappointment. The only thing that might have been worse was if he presented her with an ironing board or a toilet brush. How on earth could he be so blind? she wondered, as she fought hard to hold back the tears.

'Well, I'd better be going back to the farm now,' she said, doing her best to keep her voice even.

'I thought you wanted me to walk you back?' Eddie said, not actually making to move if he could avoid the track back to the farm.

'Ah, no, you're grand. I'd quite like the walk on my own. I'll catch up with you tomorrow. How's that?' she called over her shoulder, while she tucked the blasted, unwanted, oversized book under her arm and hoped it wasn't enough to capsize her if she came upon a slippery patch of road.

* * *

Liv couldn't remember the last time she'd been as eager to finish her shift. She was so relieved to hand her patients over to the young Libyan nurse who had arrived that she almost forgot to tell her about Mrs McDonnell in the plaster room who was waiting to be transferred up to a ward. Mind you, it wouldn't be the first time a patient had been left there for hours on end, just because A&E was too busy and staff forgot that there was someone tucked away in the plaster room out of sight.

She raced upstairs, her feet hardly touching each step. It was funny, but when she'd left Finn that morning, she'd said goodbye and had no intention of visiting him again. After all, he was on the mend now, out of the coma, and his recovery should be straightforward, a day or two to make sure there wasn't concussion or any risk of internal bleeding and he would be sent home to resume his life as normal.

'Ooh, Mr O'Connell's personal tonic.' Morgan laughed as he buzzed her through. 'According to the notes, he's hardly opened his eyes all day and when he has, he's been asking for you?'

'I obviously made a lasting impression,' she joked, but now she wondered if perhaps he was traumatised by waking from a coma to find a strange woman holding his hand. That certainly wasn't something she was going to share with Morgan though.

'Hey,' she whispered this time to announce her arrival, but Finn O'Connell was fast asleep, so she sat down next to him.

There was something quite extraordinary about watching him sleep. His chest rising and falling, his soft breath, in and out. It was calming, grounding. It was strange, but all of those other noises of the ward – the ongoing buzz of machines, the occasional bleep of a monitor recording a change, the swishing, clicking, buzzing sounds that made up this place – just faded away while she sat watching him.

'Hi,' he whispered eventually, pulling her from her trance.

'You're awake.' She smiled at him.

'It seems like it.' He tried to sit up a little, but there were too many things to negotiate, like the drip, probably a catheter, and the severe tucking in by Morgan or one of his colleagues. 'Can I have a sip of water?'

'Of course,' she said as she put the beaker to his lips gently and watched while he sipped. 'How do you feel now?'

'Super-duper,' he joked. 'Ah no, really, I can't complain; even if I was in any discomfort, they have drugged me so well, I can hardly feel a thing – good or bad.' He laughed.

'Don't knock it,' she said. 'It was a nasty accident. You're lucky to be in the shape you're in.' And of course he was; miraculously, there were no broken bones or worse.

'So, how do we know each other again?' He was watching her now.

'Well, I'm not sure we do, really…' She smiled. 'We spoke a

couple of words just before the bike hit and then I travelled with you in the ambulance…'

'My guardian angel.' He nodded as if confirming something.

'More like the other way round, actually.' She explained how he had pushed her out of the way of the oncoming bike and taken the brunt of the hit himself. It was funny, but at the time she wasn't sure she was even fully aware of what had happened; of course she'd helped the police as best as she could at the time, but it was only sitting here next to him that it had all become clearer in her mind. 'You won't remember any of it, probably.' Which she knew was just as well.

'Well, apart from the raging headache,' he said, making a joke, 'I'm glad we've met.' He looked at her intently for just a moment and she felt herself blush. Oh God, she realised, she was falling under his spell, and it was so easy. No wonder he had Estelle and M and who knows how many more women fawning over him.

'Anyway.' She spoke now with as much authority as she could muster. 'You were carrying this, when, you know…' She reached down into her bag and pulled out the gift with the tiny card attached.

'Oh?' He looked at it and she knew he had no memory of buying it.

'It's obviously a gift,' she prompted. 'To M? Perhaps you had just picked it up before the accident?'

'Yes, yes of course,' he said shaking his head, but all the same, there was something of embarrassment about the way he looked at the gift. 'Would you put it into the locker for me?'

'Of course.' She wasn't sure that he was meant to have anything in here that wasn't completely sterile. 'Actually, would you rather that I hold on to it, for now? I'm not trying to keep it or anything, but they can be a bit funny in here about people's personal belongings – they don't even allow patients to have flowers in case they contaminate the sterile environment,' she explained. 'Or I could give it to Estelle?'

'No, no – that's fine; tell you what, the best thing is if you could hold on to it for now and as soon as I get out of here, I can take it back and give it to…' He began to smile thinking of whoever the lovely M was, no doubt. 'You were very good, to hold on to it for me.'

'Not at all, I just…' How could she say that she had a feeling when she met Estelle, that no matter how striking the girl was, Liv just knew, deep down, that she and Finn were not quite the right fit? No doubt, there was room for a great mutual attraction. She was certainly gorgeous and he was… well, handsome in an old-fashioned, Mr Darcy sort of way. She wanted to ask him who M was. She imagined some sophisticated, stylishly thin, honey-haired beauty – possibly French – who would sweep along the corridors of the hospital in a cloud of heavy perfume and make heads turn wherever she went.

'So, you're a nurse? Here?'

'Yes. I was meant to be going home for Christmas, but just when I met you, all that changed and so, here I am.'

'You put off your Christmas plans for me?' He looked shocked.

'No.' Liv began to laugh.

'You could have lied, said you were already on your way?' He was teasing her.

'Don't. The thought actually did cross my mind, but then, I thought, I can still celebrate Christmas in a week's time.' She looked down at her left hand now, thinking of the romantic proposal she was missing out on.

'There's something else, isn't there?'

'Oh, it's nothing.' She shook her head.

'Go on, I won't tell anyone.' He was still smiling at her.

'It's daft, but I thought…' She began to smile now too. 'I was convinced that my boyfriend was going to propose to me this Christmas…' She knew that, compared to Finn's position of almost being killed in a bike crash, it was nothing: a marriage proposal could happen any time. 'He's a jewellery maker, you see, and I spotted a ring in his workshop. I'm certain he's made it for me; it's everything I could have wished for and…' She wasn't even sure why she was telling this complete stranger something she hadn't dared to breathe to another living soul. 'I know it doesn't sound like much of a big deal, but he's not exactly the romantic type. He's never made a grand gesture in his life.'

'That's a pity.'

'Pardon?'

'Well, every woman deserves an occasional grand gesture.'

'You're making fun of me.'

'Maybe, a little.' But he looked a little sad now. 'Hey, I'm sure that when you two meet up again, he'll pull out all the stops for you. And think of it, how many women get the ring of their dreams handmade by their future husbands?'

'That's true,' she said, but somehow the sparkle had come off the whole thing now. Perhaps it was just this place, talking about it amidst buzzers and the life-or-death balance of the intensive care unit. What did Finn know or care about her life? What on earth was she doing sitting here anyway, when she should be back at the flat catching up on her sleep?

***

When she did get back home, she could no more sleep than she might have if she'd just woken up after a long and peaceful night's rest. The conversation with Finn had somehow distracted her, as if it had obliquely knocked her off balance and now, as she looked about her little flat, everything seemed to have taken on an unfamiliar quality. Instead, she wandered about the flat picking things up and opening drawers randomly, as if checking that everything was exactly where she expected it to be. And of course, everything was exactly as it was meant to be. She'd already tidied the place, so it didn't look like quite the dump it had after Eddie had scrambled his bags together in a hurry for the week at home.

It was, she realised, actually really nice to have the place to herself – clean, tidy and fresh thanks to the window she'd opened to watch the snowflakes fall into the street below. She'd closed it quickly, and she'd shivered and pulled out the old cardigan that had once belonged to Rachel. She hardly ever wore it these days. When she pulled it on, it felt as if she had Rachel right next to her. She stood for a long time, just watching the snow fall, lost in her thoughts. When she looked at her watch again, it was almost midnight. She needed to get to bed.

It was the first night since Eddie went back for the Christmas holidays that she didn't stumble into the room and collapse beneath the duvet. Instead, she took her time, had a lovely long shower, put on rich moisturiser and her favourite pyjamas from the hot press in the kitchen. The only other thing that could make it perfect was a hot chocolate, so she padded out and popped some milk on to heat.

It was as she was pulling down the box of chocolate powder that some bills and correspondence that Eddie had been ignoring for the last few weeks in the busy run-up to Christmas fell to the floor at her feet. She shook her head, picking them up; he really needed to make it his new year's resolution to at least open his bills, she thought. She decided to leave them standing against the tea caddy so there would be no missing them when he got back, then, something caught her eye. The first letter had a handwritten note scrawled on the back of it.

What a funny place to write a note, she thought, picking it up and scanning down through the words. The writing was familiar, swirly and feminine, and it took a moment for her to understand exactly what she was reading. And then she realised, this note was definitely only meant to be read by Eddie.

8

Liv walked into the soft snowfall, tears racing down her cheeks. She was so cold, but still she dragged her heels, drawing out the journey back to the farmhouse for as long as possible. She was distraught. There was no other way of putting it. She had been so convinced that Eddie would propose. She'd been certain of it when she saw that ring in his workshop. And then, she wondered if she might have imagined it. These last few weeks, because they were short-staffed at the hospital, she'd taken on extra shifts. She was tired, agitated and, yes, maybe a bit stressed with the workload and having to organise everything for herself and Eddie and then the spectre of Barbara Quirke for Christmas.

For as long as Liv could remember, her biggest ambition had always been to be a wife and mother. It was old-fashioned and not the sort of thing she would admit to everyone, but it was the truth. She wanted to have a happy home, a big chaotic house, with home-made jam and long weekend family walks in the countryside. She wanted children, four at least and a dog, a great big daft thing that would almost jump out of its skin with excitement at the sight of her each morning. There was nothing wrong with that was there? It seemed like a simple enough aspiration; it was hardly up there with being president or Miss World. And yet it seemed just beyond her grasp.

Sometimes, she thought her life would never move on to the next stage and that made her feel completely depressed. It wasn't that she didn't value what she had. Liv knew she was lucky – she had her own flat, a job she loved and a family she treasured. She had Eddie. Now, that final thought made her heart sink like a stone. Yes. She had Eddie. She took a deep breath, stood stock-still; her face and her hair were damp now with the gentle snowflakes blowing towards her. She had to stop thinking like this; she knew it was dangerous territory. She had to remind herself how lucky she was to have him; after all, surely being with Eddie was better than being on her own?

She started to walk again, making excuses in her mind for the mix-up she'd made in thinking that tonight was the night he would propose to her. She was just tired and stressed, shattered from the last few weeks, weary from life in general. That sort of exhaustion, well it did things to you, didn't it?

Yes. Perhaps that was it? She'd just imagined seeing that ring – that very special and unique ring with a curve of emeralds arranged like shooting stars.

But she didn't imagine it. She knew she didn't, because she could see it clearly in her memory; she could still feel the coldness of the gold against her skin. It was definitely her shooting-star ring and it was definitely in Eddie's workshop.

And then, of course, she realised. He had never intended to propose to her at Christmas. Of course he hadn't. That wouldn't be Eddie's style at all. A Christmas announcement would be much too traditional for Eddie Quirke and a little part of Liv wanted to curse him for raising her expectations so foolishly, but instead she started to smile, because he would just ask her out of the blue. She didn't expect him to go down on bended knee, and there was a good chance he would do something completely unconventional, something that in his mind was a grand gesture, but to hers would be… maybe a little… less than that. But he was still Eddie, her Eddie, and she would try to love it however he went about it.

The problem was that knowing it, now she would have to spend her whole time on her best behaviour so as not to put him off track if he'd already picked out a day in his head. Oh, Eddie. It wasn't his fault; she knew that.

Clouds had covered over the moon and stars; there was nothing but a black ceiling above her, cutting off the heavens, or any shooting stars that Rachel might think of casting in her direction.

This was crazy. She needed to take the future into her own hands and make the most of the life before her. Hadn't she enough to be worrying about? Wasn't her dad's angiogram enough to preoccupy her? She loved Eddie; that was the main thing. All the other little niggling things, like how long it was taking him to propose and the fact that she still couldn't say she loved his mother – well, they were just periphery – when they were married, they wouldn't matter one bit.

And Barbara Quirke wasn't that bad; Christmas had gone off all right, hadn't it? In the end. She could live with Barbara as her mother-in-law, so long as they didn't come home too often and she closed her ears to her put-downs and curbed her inclination to tell her to mind her own business occasionally.

Liv dumped the stupid book at the back of the hall stand when she arrived home. From the living room, she heard the low sounds of a television programme playing away and, she knew, more than likely being ignored. She ran to the bathroom and scrubbed her face clean from the little amount of make-up she'd been wearing earlier and then put on her pyjamas before she looked around the sitting room door to see if anyone would like a hot drink before bedtime.

'Huh, what time is it?' Her father stirred; perhaps not really realising he'd been asleep at all. Her mother was snoring contentedly on the couch. On the TV, Batman was slugging it out with Superman – hardly her parents' cup of tea. 'Nothing for me, dear, but come in, tell us all about what's happening down in the village.' Her father hadn't left the farm since midnight mass on Christmas Eve – no need, everything he wanted was right here.

'Oh, not a lot, the usual carry-on. The older team managed to win the match, but Eddie was out in the first fifteen minutes.'

'Sent off?' Her father shook his head. Eddie had always been what her father called a 'dirty player'. He was as likely to strike out at an opponent as he was to put the ball in the back of the net.

'But there was a good crowd in Flannelly's.' She turned towards her mother who had just woken up. 'We met Anya; she seems good after the break-up. She's looking for a place to stay in Dublin.'

'Well, no better girl; I have a feeling that Anya is well able to look after herself. You didn't offer her your spare room, did you?' Her mother looked at her through narrowed eyes; her family thought she was a soft touch for every waif and stray.

'No, of course not.' She didn't mention that Maya would have murdered her if she had and she was probably right – the flat was hardly big enough for her and Eddie, never mind Anya and the extensive wardrobe that she'd acquired while she was going out with Pete.

'Good. I was never keen on that girl; always had a feeling that wherever she goes there'll be trouble not far after her,' her father said uncharacteristically. 'Don't look at me like that – I know more about the world than just sheep and lambs.' He squeezed Liv's hand affectionately.

'It's lovely to be home for Christmas,' Liv said and the words had come from nowhere. Or maybe, they were just a reaction to the disappointment that Eddie's gift had left her with. But it was nice, to be sitting here in the big old farmhouse, surrounded by the people who would love her no matter what happened.

'Aye. It is lovely, all right,' her dad said contentedly.

That night, when Liv lay in her bed, she knew she wasn't going to fall asleep easily. In the room next door, Maya slept contentedly, her head probably filled with land deeds and tort law and maybe, if she was lucky, a prosecution for something a little more dangerous to look forward to; perhaps defending a client in a big case in the New Year.

Liv snuggled down, expecting to dream of nothing more than snow falling on her face as she walked back to the farmhouse earlier, the taste of disappointment on her lips and a hollowed-out, disillusioned feeling in her stomach. So she pulled the quilt up tight around her, pretended that everything had turned out just as it was meant to and felt herself drifting off into a deep and dream-filled sleep before the clock struck the hour in the hall at the bottom of the stairs. She was woken just on the cusp of sleep by her phone vibrating next to her. She reached out to her night stand and pressed the on button to check her notifications. She hadn't really looked at it all day. She had a missed call from Pete. Damn, some friend she was after all her giving out to Eddie earlier. She'd ring Pete first thing in the morning, see what was up; probably, it was nothing more than he fancied going for lunch in the next town over.

Liv drifted easily back to sleep, thinking of Pete, and somehow a smile crept across her lips and she was contented, far more content than she had a right to be.

* * *

In the city, Liv got up the following morning, ragged. The snow on the empty streets outside brightened everything in a sterile light. It made her shiver, quite aside from the fact that the temperatures had dropped further. It seemed, within the space of a couple of written sentences, her whole life had been capsized. In a bolt from the blue it had emptied her out as easily as if she'd been tipped over and spilled across a precipice that she'd never imagined could lie so close to life as she knew it. She hadn't slept all night and if she did manage to close her eyes for even a moment, they shot wide open again with the certainty that there was no ignoring what she'd read in that note last night. At this point, she knew the words off by heart. She'd read it a thousand times over, sat at the kitchen table, unable to move any further. Shock. That was what it was, complete and utter shock.

Can't see you this week, Pete is asking questions. Too much to lose.
Don't contact me for a while,
x

Liv had known immediately what it was. Anya and Pete had been over a few weeks earlier. They'd had dinner, takeaway, because Liv had ended up working late and there just hadn't been time to cook. They'd drunk wine, probably too much, and sat talking into the early hours. Just before they left, Anya mentioned that she knew a girl who might be interested in getting some jewellery made. She'd made a big show of writing down the girl's details and handing them to Eddie. Eddie had stuffed the envelope into his pocket and, truly, Liv had forgotten about it after that.

Until now.

Now, she was sure this was the same note. But it wasn't a name and address or a phone number or an email contact for some potential customer who would keep Eddie busy for the New Year. It was something else entirely. A cruel game they were playing behind Liv's back and behind Pete's back. Pete had somehow seen through Anya, but of course, Liv had been completely blind to it all.

What had Pete said? It wasn't serious; Anya had only been fooling around. Pete had suspected it was with a married man – married? Hah! That was a joke.

True, Liv knew, she was the queen of burying her head in the sand when it came to Eddie. At about three o'clock in the morning, it dawned on her that she'd been doing just that for their whole relationship. Relationship? Had there ever even been a proper relationship there beyond what was convenient for Eddie? She had to think about that long and hard. The way they'd gotten together, the way they lived their lives – they were just flatmates, not even good friends. They were flatmates with benefits, and if Liv was being completely honest with herself, and why not at this point? The benefits weren't even all that spectacular. Sex with Eddie was just about going through the motions. Had it ever been any more than that? No.

She had worked hard, over the years, to convince herself that they were content and happy together. But honestly, now, with the stark reality of that note in her hand she had to face it. Their 'connection' had been little more than convenient for Eddie and maybe, God – and this made her feel really pathetic – but it had been fostered by her own desperation. Yes, she knew it: she was so desperate to have this ideal life she'd pinned her hopes on when she hardly knew anything about life at all, that she'd traded years of her time for something that hadn't been really worth a second glance at all. She'd always known, deep down, that this thing between them was second best. Now, she was certain that it wasn't even second best. This morning, as she sat looking across at that note on the table opposite her, she had a feeling that it might have freed her from the most toxic relationship she had ever forged and she wasn't just thinking about Eddie, she was thinking about his mother just as much.

Maya had seen it from the start. She'd tried to tell Liv so many times, but in the end, she knew that even she couldn't convince her sister that this thing was not right. But it had gone on so long. How on earth had she let it continue for almost six years? And then, she got really cross with herself, why on earth had she sold herself so short? For so long.

And she'd have married him. She'd have slipped that ring on her finger, with the deluded notion that because it looked like something that meant something to her, it would all be well and she and Eddie Quirke – and his awful mother – would live happily ever after.

She was so mad!

She was angry with herself, with Eddie Quirke, with Anya and even with Maya for not making her see sense sooner, which she knew was completely unreasonable. She had two hours before she was due back at the hospital. She had just two hours to scour this flat from any trace of Eddie Quirke. She started with refuse bags, everything from their bedroom that was his, which basically meant his shoes and clothes, because he'd never gone out and bought so much as a dish cloth since he'd moved in.

She cried and wailed while she was stuffing in socks, jumpers, jeans and underwear, then she moved towards the bathroom and continued to drop things in, aftershave, body spray, hair gel – so many products. She looked at the towels on the rail. They would all have to go. She'd buy all new towels and sheets in the January sales. That thought made her cry even louder, so by the time she made her way into the living room, she was almost spent, just that racking, uncontrollable breathing that she'd perfected as a child and then stopped somewhere around the teenage years; she had forgotten that she could cry so much, but then, these were tears filled with rage as much for her own stupidity as they were for the loss of Eddie Quirke.

Finding little tell-tale signs, like Anya's eye pencil buried between the cushions on the couch and a pink cigarette lighter tucked out of sight beneath the mattress on her bed, made her want to throw up. But it confirmed that Eddie had brought Anya here, probably on the nights when Liv had been working, and that hurt her even more. The idea that they would be here, together in her lovely flat; how on earth had she been so blind?

She would ring Maya on her first break. She'd rather wait, for another day or two, but Liv knew there was a good chance her mother would try to recreate Christmas Day when she got home at the end of the week and the last thing she wanted was the Quirkes looming like spectres on the other side of their family table.

She managed to make it to the hospital with seconds to spare. She'd left the flat with a line of black refuse bags taking up the tiny utility room. Later, tonight, she would take them to Eddie's workshop and leave them there. Where he lived, or indeed how he lived, was no longer her concern. That thought gave her a huge pang of loneliness and yes, she hated herself all the more for it.

The truth was that after six years together, their lives had woven into each other; and then she shook herself out – because whose fault was that? It certainly was not Eddie Quirke's. He may have lived in her flat for free, eaten the food she'd put in the fridge and allowed her to let him take her for a complete fool, but to be fair, he'd never made any promises. There had never been a declaration of any sort – love, lust or even enduring partnership of any kind.

But, he had taken everything she'd so willingly given and he must have known that in her mind things between them were very, very different to what they'd put into words.

* * *

'And you haven't told him yet?' Maya had said after she'd called her. Liv knew she was choosing her words carefully.

'No. I know I should have, but I needed to get my head around things first. I needed to get everything sorted.' The last thing she wanted was Eddie Quirke arriving back in Dublin to convince her that it was all some misunderstanding when she knew in her gut that throwing him out of the flat was the right thing to do. It was the only thing to do. 'I'll ring him when I'm good and ready. Let's face it, I don't owe him any favours at this stage.'

'Of course,' Maya said. 'I know you won't want to hear this, Liv, but I really think you should be absolutely rejoicing. You've had the luckiest escape from him – he's only ever been a leech. He'd have made you completely miserable in the long run.'

'Or I'd have made myself miserable more like.' Liv knew that it took some sort of action for another person to have any effect either way on you. And the fact was that Eddie didn't care enough to make her feel bad, unless it was by deflection of following his own interests. The more she thought about it, she realised, all she'd ever been was a wave to his tidal direction.

'And as for his awful mother, yikes!'

'Yes, at least Dad will be the over the moon on that front – no need to worry about any more not-so-cosy get-togethers with the Quirkes.' Liv was keeping her voice light, but it would be a lie to say she wasn't hurt and sad at the end of things, even if it was just the end of her idea of things with Eddie. She imagined Maya telling her that she'd equally miss a headache, if she'd put up with it for over six years too.

'No, Liv, he definitely won't be over the moon, not if he thinks

Eddie Quirke hurt you in any way. You know Mum and Dad, they'd put up with anything if they thought it made us happy, even the devil himself, or his incarnate: Barbara Quirke.'

'Listen, don't say anything to them, not until I get home, at least. I'm going to offer to do some more shifts here, just so I have time to think and I want to sort the flat into an Eddie-free zone!' She was going to call Pete next, tell him the truth about Anya's affair, and ask him to keep it to himself too – for now, at least. The last thing she needed was to go home and bump into Eddie and Anya at every turn. She could just as easily take her Christmas holidays when everyone had gone back to work and it would take her out of the city when they returned.

'Do you want me to come and stay with you for a few days? I'm pretty handy at changing a door lock, among other things,' Maya said.

'No. Not yet, Eddie isn't going to turn up here for at least another week. By then, I'll have straightened myself out and given him the news that I've moved him out of the flat,' she said. At least knowing that, probably, Eddie would be more bothered about not having anywhere to live than the idea that things had finished between them made throwing him out a lot easier.

That evening, when Liv's shift had finished, she walked towards the stairs. She should look in on Finn O'Connell, really, just to make sure he was doing okay, but she couldn't face it. Probably, he wouldn't expect her to show up every evening. If there had been any change for the worse, Morgan would have let her know.

She turned away from the stairs and headed towards the front door instead and out into the driving snow. They'd been lucky with the weather so far. It was soft underfoot and although there were occasional icy patches, for the most part it was easy enough to walk on. Outside the hospital, as she waited for her bus in the cold, she thought about that evening of the accident and it felt as if it had been almost the starting point to what was coming next, even though she hadn't realised it at the time.

She'd made a snap decision. The right decision, she was certain of that much, but it was bringing her down a road she didn't want to travel, even if she knew it was exactly where she'd always needed to go. With that, she looked up towards the sky. The clouds had been driven back for a short reprieve and the moon, silver and full, was suspended low in the sky. She counted seven stars. Just seven and she wondered what that might mean, if they were a message from Rachel. As the bus pulled in to the stop, she realised that perhaps they meant nothing at all; they were just stars in the sky and if Rachel was really looking out for her, all she had to do was trust that everything was working out for the best.

Just as the bus was pulling away, she thought she saw Estelle walking up the avenue towards the hospital and a little part of her was glad she hadn't gone to visit Finn. She wasn't sure she could cope with seeing him and Estelle together now. Not when she felt so thoroughly on her own.

9

Liv woke the following day and tried ringing Pete first thing, but there was no answer, which was a pity, because Pete always pulled her out of the doldrums. Still, she was determined not to wallow. So, last night had not been *the* night, but she knew that there had never been any guarantees that it would be. The main thing she had to keep reminding herself of was that Eddie had made that ring for her, whatever that meant – whether he was planning on a Christmas engagement or not, it meant that he loved her.

It was mad, really, but as she tramped out across the farm with the dogs in the cold morning air, it niggled her again, the fact that Eddie had never actually told her that he loved her. She'd told Maya once, who'd laughed. And then of course it all made complete sense. How could Eddie be anywhere near halfway normal about his emotions with a mother like Barbara Quirke?

But it mattered to Liv some days more than others and it mattered today. She wouldn't mope, because it would only worry her parents, but there was no harm getting it out of her system with a long walk and a little cry along the way if she felt like it.

Of course, she realised that she would have to make peace with Eddie. Not that she'd fallen out with him exactly the previous night, but she'd hardly even said thank you for the book. Instead, she'd tried to swallow her disappointment and made her escape as bluntly as possible. She pulled her phone from her pocket.

'Hey,' she said and she knew she sounded *too* bright.

'Huh?' Eddie sounded as if he was still half asleep.

'Sleepyhead, late night?' He'd have gone back to Flannelly's, probably hadn't even eaten dinner. Honestly, Liv thought, if it wasn't for her making sure he ate three meals a day, she wondered if he'd survive at all.

'Yeah. Too late probably.' She heard him scrabbling. 'What time is it?'

'It's after nine.' She smiled.

'Flipping hell, Liv, don't you know it's the holidays? What on earth has you up and ringing me at this hour?' he groaned.

'I just wanted to say thanks for the gift.'

'The gift?' He hadn't the foggiest idea what she was on about. She imagined him, bleary-eyed; probably wearing the T-shirt and boxers he'd worn the previous day, his hair messed up and sleep still in his eyes. She knew him well enough now to know he wouldn't actually be fully awake until he'd had a shower and a strong cup of black coffee.

'My book, it's lovely, thank you.'

'Oh, that, right...' He was obviously waiting for her to hang up.

'Anyway, I thought maybe we could do something today. A walk on the beach?'

'Oh, I don't think so. I need to rest up,' he began and she started to laugh.

'Come on, Eddie, you're not that old.'

'No, but neither is Ronaldo, and you don't see him killing himself out the days after a game.'

'And you're not a premier league player either. A walk on the beach is just what you need. We can have breakfast in Diane's first and then take a gentle wander afterwards.'

'Well, if you're paying for breakfast?' he checked crankily.

'Of course,' she said.

'Fine. Not that I'm hungry, but I probably need something to line my stomach. I told the lads I'd meet them for the hair of the dog later.'

*

Diane's was busy. Mainly the local old dears on their way from mass, with nothing else to do but sit and drink tea or increasingly sweet variations of coffee for an hour before their next planned activity. Eddie ordered the full Irish breakfast with a large mug of tea on the side, which he took outside while he smoked his (she guessed) third cigarette of the morning. She'd given up telling him how bad cigarettes were for him after he'd told her once she sounded like his mother nagging on and on about them. But she still hated that he smoked, even if she didn't say it anymore.

'It's flipping freezing out there,' he said when he sat at their table again and she could feel the iciness from his clothes as he took off his jacket.

'So, what did I miss last night?' She knew it wouldn't be a lot, but felt compelled to make small talk all the same.

'It was quiet. Just a few pints, the usual crew, minus Mick,' he said as Diane's daughter delivered his breakfast to the table.

'Has there been any word on his shoulder?' Mick Divine had been taken off with a suspected fractured collarbone halfway through the match.

'Broken shoulder. He'll be off work for a couple of weeks.'

'That's a pity. Poor Mick,' Liv said automatically, although it was hard to figure how he couldn't still teach in the secondary school in the next town. You hardly needed to put your back into standing up in front of a dozen kids and going through the course curriculum for Irish. 'Anyone I'd know call in?' she asked, wondering about Pete, although it was unlikely he'd turned up – he wasn't exactly a pub man.

'Yeah, Anya came in for a while. We had a drink together. She's taking it all very badly, about the coffee shop, you know.'

'Did she mention Pete at all?' Because it seemed to Liv that losing a man like Pete should cause her much more pain than losing her business.

'Haven't seen sight nor light of him, but then, that's Pete, isn't it?' Eddie mopped up some runny egg with black pudding before eating it.

'Isn't she cut up about the relationship ending though?' Honestly, men, they could be so obtuse sometimes.

'Yeah, well, I suppose she is, too, but you know…'

'No, go on tell me.'

'Well, when it's over, it's over, isn't it?'

'So, she's not eager to get back together then?'

'I... I'm not sure. I suppose so, I mean, look at the pair of them; it's unlikely Pete's going to find another Anya, isn't it?'

'He seemed to be crazy about her all right.' Liv sipped her coffee, but still, she couldn't imagine ending a relationship with someone and not feeling something more than just worry about their shared financial commitments – surely there had to be more to love than that.

'I think he was a bit of a shit to her to be honest,' Eddie said.

'How do you mean?' The comment caught her off guard. Okay, so she knew Pete could be hard to get to know, but he was a good bloke. Liv asked, mainly because it was so unlike Eddie to offer any information beyond the bare essentials.

'Oh, I don't know, apparently, he could be very possessive, not letting her meet up with friends, accusing her of seeing people behind his back.'

'Well, apparently he had good cause,' Liv said softly. 'She was having a fling with someone else after all.'

'You see, that's it exactly. A girl like Anya, as soon as she talks to another bloke, it's like she wants to fall into bed with them. It's not right judging her just because she's prettier than most.'

'I don't think Pete would ever do that,' Liv murmured, but his words stung, as if he was admitting that Anya was so much more striking than anyone else.

But that was silly of her. Eddie loved her; what was she doing feeling jealous of Anya?

'Humph,' he said as he put his cup down. 'Well, from what she said last night, it sounds as if he's just being small-minded, going after the shop, throwing her out of the flat. It's as if he's trying to get back at her for something she didn't do to begin with.'

'I'm sure Pete has given her plenty of time to find somewhere else.'

'It's hardly a renters' market out there at the moment,' Eddie said. He was examining his fingers now, wrapped around the mug, as if he was thinking about something much more personal than the current housing crisis. 'And so, you can see how she'd be in a bad way about the coffee shop?' Eddie said.

'I suppose, it is her livelihood.' She didn't add that she wouldn't have had it in the first place if it wasn't for Pete. 'But couldn't she get some sort of loan and buy his interest out of the place? If it's doing as well as it seems to be, I'm sure that there are plenty of investors who'd be jumping at the chance for a share in the place.' The café always looked busy despite the exorbitant price for a cup of coffee Anya charged.

'I'm not sure that's Anya's area of expertise.'

'But there are people, agencies to help with all that sort of stuff, surely…'

'I think she's just hoping that he will continue to keep the place afloat until she can figure out something else.' Eddie put down his knife and fork and belched loudly. 'God, I needed that,' he said sitting back in his chair contentedly. He looked rough, as if he'd spent half the night in the pub and the other half of it sleeping somewhere he shouldn't have been.

'You okay?'

'Sure. I'm just a bit worried about Anya.' He lowered his voice. 'She has nowhere to live and she has to go back to open up the coffee shop again.' Anya's coffee shop was bang smack in the centre of the banking district. It wouldn't be busy for Christmas – her customers would survive without her – but she would have to open her doors soon.

'No, but I'm sure she'll figure something out before too long,' Liv said thinking of her mother's warning the day before. There simply wasn't room in her little flat for Anya and if she was completely honest, even if there was, Liv wouldn't fancy sharing her home with the girl; they just didn't click. And then there was Pete. At the end of the day, he was her best friend and while she didn't want to fall out with Anya, neither had she any intention of making things awkward with Pete. 'Come on,' she said then, changing the subject, 'you can have a cigarette and I'll pay for this, then we'll go for a short walk across the beach.'

'Uh, do we have to?'

'Yes. It's how you're going to pay me back for breakfast and you'll feel much better if you can clear your head before you go back to Flannelly's and get pulled into another mad drinking session.'

*

It was windier today, the waves crashing against the sand with a tightened ferocity that would put off even the most committed wild swimmer. The breeze whipped sand up around their calves as they walked. It was one of those days when only the locals would brave walking along here. As it was, she spotted a few walkers ahead of them, dogs running happily in and out of the water and one desperate surfer enjoying waves that were high enough to be worth chasing.

'We could ask her to stay with us,' Eddie shouted above the breeze.

'Who?' Of course she knew exactly who he meant, but she was playing for time.

'Anya, of course, who do you think? The queen of England?'

'Oh, no, Eddie, I don't think that would work at all.'

'Why not? It would only be for a week or two.'

'She might say that now…'

'Is that a dig at me?'

'No, of course not, that was completely different.' She shook her head. They'd had this out before. It annoyed Eddie that the flat belonged to Liv, her name on the deeds. She had looked into changing it because he'd pestered her so much, but her parents had been dead set against it and then, when she asked Maya, it turned out the legal costs alone were nearly as high as the national debt. 'You and I, that's different.' She put her arm through his, but he shrugged it off and suddenly, she thought of the night before, the idea of that lovely ring, maybe sitting in his pocket right now. Was this a test? Was it some crude way of gauging if they could be together forever?

'It seems a bit cold to me, owning your own flat and leaving poor Anya homeless when she could as easily bed down on the couch for a couple of nights.'

'But, Eddie, it wouldn't be just a couple of nights, would it? I mean, it takes time to find a place and then, there's waiting until you can move in – I mean, if her business isn't making enough money, can she even afford the deposit on a place?'

'Oh, don't be so naïve, of course she can pay for a roof over her head.' He was sulking now – had he already promised Anya a place to stay? For some reason, this irritated Liv beyond reason.

'And then there's all her belongings – the flat is hardly big enough to hold our stuff – I mean, I've never seen Anya wear the same outfit twice. I'd say her clothes alone could fill up the whole living room.'

'Bitchiness doesn't suit you at all. Do you know that, Liv?'

'Eddie, I'm not being a cow here, really. You have to see this?'

'I'm done walking,' he said pulling away from her and heading back towards the village. He left her standing there, open-mouthed and not entirely sure what had happened between them. This holiday was going nothing like how she had expected it to.

* * *

It took three hours, two taxi journeys and too many black refuse bags to count, but by nine o'clock Liv was back in her little flat and there was an undeniable sense of contentment about her, albeit sitting alongside a digging sadness at the idea of ending something that had taken up six years of her life.

A headache – isn't that what Maya would have said? Could she really compare her relationship with Eddie to an enduring migraine? Anyone would miss a headache if they'd suffered with it for as long as she'd stayed with Eddie. And now, sitting here, sipping a large mug of hot chocolate, she realised that she had stayed with him. He hadn't made any huge promises. There'd been no agreement between them. She'd just clung on, hoping that it might materialise into something more. She'd held on to something that wasn't actually hers. All this time, she'd blinded herself to the reality: that she and Eddie were no more compatible than salt and sugar. This was an epiphany and although, initially, it made her wail like a banshee, facing up to it actually made her feel a lot better.

She grabbed a wet wipe from the bathroom and cleaned off her face roughly. Her skin stung and her eyes felt as if they'd dried up with all the crying, but somehow, this sense of being emptied out almost felt as if she was done with getting past the worst. She needed some cheer and, as her little celebration of Christmas had never actually happened, she lit the fire log that had been buried beneath a tonne of Eddie's old shoes and then switched off all the lights in the flat so she could enjoy her open fire again after all these years. When it took off, she sat back on the sofa, enjoying the flames dancing, the candles lit on the mantelpiece, the peace and quiet of having the place to herself, and yes, maybe she took a certain amount of pleasure in the serenity of knowing that somehow life had just become more authentic for all those tears.

*

The following morning, the alarm clock woke her to the unusual brightness of new snow covering the streets beneath her window. There were a number of things she had to do today, if she was going to make a clean break of things and start this new life that she hoped would open up in some way, to give her, if not the dreams she'd dreamed up until now, then at least a new contentment within herself.

First things first.

It was almost nine o'clock in the morning and she'd promised Francine she'd cover a split shift for one of the agency girls who wanted to finish early. She didn't have to be at work for another hour, so, after her shower and pulling back the curtains in the flat, she switched on her phone.

'Eddie,' she said with a lot more poise than she felt. Inside, her stomach was doing somersaults for all her earlier bravery.

'Huh?' It had clearly been a very late night. 'What time is it?'

'It's early, but I needed to talk to you. Are you awake yet?'

'Huh? Yeah, I don't have much of a bloody choice now, do I?'

'No, you don't. I rang you because I'm finishing things between us!'

'You're what?' She could hear something vaguely resembling wakefulness abruptly come into his voice. She'd like to think he shot up in the bed, shocked and devastated, but this was Eddie, and she knew he was probably too hung-over for devastation to set in.

'Yes. I'm sorry to spring it on you, by phone, but really, it's better this way. It gives you time to sort out somewhere to live when you come back to Dublin after the holidays.'

'You're throwing me out of the flat?' He was stupefied and she almost felt a little bad for catching him on the hop, until she remembered the note from Anya. 'Hang on a minute there…'

'No. You hang on. I know you've been sleeping with Anya and regardless of what you believe, I'm not a complete doormat.'

'You can't just throw me out of my home. I have rights.'

'It's my flat, Eddie.' She felt a tremor of fear slip over her as she looked about her newly tidied living room. Could he try and make some sort of claim on the place? Squatter's rights? She couldn't bear that, because she realised just how much she loved this little place. It had been her haven when Rachel died and she'd felt exactly the same comfort the previous evening as she'd sat watching the flames lick up the chimney. Why had she taken it for granted over the last few years? It was as if it had turned into little more than a place to sleep, a place to share with Eddie and his vast collection of trainers and video games. It could do with a lick of paint. Everything about it had sort of grown shabbier over the last few years. How had she not noticed that until now?

'It doesn't matter who owns it. I've been living there for over six years; you can't just leave me homeless. There are laws about that sort of thing,' he said and she'd never heard him so vehement before. His words, spitting down the phone, actually made her feel as if her chest was tightening just a little more with every syllable. It was scary, hearing the reality of what was ahead of them coming from his bitter words.

'Oh, I think you'll find I can. I've spoken to Maya.' It was a complete lie.

'Oh, of course, perfect bloody Maya; well, she would have something to say about it. She never much liked me anyway, did she? I was never quite good enough.'

'That's not true.' But Liv knew it was true. It wasn't time to think about that now, but later, she could reflect on the fact that Maya had always worried about her relationship with Eddie. It turned out she'd been right to be concerned.

'It doesn't matter. All my stuff is there. I still have my keys and you have no right to ring me up and just decide that you're going to...'

'Can't you hear yourself?' It had just dawned on Liv: Eddie didn't give two hoots about the fact that she knew about his relationship with Anya. All that bothered Eddie was that he had to move out of the flat. 'Don't you care that…' She stopped herself, because she wouldn't do this. She'd let herself down enough. Now it was time to gather whatever bit of self-respect she had left about her and move on with her life.

'Some of us don't have the luxury of caring about much more than making ends meet at the end of the week.'

'Oh, Eddie,' she said. God, she'd been taken for a complete fool. She'd paid all his bills. She'd put a roof over his head, for free, and yet, he always had enough money for designer trainers and to spend his Christmas holidays from opening to closing time in Flannelly's pub getting drunk with his mates. She wanted to ask him about that ring, but she had some small sense of pride left. She needed to forget she'd ever seen it, pretend that some small part of her didn't believe he'd made it for Anya.

'Don't Oh, Eddie me, who on earth do you think you are? First off, you don't even bother to come home for Christmas and even if you had, it's not as if you'd want to do anything with me.' His words fell off. The only place he ever wanted to spend time in Ballycove was at the pub. 'And then, you ring me up and accuse me of…'

'I know you were seeing her.' She held the phone away from her while he absolutely lost it on the other end, but the more he spoke, the more she knew this was the right thing to do. At the end of it all, when he'd played himself out, she waited a beat before she spoke. 'You're right about only one thing, Eddie. You still have the keys to my flat and I'd like them back. I've moved all your stuff out. I've left everything in the workshop. I still have your keys for there by the way, so I propose we do a swap – otherwise… well, I'm going to have to ask Maya to step in.' And, with that she ended the call. She absolutely wouldn't put it past him to turn up and let himself in after the holidays, and she knew the sensible thing to do was change the locks; perhaps Pete would help her out with that.

The call shook her. She wasn't completely naïve – she hadn't expected it to be easy, but she knew she had to tell him while she was fired up for it. The thing about working in A&E was that you never knew what the day would bring and even a very short shift could empty her out, so making a call like that would be impossible afterwards.

She sat in the tiny alcove by the window. Maya had made this into a window seat for her – they'd bought the deep velvet cushion together. She sat there for a long time after she hung up the phone on Eddie. Her thoughts raced away from her. She supposed it wouldn't take long for word to get round the village that she'd called time on their relationship. She imagined Eddie, sitting in Flannelly's for the next few days, milking his sorrows for all they were worth. She pictured his mother, pursing her lips and making nasty insinuations about how she'd never thought much of those Latimer girls anyway. The only blessing was that anyone decent in the village had the measure of both sides a long time before this happened. And then, Liv thought of her parents, having to put up with the Quirkes for Christmas dinner while she'd been up here working without any idea of what was going on right under her nose. She had to speak to them next.

Liv went to the bathroom and brushed her hair, while trying not to make eye contact with herself in the bathroom mirror. She knew she looked terrible, but if she sat with her back to the light, she might just fool her family into thinking that there was nothing to worry about and she was taking this in her stride. She smeared on some rose lip balm and a hint of blusher and then she went back to the window seat and called her mother on FaceTime.

'Good morning, darling.' Her mother looked as if she'd just come back from a walk outside; perhaps she'd been down checking on the lambs and this idea sent a now almost familiar pang of loneliness through Liv.

'It is a good morning,' Liv said, not sure how she was going to tell them why she rang. 'Is Dad there?'

'I'm here.' He peered into the screen at her and her heart flipped with the love she felt for them both.

'Good, perhaps you should sit down for what I have to tell you next.'

'Oh, dear.' Her mother's face broke into a thousand furrows. 'What is it? Is everything okay? What's happened?'

'It's not that bad, but you need to know. I've just spoken to Eddie…'

'Oh God, is he all right?' Her mother again; perhaps her father expected bad news about Eddie as a default.

'He's fine. Hung-over, as usual since it's Christmas, but I've broken things off with him.'

'Oh?' Her mother's voice was high-pitched. It was, Liv realised, the very last thing she expected. Well, it was the last thing Liv had expected to happen this Christmas too.

'It was time,' Liv said simply. There was no point telling them about Anya. They would only worry too much. Maybe when she went down for a few days closer to the end of the week, she would tell them then.

'How are you, darling? It's…' Her mother's whole expression had drained. It was an expression Liv had seen many times in A&E on mothers' faces as they watched their child fight their way out of whatever had brought them there in the first place.

'I'm actually fine.' Liv smiled and in that moment, she actually was. 'I've had a big clear-out of his belongings. I needed to get the flat back to myself and I'm…' What was the word…? She couldn't call herself happy at this point, but there was something else.

'Relieved?' her father put in. He knew her so well.

'Yes, Dad. That's exactly how I feel. It's like a huge weight has been lifted from my shoulders and I can breathe again for the first time in a long time.'

'Thank God.' Her mother breathed.

'What your mother means is, she's delighted that you're all right, not that this has happened,' her father put in hastily.

'I know exactly what she means.' And Liv did, because they'd probably all be a bit relieved that Barbara Quirke was finally out of their lives for good.

'He won't be happy,' her mother said, because of course, she knew without ever saying so that Eddie Quirke had been on to a good thing.

'It doesn't matter what he'll be now,' her father said. 'As long as our lovely Liv is okay, that's all that matters to us,' he said and Liv thought she'd burst with gratitude for having both of them as her parents. Really, after all this time, what more could she possibly ask for?

10

'Hello, Liv?' Barbara rang that afternoon, which was unusual, because normally when she rang Eddie, it seemed she made a point of not even asking after Liv, much less actually speaking to her and certainly never ringing her up for a friendly chat.

'Yes, Barbara, how are you?' Liv was just washing the dishes after lunch. Her parents had ambled out for a walk about the farm and Maya was still at the office.

'Well, I'm not great, obviously,' Barbara said and Liv wasn't sure what to reply next. 'I'm stranded here without so much as a drop of milk and I'm too nervous to walk up to the supermarket with the state of the footpaths.' It had frozen over the night before, although, it seemed to be thawing a little more now the winter sun was shining.

'Oh.' It took a minute for Liv to realise what she was meant to say next. 'Well, would you like me to pick up some shopping for you and drop it off?'

'If you wouldn't mind?' Barbara snapped. 'Only, Eddie had to go on an errand and I don't know when he'll be back.'

'An errand?' Liv asked a little guiltily, because she didn't want to alert Barbara to the notion that he might have done a disappearing act after their disagreement on the beach earlier. He regularly did that in Dublin – stormed out after an argument, probably went to the pub and then slept on someone's sofa for a day or two until he needed to come home for clean clothes and a proper bed to sleep in. In the beginning it had really upset Liv – the idea that he could just walk out the door and leave an argument hanging for days on end, but like everything else about living with Eddie, she'd gotten used to it, and now it didn't bother her so much.

'He was bringing Anya back up to Dublin. She has to move out of her apartment apparently.' Barbara had even less interest in Anya than she had in Liv, presumably. 'Just so you know, I'm very particular about my shopping…'

It was no surprise that the list was a lot longer than just a bottle of milk and a pound of butter. Outside, snow had fallen even more heavily, so once she had the list taken down, with each of the specific instructions about each item, Liv grabbed the keys of the jeep and headed for the village. Ballycove was breathtakingly pretty this afternoon, Liv thought, as she drove onto the main street. Everything was so crisp and white, idyllic really, beneath another layer of freshly fallen snow. But underneath it, she knew that the ground could be treacherous. She'd already felt the jeep sway on an icy patch as she'd rounded some of the bends on the journey from the farm.

The supermarket was fairly quiet, so Liv grabbed a trolley and began to fill it with the items on the list. Barbara really was very particular; everything was specified down to the last millilitre and flavour. It took an age to get exactly everything on the list.

'Finally,' Barbara said as she opened the door for Liv when she arrived with the first of the bags of shopping. 'Really, where on earth did you go? Timbuktu?' she said closing out the door and ferrying Liv into the kitchen. Then, because Barbara made a scene about her back apparently playing up, Liv knew she had no option but to put everything away, which was a nightmare, because of course, again, Barbara liked everything just so. By the time everything was packed in the cupboards Liv felt the onset of a nasty migraine. She pulled the receipt from her pocket. The total came to over a hundred euro. 'Oh, I can't possibly pay you now,' Barbara said falling into her seat.

'Are you all right?' Liv asked, because the woman looked as if she was taking some sort of turn.

'No. I'm not all right!' she snapped. 'I've been sitting here waiting for two hours for a pint of milk to make a simple cup of tea and all you're worried about is your money.'

'I'll make the tea for you,' Liv said, although all she wanted to do was get out of here.

'And you can pick up what I owe you for the shopping from Eddie. I'll let him have it when I'm feeling a little stronger,' she said weakly, although from what Liv could see, there wasn't a lot wrong with Barbara. 'I might take some toast as well,' she said then, 'not too brown, just slightly golden all the way round.'

'Now,' Liv said when she'd popped the tea and toast before Barbara. 'I'd better get going; my mum needs me back at the farm. I was only meant to be gone for half an hour.'

It was a lie, but it was her only chance of getting out before Barbara had her doing a spring clean of the entire house. She had already given two broad hints about the fact that her vacuum cleaner was broken and she really couldn't see her way to going down on her hands and knees in the sitting room to pick up the crisps Eddie had accidentally spilled the previous evening. 'Don't worry; I'll pick up the shopping money from Eddie,' she confirmed gaily as she left Barbara chewing thoughtfully on a slice of toast.

She knew she wouldn't of course, not unless Barbara actually thought of handing the cash to Eddie and then, Eddie actually thought of handing it to Liv. That was the problem with artists. Eddie was so wrapped up creating beautiful things that the microeconomics of the real world never really occurred to him.

'Ah, so you're doing house calls now?' she heard a voice call to her as she made her way back to the car. She looked up to see Pete making his way along the road. Liv felt her heart lift when she spotted him.

'Yes, next stop the maternity ward!'

'Seriously?' He looked confused.

'No, of course not. I'm headed home to check on the newborn lambs.' She enjoyed teasing him. 'It feels as if I've met everyone in the village except for you since we got back.' She reached out and touched his arm.

'Actually, I'm glad I ran into you. I've been trying to call you, only I just...' He looked up and down the road now, as if checking to see if anyone was watching them.

'How have you been? Well, the word is out about you and Anya.'

'It seems the whole village has heard about me and Anya, but they've only heard half the story. I think I've had a lucky escape actually.'

'Well, as long as you're both doing okay.' Liv couldn't help but feel a little disappointed on his behalf. Perhaps it was because he'd seemed to be so besotted by Anya, certainly at the beginning at least.

'I have a feeling that Anya will always be *doing okay*,' he said wryly.

'She was worried about the café and the apartment,' Liv started. 'I met her at the football match…'

'Look, I know everyone probably thinks that I'm just walking away from this, but really, I've no intention of dropping her in it with the coffee shop. We were having problems for some time. She…' He stopped and looked up and down the street. 'Finding out she was having a fling behind my back was the final straw, maybe just what I needed to know that things weren't ever going to be right…'

'Still, it doesn't make it easy, for either of you.'

'Strangely enough, in the end, it made it very easy for me.' He smiled now and she supposed it was probably a relief to be free of the relationship if it was making him miserable.

'And this other guy… will she stay with him now?' She wanted to add, *asking for a friend,* because it seemed much more realistic that Anya would move in with her new boyfriend than expect to move in with her and Eddie. She didn't say that, of course, because what was the point in adding any stress to Pete – he'd probably already had enough.

'I doubt it; otherwise, she'd probably have left months ago.' He shook his head, wiser but surprisingly chipper. 'I think he's probably married or with someone else. Right up to the end she was denying there was anything going on, but when you know, you know, right?'

'I suppose so,' Liv said and she looked at him now, properly looked at him. He'd changed – she hadn't noticed in the dark of Christmas morning when he'd driven her home. He'd lost weight, but maybe it suited him. He looked more like he had when they were younger, apart from the designer glasses and expensive casual clothes. Of course, Pete had never *really* changed. He might look more polished than he had at school – sometimes Liv caught herself looking at him and wondering when he'd turned into such an attractive man – but underneath, he was still good old Pete. She knew that some people – well, the Barbara Quirke set at least, thought he was aloof, that his success had gone to his head. He might look uber confident, but he was actually quite shy and very funny, when you got to know him. 'It's just good to see you're doing okay,' she repeated.

'To be honest,' he said, leaning into the jeep, 'it's a big bloody relief. Who wants to live the rest of their life with someone who only wants to bleed them dry and treat them like second best?' He held her eye for a fraction too long.

'Who indeed?' she said. But those words resonated with her later as she started the engine before she drove back out of the village, her thoughts far more tangled than she could understand why.

* * *

'We'll be throwing him out today,' Morgan said when she made her way up to ICU on her first break.

'Well, that's good news.' Liv looked down at Finn who had just woken. Estelle was sitting next to him, in the most luscious green velvet coat, perfectly poised, groomed and wafting expensive, suffocating perfume. It seemed to Liv that the frightened girl she'd met that first evening had been transformed into a woman who might have strode from a centre spread of *Cosmopolitan*. She made Liv feel so dowdy by comparison with her hair scraped back and wearing her polyester uniform and sensible rubber-soled shoes.

'You're awake, darling?' She bent over him and kissed him lightly on his forehead, rather than causing any pain where he was bruised along his cheek and jaw.

'Yes, yes, oh…' He stopped, surprised perhaps to see Liv standing once again at the end of his bed. 'No need to worry. They've said there's no concussion and no lasting damage,' he said cheerfully, although Liv knew that from the bruising and the bashing he'd gotten, he must be in some discomfort.

'Yes, well, your consultant will likely transfer you to a general ward and they might just keep you in for another day, to be sure,' Morgan said carefully, because there was no telling with a head injury.

'It'd be nice to get home though; it is Christmas, after all,' Finn said.

'Tell me about it, mate.' Morgan slipped his chart back on the trolley.

'Sorry, I forgot, neither of you have had much of a Christmas either,' Finn said, looking from Morgan to Liv.

'Not so bad for me – I only live down the road and my wife works shifts too, so we'll just have our Christmas Day a little late,' Morgan said moving on to the next patient.

'And what about you?' Finn fixed those blue eyes on Liv.

'Usually, it's Christmas at home with my family, but well, maybe it's a January Christmas celebration this year…' It sounded rather parochial, but she loved it. Every year, just the four of them – somehow, it felt as if Rachel was still there with them. Probably very different to the grand plans Finn and Estelle would have in the city.

'Home?'

'Ballycove. It's in the west…'

'I know it, I've been there.' He smiled, perhaps remembering. 'It's a long way to travel for a slice of turkey though.' He was laughing now.

'I suppose it is, but like you, my plans were thrown up in the air on Christmas Eve, so I'm just going to make the best of it.'

'I'm sorry you missed it.'

'Don't be. We had mince pies on the ward and carol singers dropping by at all hours before the holidays and anyway, this year, I'm actually glad I was here…' she said thinking of finding that note and the fact that if she hadn't she might have spent years never seeing through Eddie for what he really was.

'I'm pleased you were here too,' Finn said.

'Don't be too happy about it, if it wasn't for me, you mightn't have ended up underneath the wheels of that motorbike.' It was the truth. Finn had thrown her to safety out of its path and taken the brunt of the collision.

'I'm still glad,' he said hoarsely. And for a moment, when their eyes met, there was that uncomfortable feeling that perhaps something more was being said than either of them meant. She was saved from making a complete fool of herself by Estelle's mobile phone going off.

'Oh no, I must have forgotten to switch it off. I'm so sorry.' It was one of the topmost cardinal sins of ICU – no phones. It was right up there with don't visit if you have a vomiting bug.

'Go on, go and answer it outside before you set every heart monitor off in the place,' Finn said, laughing.

Wafting a heady scent of expensive perfume after her, Estelle glided easily between them and towards the foot of the bed. 'Behave yourself when I'm gone, you.' Estelle was unrecognisable from that frightened girl who'd turned up that first night. It seemed that as Finn's condition had improved her confidence had grown and she'd become older, sexier and territorial.

'Not much chance of anything else.' Finn laughed.

'I probably should be getting back on shift.' Liv went to follow Estelle out of the unit also.

'Really, is that all you get? Five minutes and then they need you back?' He was smiling at her, almost challenging her to wait a little longer.

'No, of course not, but I'm sure you'd much prefer to spend the time with Estelle than having to make an effort with a perfect stranger at the moment.' The truth was, Liv wasn't even sure why she'd come up here. After all, he was obviously on the mend, and there wasn't much more she could do for him now, apart from handing back the gift she'd been holding for the mysterious M as soon as they released him onto the main ward.

'I like having you here,' he said easily. 'It's…' he paused, then settled on: 'distracting.'

'Well thanks so much. You make me sound like a pothole in the road!' She liked being here too, for some reason, even now that he was awake. It reminded her of being with Rachel. It was a strange feeling, as if she'd come home again. She couldn't explain it if she tried, but it almost felt as if her world had turned in some indefinable way when she'd met him. It was ridiculous of course, to think that three seconds could change your whole life, and yet... Here she was; her life had changed beyond anything she'd have imagined before she put her finger on that button to cross the road. Hadn't she spent the days in the run-up to that, thinking of little more than Eddie proposing to her and that engagement ring and, maybe, a version of a happy ever after that she'd always craved?

And now, well, after finding that note, she knew that if she was ever going to find her happy ever after she'd have to start looking for it without Eddie in the picture. Maybe, she realised too, it wasn't that Finn reminded her of Rachel, as much as he somehow reminded her of herself. And possibly, that was just what she needed at the moment.

'Oh no, not like a pothole.' He was laughing now, jerking her out of her thoughts. 'You're much more entertaining than that. And to be honest, even if you weren't good company, it's just nice to have someone to talk to; seriously, it's a long time to be tied here to these machines.' He shook his head. 'Perhaps, if they transfer me onto a recovery ward tomorrow I'll be able to go walkabout,' he said now.

'I'm sure you will, in no time. For now though, you just have to rest.'

'Would you let me buy you coffee on your break, if they allow me out of here?' He was pulling himself up to watch her and she leant in to straighten the pillows at his back.

'Sure, but it's a much longer walk than you might think.' She knew that getting out of bed that first time might take a lot more of his energy than he realised and the coffee shop was at the furthest end of the hospital from the general wards.

'Well, if they'll let me out, I'm holding you to meeting up for coffee tomorrow on your break!' He looked beyond her now to where Estelle was coming back onto the ward. 'Ah, that didn't take long,' he said changing the subject and winking at Liv.

'I'd better be getting back,' Liv said, not entirely sure what she'd agreed to, but suspecting that Finn wouldn't be telling Estelle about their coffee. On the way downstairs, she shook herself out; after all, it was just coffee. What harm could having a cup of coffee with him do – she wasn't planning on running off with him, or anyone else for that matter.

*

There was something about seeing Finn and Estelle together that sparked something in her. She'd been putting it off since she'd found that note, but she knew now she couldn't put it off any longer. She walked down the three flights of stairs to the huge foyer that was normally packed and noisy with people coming and going, but today, it was silent apart from the furry indistinct sound coming from speakers in the tiny gift shop next to the entrance.

She'd have to ring Pete. She'd thought that night when she found the note that the worst part would be having to tell Eddie that it was over; that she knew, that there was no going back. She'd been wrong. She'd known as soon as she heard his voice, bleary from the previous day's booze, that telling Eddie would not be the worst of this mess. Telling Pete was the bit she was absolutely dreading. Then she thought of those Carry On movies and Hattie Jacques administering foul medicine, and she knew that was what she had to do now: she had to take her medicine, make the call that would break her best friend's heart. She couldn't put it off any longer.

As usual, Pete answered on the second ring.

'What can I do for you Mrs Tucker?' That was Pete, always in good form, quoting from *Carry On Matron* again.

'Ha ha…' she said, because she knew really this wasn't a call for making jokes about. 'Listen, I wanted to talk to you. I've found something…'

'Go on.' Pete was suddenly serious. He had the uncanny knack of being able to see right through her, even when he was over a hundred and fifty miles away; perhaps he picked it up in the silence as much as the words. Liv imagined him, sitting forward, pushing his glasses higher up on his nose. 'Is everything all right?'

'I hope you're sitting down for this, but it's Eddie and…'

'Anya?'

'You already knew?' Liv hadn't expected that.

'No, sorry, not about Eddie, not until you called just now.'

'God, no, I'm sorry. I feel as if…' She felt weirdly as if it was her fault, but that made absolutely no sense at all. 'Are you okay?'

'I'm fine,' he said and she knew from the way he said it that he actually was; perhaps knowing the full truth was a bit of a relief, better than wondering at half a story. 'I'd be more worried about you. You and Eddie were together a long time. How are you?'

'Believe it or not, much better than I'd have imagined, if I'd ever thought this could happen.' She laughed, because honestly, never in her wildest dreams could she have thought that Eddie and Anya would do something like this.

'Are you still in…?' He stopped for a moment, trying to get

his bearing perhaps. 'Oh, God, you're not there on your own, are you? Will I come up? Help you sort things out?'

'No, absolutely not – you need to get yourself sorted. It's sort of settled on me now. I've moved all Eddie's stuff out of my flat and told him it's over. The worst is done.' She laughed, a nervous sound in the back of her throat. Overhead, she saw the clock was just about to fall on the hour. 'Listen, I'm sorry to do this in such a rush, but I'm due back on shift now. I'll call you later, okay?'

'Sure, no problem, Liv…' There was so much more to say. There would be so many more conversations about this, probably over the next couple of days, but for now, Liv knew there was only one thing she wanted to ask.

'Will you be okay?'

'I'll be fine. Honestly, Liv, it doesn't change anything for me and Anya – it was over anyway – but it was hard to see a way out of it with the coffee shop and you know…' He didn't need to say any more. 'Liv?'

'Yes?'

'Mind yourself, yeah?'

'Of course and you too.' She smiled before swiping the call to end. And she realised that far from being more miserable after the call, she actually felt relieved. Another piece of the past put to rest.

*

Francine was sitting in the nurses' station when she returned to A&E. It seemed they were having a brief reprieve. 'The calm before the storm, no doubt.' Francine chuckled. 'So, what's been going on with you this Christmas?' She looked at Liv with the sort of knowingness that negated any lies.

'Oh, just your usual kind of Christmas fun and games…' Liv thought she might as well be honest; until now, there hadn't been five minutes on the ward to talk to anyone about anything much more than being on the job. 'I found out that Eddie has been seeing someone else…' she said.

'Oh, no. I'm so sorry,' Francine said and she reached out and patted Liv's hand. 'And you've been stuck here, on your own for the whole holiday.'

'Yes, maybe it was for luck, being here for Christmas. If I'd gone home, I'd probably be none the wiser.' She shook her head, because honestly, she was glad she'd found out, even if it hurt, somehow knowing was almost like having the fears that she'd buried at every turn confirmed and it was a surprising release. 'Anyway, I've told him it's over and…'

'But maybe…'

'No, Francine, it was meant to be. We've never been right together, Eddie and I – it's never lived up to what I always wanted.' She just hadn't been brave enough to admit it before. 'And I think finding this out… well, it's given me the courage to do something about it.' She smiled. 'I've moved all his stuff out of the flat.'

'Can you just do that?'

'I don't see why not. It's my flat and he's only ever been staying with me. He's never made any contribution towards the mortgage or anything like that so…' She didn't add that she couldn't stand the idea of him coming back to live there now. 'Actually, I'm glad to have it back to myself again, moving his stuff out and generally tidying the place up, I'm going to redecorate in the New Year and…'

'Well, I can help you there.' Francine smiled. 'My Dave just retired in November. He's sitting at home twiddling his thumbs all day long. I'm sure he'd love to give you a hand.'

'Oh, Francine, I couldn't possibly let him do that.' It was a fabulous offer; Dave had spent his whole life working as a painter decorator. Liv knew he'd have her flat whipped into perfect colour in no time.

'Don't be daft. It'll get him out of the house, sure what else would he be doing on damp January days!'

'Oh Francine,' Liv laughed, because she knew Francine managed her husband as if she was managing a child sometimes and he seemed very happy to have her telling him what to do.

'Well, good, that's settled so. You pick out the colours and I'll have a chat with Dave. All he'll need is access to a kettle and a clear room to get started.'

'Really? That's such a kind offer, but listen, you'll have to check with him first of all, see if he doesn't mind.'

'He absolutely won't. He's been going up the walls with boredom and you know what January is like – it's probably just going to be one miserable raining day after another.'

'Well, if he doesn't mind, then it'd be great – thanks, Francine.' Liv threw her arms around her boss. It really was the nicest gift she'd gotten in a long time.

11

Liv had the worst feeling. It hit her that evening as she sat watching TV with her parents. She hadn't heard from Eddie since he'd stormed off the beach and left her there. What if Eddie had moved Anya into the flat anyway? Not that she didn't like Anya – she seemed nice enough – but she knew that Anya, with her perfectly groomed hair and fashionable wardrobe, would take up a heck of a lot more space in her tiny flat than just one night in the spare room.

In her mind's eye, Liv imagined Anya would arrive with a tonne of bags and boxes. She imagined her kitchen cluttered up with hair straighteners and nail dryers and God knows what else plugged in at every socket. Anya would fill up the tiny bathroom with products and long blonde hair would clog up the drains. She would be the sort of woman who would use four bath sheets at a time and then leave them all sopping wet on the floor.

Liv knew she was being unkind, but she remembered that when Anya had moved into Pete's he'd had to employ a cleaning lady after the first week. There would be tan on the sheets and nail varnish on the couch and then there was the fact that Liv worked shifts at the hospital. She liked to come home to her little flat and potter about and sleep for eight hours before going back in to work that night. Having Anya there would mean extra noise, extra traffic through the place and ultimately, less time and space for Liv in a flat that Eddie had already managed to shrink around his own needs. No. No. No. She pulled out her phone and dialled Eddie's number. No answer. She dialled again.

'Everything all right?' Her mum looked across at her.

'Yes, I'm just…' She shook her head. 'I'm being stupid, that's all.' Her dad switched the volume down on the TV. 'It's Anya. I'm afraid that Eddie is going to empty her stuff out of Pete's apartment and let her move into the flat.'

'He wouldn't do that, not without asking you first,' her father said.

'That's the thing – we had a row about it today.' Or as near to a row as it was possible to have with Eddie before he stomped off in a huff, Liv didn't add. 'And then, when I dropped off the shopping at Barbara's she said that he'd gone to help Anya move her stuff.'

'Well, if he has, it's very simple; he'll just have to move it back out again. You can't have three people in that flat; it's far too small and Anya is well able to go out and get her own place,' her father said smiling at her. 'Tell you what, love, if he has, I'll go up there myself and move the two of them out for you.'

'Ah, Dad.'

'He's joking.' Her mother laughed. 'Don't worry, love, I'm sure Eddie wouldn't go moving her in if you've already said no.'

* * *

Still, something of that uneasiness would not leave her. She imagined Eddie, showing Anya around the flat, but then, she thought of him hoicking boxes, bags and crates up the three flights of stairs and suddenly, the whole idea seemed to be completely mad. For one thing, Eddie complained about having to bring home the groceries if she rang him at work; he was hardly likely to go carting all of Anya's worldly possessions across the city and then up three flights of stairs in the middle of his precious Christmas holidays. And yet, he had travelled all the way back to Dublin with her, hadn't he?

Perhaps he had things to do in the workshop. Perhaps he was fixing her up with some mate of his or someone he knew through college who had a spare room they were prepared to let out to her. That would be it. Some pal of Eddie's would be pinching himself at this very moment when he realised what a gorgeous new roommate he'd managed to bag himself.

And then, Liv began to feel really guilty. After all, perhaps it *would* only have been for a couple of nights, until Anya got sorted properly. She'd have to go back to work before any of them to open up the coffee shop. Regardless of what was going to happen to the business, Anya would certainly want to make as much money as she could to continue paying the rent for as long as possible. God, but she was a terrible human being – not allowing Anya to stay on her sofa; after all, what difference would a couple of days make to her, while it could mean the world to Anya?

She couldn't settle for the rest of the evening. A strange feeling niggled at her, as if she was missing something that was just under her nose. 'I think I'll head off to bed now,' she said as she got up from the chair.

'But, it's only early,' her mother protested.

'I just fancy snuggling up with my book before I go to sleep.' Liv bent down and kissed her mother on her forehead.

'All right, love, well, sleep tight.'

It was lovely to be back at the farm again, she had a few more days before she was due back on shift at the hospital and it had been far too long since she'd been home last time. It seemed that there was always something to be done on her days off recently. Between helping Eddie with the workshop and then trying to keep the flat tidy, the fridge filled and the dishwasher emptied, she hadn't been home in months.

Liv pulled out the book Maya had pressed into her hands earlier. She was looking forward to this. There was nothing like the silence of the farm to really relax with and enjoy a good book. She'd just snuggled beneath the quilt when her mobile rang. Eddie, or at least, that was who she assumed was calling her, until she looked at the caller display.

* * *

'I just wanted to let you know that I'm back in Dublin, I thought it would be good to get back to normal and I had things to tie up, before the New Year,' Pete said when he called her that evening. Usually, he texted, so she had a feeling that maybe he just needed to talk. Had he come back earlier for her? In her hour of need? It'd be typical Pete, always thinking of everyone else.

'Well, if you're not doing anything I've got some curry dinners in the freezer?'

'That sounds like a plan.'

A few hours later, he arrived with beer and brought the freezing cold night air into the cosy flat with him.

'So?' Liv asked as she popped his plate into the microwave for a final blast. She'd made the curries just a week before Christmas, thinking at the time that it would be good to have something easily to hand when she and Eddie got back from Ballycove after the Christmas break. It seemed like a million years ago, as if that had been someone else's life she'd been living by mistake.

'So, yourself,' he said taking the top off a bottle of beer and handing it to her. She understood; of course she did. He didn't want to be fussed over, having people looking at him as if there was something wrong with him, waiting for him to break down because things were finished with Anya. It must be a relief to be back in Dublin. He just wanted to chill out and shoot the breeze.

They sat companionably on the old sofa watching one of those movies that turns up every Christmas, and they ate their chicken curries in comfortable silence.

'I like what you've done with the place,' he said in the ad break.

'What, emptied out half the crap that I hadn't even realised was here?' It was true; the flat felt bigger, more hers somehow now that all of Eddie's belongings had been removed.

'Have you changed the locks?'

'Not yet. It's on the to-do list,' she said and maybe it should be, because the last thing she wanted was Eddie dropping in when he felt like it.

'I can do that for you, if you want,' he said sipping his beer.

'I'm sure you have enough to be doing as it is.'

'The real fire is great; it really makes the place feel like home again.' He pointed his fork towards it. It was burning away gently in the grate. She'd picked up another fire log and a bag of kindling in the corner shop. 'It's nice to see it lit again.' He was smiling, probably thinking back to the day when he had cleaned the chimney after Rachel begged him when they'd first moved in.

'Yes, I had almost forgotten it was there, to be honest.' Which, she knew, was probably the story of her whole relationship with Eddie; somehow, she'd lost sight of all the lovely things she had in her life. The fireplace was only the beginning of it.

'You're probably going to have to hang a stocking from the mantelpiece next Christmas.' He was making fun of her.

'Not likely. I intend to be home in Ballycove next Christmas, with a little luck,' she said because she'd missed her family this year. Actually, sitting here with Pete was probably the first time she wasn't lonely since Christmas Eve.

'It was a fairly crap Christmas for both of us. Don't worry, odds on next year being a thousand times better,' he said and she caught that underlying, quiet optimism that had always marked him out. It had buoyed her through her darkest days and she was glad to have him here with her tonight.

'I'm glad you came over, Pete,' she said.

'That's me, always at your service.' He was joking, but he reached out and touched her hand, held it for a moment. 'You know, he was never good enough for you.'

'Ah, stop it,' Liv said, because she knew he was only trying to make her feel better.

'I'm serious – everyone thought it. It was different with me and Anya. People looked at us and I knew they thought I was punching far above my weight. She was so beautiful, while I'm still…'

'I never thought that,' Liv said, although, honestly, when

she looked at him sometimes she still saw that geeky kid from school. He'd been all teeth, arms, legs and glasses.

'Maybe not, but other people. I know, they thought Anya was only going out with me for my money and…' He looked away from her now. She had a feeling that the break-up might hit him harder than he expected after all. 'But I really thought, in the beginning…'

'Listen to me, Pete. Anya was very lucky to get you. You're sincere and funny and…' She looked at him now, as objectively as she could. He wasn't the same boy she'd grown up with anymore. He had turned into one of those men who wore his good fortune with unassuming ease. He had turned from a geeky kid into an attractive, successful man – and she'd never really noticed it until this moment. 'The problem with you, Pete, is that you're operating in life as if you're still that geeky kid. You don't seem to realise that Anya was lucky to get you. Together, you made a really striking couple.' Then she smiled and sipped her beer.

'What?'

'I don't know if I should tell you this, really, you'll probably cast it up to me forever more.' She shook her head, then keeping her gaze on the fire that nestled gently in the grate, said, 'The first time I saw you together, I had to do a double-take.' She smiled at him. That's what friends are for, after all: making you feel better about yourself when you need it most.

'Huh?'

'Yep. I remember that first night we bumped into you both at the cinema in town. I noticed you first, sitting before us. I didn't recognise you; you know how it is when you see someone you know out of context? But, you just seemed to be so… striking, you turned heads.' It was true. She'd spotted their silhouettes first, but there was something in the way they carried themselves and then later, she'd waited to see them, hadn't recognised Pete at first. They had been walking towards the exit and it had taken a moment to realise it was actually Pete. He'd looked like one of those men you see hanging about the Kilkenny Design Centre, all expensive casual jacket, good hair, attractive and intelligent-looking and then, of course, the spell was broken, when she realised it was just Pete.

'You're making fun of me now. Anya was the stunner more like,' he said to deflect any embarrassment from himself, but still, she was glad to see, the compliment had perked him up.

'Well, she certainly managed to turn Eddie's head,' Liv managed to quip.

'I'm sorry. You don't want to hear this, probably, but, I never really liked him very much,' Pete said. 'You always knew that?'

'You were just chalk and cheese.'

'I made the best of things because you two were together.' He leant forward on the sofa; the movie was firmly forgotten about for now. 'The truth is, Liv, he was never good enough for you. I have a feeling if Rachel was here, she'd have made you see sense a lot sooner.'

'Stop it. You sound like my dad, trying to make me feel better.'

'I'm not just saying it because you're Rachel's sister or because we're friends, but you were too kind, too caring and far too bloody soft for the likes of Eddie Quirke.'

'Oh, Pete, that's so nice…' Because although it was a long time ago, Liv could remember what it was like to be invisible as a teenager. She looked at him now; he was very close and then, before she realised what was happening, they had leant towards each other, their lips just brushing together. It felt as if everything came crashing in simultaneously. Her senses were suddenly on high alert, her stomach turning somersaults and then they kissed and she was, for that protracted exquisite moment, lost.

Pete pulled back. 'I'm sorry, I shouldn't have done that.'

'It was…' She wanted to say perfect, but she couldn't quite put the word together.

'You were so… saying all those things and I've just messed everything up,' he said standing so quickly he knocked over her bottle of beer. 'Shit.' Then he was grabbing a towel, drying up the mess. 'I should get going. I'll call you, if it's not too… awkward?' He bit his lip and then he was gathering up his coat and Liv was left looking about her and wondering if it had really happened at all.

12

It was Barbara.

'Hi, Barbara, is everything okay?' Liv asked wearily, knowing only too well that if everything was hunky-dory, the last person Barbara would be contacting was Liv.

'Of course everything is not okay. I'm here on my own and there's someone down at the end of my garden.'

'Do you want me to call the guards?' Liv squinted at the clock on her nightstand. It was three o'clock in the morning.

'I've done that already, but everyone knows they are worse than useless. Last time it took them almost an hour to get here.'

'Last time?'

'Never mind that now, just come over here and see for yourself. There must be ten of them in it, smoking cigarettes and probably drinking too. I'll wager not one of them is over fifteen.'

'Right,' Liv said pushing herself out of her lovely cosy bed. She moved automatically, slipping into her clothes and shoes, grabbing a flashlight – although there was always one in the jeep – shrugging into the warmest coat she could put her hand on in the porch before venturing out into the pitch-black of the night.

The jeep cut through the silent village like a roaring storm trooper pushing through pristine snowy silence. She dialled the local Garda station only to hear the call being redirected to the larger town three villages over. Barbara was probably right. It would take the squad car an age to get here. Liv hung up before they answered – what was the point in wasting everyone's time, especially if it was only kids? This was Ballycove after all; it wouldn't be much more than a couple of fourteen-year-olds. Liv was used to dealing with far scarier night owls in A&E on any given Saturday night.

When she pulled up outside Barbara's door, it hardly looked like *CSI Ballycove*. If anything, the road and all of the gardens looked as peaceful as the graveyard just a short distance away. She decided to investigate before going inside to check on Barbara and she set off around the perimeter of the house, letting herself in through a side gate that probably should have been properly locked to begin with. She stuffed her phone inside her jacket. The torch, apart from making her feel like Nancy Drew, picked out the uneven path easily. The garden, which had probably once been quite productive (Eddie told her his dad had spent many hours here, growing vegetables and pottering about), was faded now. It was a long stretch of overgrown grass and weeds on either side of the path, uneven where drills had once been dug out, but flattened out roughly with each passing season of neglect.

At the end, a shed, made of scrap pieces of wood and corrugated sheeting, hunkered back against the wall. The door, swinging open in the breeze made Liv jump but she managed to stifle down a small surprised squeal. There was no-one there. It seemed the culprit was just an old door that someone had forgotten to close. She checked inside, flashing her torch around the little shed in case there was a stray cat or dog huddled safely from the falling snow. The last thing she wanted to do was lock some poor sheltering animal up for perhaps days or weeks on end. She had a feeling that no-one came near here from one end of the week to the next, not Barbara and certainly not Eddie.

There was nothing more than dirty and rusting gardening tools and a single string of rotting onions hanging from the roof. She pulled the door out securely behind her, feeling an odd sadness for the notion that this place might have been very different if Eddie's father had not died at such a young age. She hardly remembered him, really, but it was only a few years before she and Eddie had gotten together. Her father had said once that Tim Quirke had chosen the easier path. Was suicide really easier than living with Barbara? She shivered now and wondered if it was the winter cold or some spirit that had brushed too close to her as she turned to walk back up the path towards the house.

It took Barbara a few minutes to answer the door and for all her worry on the phone earlier, Liv couldn't shake the feeling that the woman had managed to go back to sleep again.

'The shed you say? Left open – yes, that would probably account for the noise,' she said standing solidly in the doorway. It was obvious that now the problem was sorted, Barbara was not in the mood for chit-chat.

'So, it's happened before?' Liv was fighting the urge to

lose her temper. After all, if it was just a simple question of checking that the shed door was locked at night, surely it wasn't too much for Barbara to do a simple job like that herself?

'Oh, yes, it happens all the time; someone pops in for something and then forgets to lock it up. Honestly, you'd think the Vikings were making a return assault with the noise in the middle of the night. It's enough to bring on one of my terrible migraines; I could be out for days with it...' Barbara said closing out the door slightly. Liv knew only too well what that was like, so perhaps, she could forgive Barbara this once. She turned back towards the jeep, had hardly reached the gate when she heard the soft click of the Quirke front door closing behind her. Then there was the rattle of the chain lock being pulled over to ensure that no intruder could make their way back into the house for the rest of the night.

It was only when Liv sat into the jeep that she began to wonder again where Eddie was. There was no sign of his van parked outside the house. Surely, he wasn't in the pub until this hour. It was almost four o'clock in the morning. He couldn't still be in Dublin with Anya, could he? Out of the blue, a sly film of sweat eased through every pore in her body, a tightening of her stomach muscles and the feeling that it was hard to catch her breath. Where on earth was he? She couldn't turn around and ask his mother if she knew where her son was; it would only give Barbara the satisfaction of being able to place a gnawing question mark forever between them.

And then, she realised what it was that had been lurking

beneath her thoughts since they'd had that disagreement on the beach. She had only half given it words earlier with her parents, but now she was almost certain. He had decided to take matters into his own hands and invite Anya to stay in the flat anyway. Surely, he wouldn't do something like that, not without both of them agreeing to it, not when she'd been so clear about the fact that it just wasn't a runner. And then, her breath caught up and she felt for a moment as if she might never catch it again. This was ridiculous. The only thing that had caused it was the realisation that of course she'd let Anya stay, because otherwise, Eddie might just take her lovely ring and leave her all alone again.

She felt hot stinging tears of humiliation and some small part of her wondered how had she turned into such a needy, dependent woman? She shuddered. Rachel would turn in her grave if she could see her bending over backwards to Barbara Quirke, never mind putting up with half of Eddie's antics. She quickly pushed the thought from her mind. No. This was all her own fault. Why on earth couldn't she just have said *okay*? If she'd just said Anya could stay everything might be fine now. But no. She so badly wanted to get married and have a family – she couldn't bear the idea of Eddie taking off and leaving her.

What was she turning into? And she knew it was pathetic, but there was no changing that now, was there?

*

The following morning, when she finally woke up back in her bed at the farmhouse, her adventure, if that was the name for it, almost seemed like a dream or a nightmare. Except, she knew it was all too real. Her eyes were sticky with tears that she had a feeling kept on coming long after sleep – however short and unsettled – had finally shrouded her.

Pete's call at eleven was a pleasant surprise. She needed something, or someone, to distract her from the maelstrom of emotions that Eddie's worrying silence was evoking in her. She'd tried his mobile several times, sent texts that she'd edited as much as she could to make sure there was no ounce of neediness contained anywhere between the lines. It was simple; she just needed to hear Eddie's voice. To know that things were okay between them. She needed him to tell her that he loved her, even though part of her wondered if he ever would. But still, just knowing that they were together, even if he couldn't say the words, was as much as it would take for her to quell this terrible feeling of emptiness within her.

'Hey, what are you up to?' Pete sounded good and if she thought there was an undercurrent of worry in his voice, she simply put it down to her own black mood.

'Not a lot, just hanging about here, quite content and happy with a new book.' First lie of the day: she felt anything but content or happy.

'How are those lambs? I thought I might go and see them – if you had time to spare, you might even treat me to a cup of tea?'

'Sure, not that I'd expect you to know one end of a lamb from the other.' Pete had grown up in the village – his father was a barber and his mother worked in the local supermarket – but as soon as he moved to the city when he went to college, Pete became a townie.

He arrived within minutes, loaded down with a six-pack of fancy craft beer for her dad and chocolates for her mother, smiling and full of his usual friendly banter, but Liv knew immediately that something was wrong. She dragged him from the warmth of the kitchen out to the little shed where there were now sixteen lambs bleating loudly.

'What is it? What's happened?' Her gut felt heavy with anticipation; she just knew it was bad news.

'It's nothing. It's…'

'It's not nothing. I can read you like a book, remember?' They'd been through too much together watching Rachel die for there to be room left for secrets or half-truths between them.

'Fine, I just… I don't know how to say it, but…' He walked towards the far end of the shed, picking out his steps – she had a feeling he was even more carefully picking out his next words. He seemed to be purposely keeping his silent stare on the ground, as if he couldn't quite meet her eyes. She knew then it must be really bad, because they'd shared the worst news and never had there ever been a time when they couldn't just blurt out what they were thinking.

'Oh, God, it's Eddie, isn't it?' Liv wasn't sure if she expected him to be dead, or worse. And then she mentally corrected herself, because nothing could be worse than losing someone like she'd lost Rachel.

'Yes. He's…' Pete looked at the ground for a moment, considering the best way to put what he had to say next.

When he met her eyes again, she knew this was excruciating for him, as hard for him as anything he'd had to tell her.

'Just say it,' she whispered.

'It's Eddie. He and Anya, they're seeing each other. I mean, behind our backs, they've been…'

'No.' Liv put up her hand to stop him. She didn't want to hear this. 'There's some mistake. I mean, I'd know, wouldn't I?' And then she thought about all those times when Eddie had walked out the door, how he'd never once told her he loved her, when he'd joked about never being tied down. Not so funny now. Now maybe, if she let herself, she could see it. It wasn't what he'd done, was it? It was what he hadn't done. Liv turned away, tried to focus on the old stone wall opposite, but she couldn't see anything. Her eyes had filled with tears that she willed not to fall. Everything was a complete blur; every part of her was disintegrating into a maelstrom of emotion; all the pathetic feelings were rising up in her. She didn't want this to be happening to her; she didn't want to lose Eddie. She wanted to get married, have a family and a nice house and… She was thirty-six, for heaven's sake. She felt too old to start over again. 'No.' Liv heard her own voice, coming from some resolute part of her. 'No. I don't believe it. He wouldn't. There must be some mistake.' She turned back towards Pete again.

'I'm sorry, Liv. I know it's awful, but… See for yourself. She's sent me a text by accident… Look, if you don't believe me. It's meant to be for Eddie, but… somehow, she must have…' He held out his phone to her.

'No. I'm not looking at that. There's some mistake; it's another Eddie. I'd know.' And then, she felt something strange happen to her features. 'He'd never do this to me.' Her voice sounded a lot more confident than she felt. She turned away again, not willing to face either Pete or this terrible news. She closed her eyes, fixed her hair and then turned up the corners of her mouth into the nearest she could manage to a smile. Of course, she was smiling; it was an unreal contortion of her features, but she hoped it would be enough to make Pete stop with this thing he thought he was setting in motion. 'We're getting engaged, Pete. So, it can't be real. You've gotten him confused with someone else – that's all, a simple mistake.' And she started to laugh, because, really, that's all it was – crossed wires, something innocent that had become all mixed-up.

* * *

Even though Liv's mind had been full of that kiss when she'd fallen asleep and when she'd woken in the morning, it was the engagement ring in Eddie's workshop that filled her dreams. Now, as she picked her way back up the avenue to the hospital, she wondered if she had imagined coming across it that afternoon. But she was quite sure she had seen it. She could remember her surprise, a feeling that mixed up the idea of something she'd always wanted with a nagging doubt that she hadn't been brave enough to face until now. Eddie had made that ring for someone – the question that she really wondered about now, was if he'd made it for her or for Anya. Of course, the truth was, he could have just made it as a commission, but it was the way he'd hidden it away in a drawer and he'd never once mentioned a commission with emeralds or that unique motif.

The hospital was a little busier today; filling up now with relatives popping in to see patients and no doubt the A&E would be busy with more seasonal-related incidents like ice skaters and new trampoline enthusiasts who had come a cropper over the last few days. Liv was early for her shift, so she decided to check in on Finn before she started. She had almost an hour to spare. Morgan told her he'd been moved to male surgical overnight; apparently, there weren't enough beds in the general ward at present.

'Hey,' he said, smiling when she popped her head around the door. 'You found me.'

'It wasn't that hard. You all but sent me a map and I do work here.' They'd given him a bed in a room with three others.

'Come on.' Finn pushed himself out of the chair. 'The doctor says I need to get exercise.' He was walking perfectly – no limp – and he seemed to be back to normal apart from the nasty-looking bruise on his head. He had to be in some pain though, even if they had medicated him to minimise it.

'Coffee break?' she asked, looking at her watch. It was just before eleven. She was due on shift at twelve.

'I was just about to suggest the same thing,' he said setting off with her at a slow pace.

The coffee shop was busy, but they managed to nab a table near the window and Liv queued for the coffees while Finn looked out at the comings and goings at the front of the hospital. She had a feeling he'd need to catch his breath after the walk, even if it looked as if he wouldn't admit it. They chatted for a while, easily covering over the daily pleasantries while occasionally dipping into the fabric of each other's lives. Finn, it turned out, was a writer. He wrote young adult books about witches and warlocks. 'No. Nothing like Harry Potter, nowhere near as successful, but good enough to allow me to dodge any real work.' She discovered he had stayed in Ballycove a couple of times; renting a cottage in the winter months, just to write in peace. 'It's beautiful there, desolate and thrilling, perfect really for what I'm writing when the wind howls and the mist covers the land for as far as the eye can see.'

For most of the time, he lived in Dublin, in a little house near the docks. He'd been married, once to Mena Swan, but that had ended and there had been no-one serious since. Liv knew Mena Swan. Everyone knew Mena – she'd spent the last couple of years propping up Ireland's longest-running soap opera, but she'd recently announced that she was leaving to pursue other projects across the pond, so she was cutting her ties to Dublin and presumably to her ex-husband also. There hadn't been anyone serious since his marriage ended.

'Does Estelle realise that?' The question slipped from Liv and she knew as soon as she said it she was wrong to ask. 'I'm sorry, just ignore that.'

'Estelle?' He threw his head back and laughed.

'What's so funny?'

'Sorry, no.' He put his hand on his side; laughing isn't always the best medicine. 'No. It's a valid question – after all, you did buy the coffee, it gives you a right.' He was joking with her now, but when he began to speak again, his voice was gentler, more thoughtful. 'The truth is, Estelle and I?' It was an unanswered question.

'She's very beautiful.'

'She is, but she's like my sister. I've known her forever. She grew up just down the road from me and she spent as much time in my house as she did in her own. My mum used to babysit her while her parents were at work.' He examined his coffee cup as if he might find the next sentence hidden in the logo on the side. 'She pretended to be my nearest and dearest because she knew my parents were away and she wanted to make sure I was going to be well looked after.' He pointed towards the bandage on his head. 'Sometimes it feels as if she's almost taken ownership of me, but the fact is, I'm probably the nearest thing she'll ever have to an older brother.' It was true. Estelle had all but taken up residence at his bedside. She'd have had to lie to the nursing staff on duty too; otherwise, they'd never have let a casual girlfriend or friend into ICU. Wouldn't Pete have done exactly that for her, if they were in the same situation?

'No, I get it. She's been really worried about you. Sometimes hospital rules are meant to be broken.'

'Exactly. Now my parents are here, I'm hoping that she'll take a step back and enjoy what's left of Christmas with her own friends and family.' He smiled.

'What about you? Aren't you meant to be getting engaged one of these days?'

'Oh, you don't want to hear about my love life.' She laughed in spite of herself, but he was still waiting for an answer. 'Okay, here it is; I'll give you the edited highlights only. I've been with someone for years, that is until a few nights ago when I went back to my flat and discovered that he's been seeing my best friend's girlfriend behind my back, probably for months.'

'Ooh, painful.' Finn raised his cup in toast to her. 'I'm sorry; it really has been a crappy Christmas for you, hasn't it?'

'You could say that, or you could say that I'm looking forward to an exciting new year.' Liv leant back in her seat and she felt the glorious winter sun penetrate the glass window at her back. 'I'm surprising myself when I say this, but I'm actually looking forward to a new start. Things with Eddie, well, perhaps they were never really right to begin with.'

'How do you mean?'

'Long story, but the simple truth is, at this point, I actually feel as if finding out about him and Anya is almost a relief. Does that sound crazy? I mean, it was terrible in the beginning and still, there are moments when I feel so betrayed, but somehow, it feels as if I have hope of something better for the first time in as long as I can remember.'

'Not at all, if it's how you truly feel.' He smiled at her and they sat there for a while, both lost in their own thoughts; perhaps they were both getting a second chance. 'What if, in the spirit of new starts and by way of saying thank you… what if I was to ask you to dinner?'

'Oh, I don't know.' There were too many reasons not to go, chief among them being the fact that she'd been his nurse and he'd been her patient – if only briefly. There was also the reality that regardless of how she felt at this particular moment, she knew, so soon after Eddie, she was in no fit state to go getting involved with someone new, certainly not someone like Finn O'Connell who really could break her heart in two with just the toss of a coin.

'As friends, just as friends, we could celebrate our own late Christmas; it seems such a shame to have missed out on this one,' he added.

'As friends?' She smiled at him, because as long as that was clear, where could the harm be? She didn't want to tell him she just wasn't a casual sort of girl, but then, she looked at him and she had a feeling that maybe Finn O'Connell wasn't a casual sort of bloke either, not if the right woman came along.

13

There had been some kind of crazy mix-up. Pete or someone had gotten their wires crossed; there was no way that Eddie was seeing Anya behind her back. No way, not Eddie. Liv took a deep breath. But then that small traitorous voice in her head asked: *So, where is he now?* Exactly. *Where has he been for the last two days?* Off in Dublin sorting out where Anya is going to live, that's where. He was looking out for her – that's all it was, Liv told herself sternly. He was looking out for her, just like anyone with a scrap of human kindness would. She was sorry now that she'd stormed off on him, sorry that she hadn't asked him for more details; maybe if she'd done that she could put this whole silly notion out of her head. Maybe. What on earth was wrong with Pete, though? That was the question.

Liv felt terrible, as if she might get physically sick at the idea of what Pete had suggested. He was wrong. She had to convince herself of that, otherwise – well, she couldn't contemplate otherwise. There was no otherwise.

Eddie and she were good. Fine, so their relationship had never exactly been what she'd always dreamed of, but she wanted to marry him. She wanted to spend the rest of her life with him – didn't she? Now that it felt as if it might be slipping away from her, Liv felt it more keenly: this idea that she wanted to settle down, have a family, buy a proper house, start the next phase of her life. With Eddie.

She was sure of it. The more that niggling little doubt dug into her thoughts, the more she imagined herself stamping on it, like a smouldering fire that she couldn't possibly allow to take light in her imagination.

She would have it out with him. She had to have it out with him; she needed to hear him deny it. She needed him to tell her that he loved her, just this once. She needed him to go down on bended knee and convince her that she hadn't wasted years of her life on him.

And yet, in her mind's eye, she just couldn't see it.

She couldn't see him on bended knee. She couldn't imagine him waiting at the altar for her. She couldn't even imagine him in a dress suit – never mind actually standing there and proclaiming to their families and friends that he loved her and he wanted to spend the rest of his life cherishing her. Hah.

He'd never cherished anything more than his time down in Flannelly's with his mates, getting paralytic on too much beer and old stories that had been told far too often already.

Liv marched back up the farmyard. Bloody Pete. Why on earth did he have to come here telling her this today? She was so angry with him, too angry to be able to see that he'd only been looking out for her. Too angry to realise that coming here, giving her this awful news, was the mark of a real friend.

She pulled out her phone and stabbed at Eddie's number to call. It rang out. She wanted to scream, but the truth was she could hardly breathe. 'Oh, Eddie, what have you done?' she said out loud. The truth was beginning to dawn on her. She began to put together a text. *Where are you? Eddie, please call me, there's something I need to...* She stopped. What did she need to do, ask him or tell him?

Maybe she already knew, even if she didn't want to admit it to herself. Instead, she rang Barbara.

'Yes?' Barbara sounded sniffy.

'Hi, Barbara, I'm trying to track down Eddie. You don't happen to know where he is, do you?'

'I haven't seen him since yesterday, when he went off with Anya,' she said coolly.

'Hasn't he called you?'

'He's a big boy now, Liv; he doesn't ring me every five minutes.'

'Of course,' Liv said. If it wasn't for the fact that she was probably in complete shock, Barbara was the last person she'd have rung.

'You should know as much as I do; you are meant to be his girlfriend after all,' Barbara said.

'Of course, but I just wondered if he'd been in touch. I haven't been able to reach him and what with the icy roads and everything...' It was the best she could manage at the moment, but then she thought, if Eddie had been playing away with Anya, the icy roads would be the last thing he needed to worry about when she got her hands on him.

'Well, that's nice to hear.' Barbara's voice oozed sarcasm.

'I won't sleep a wink tonight now, thinking of him in that van.'

'Sorry, I'm sure there's nothing to worry about, but if he does call you, will you ask him to ring me? I just need to check something with him.' As she hung up the phone, she spotted headlights snaking their way along the drive. Maya, home from work. Liv wiped the tears from her eyes – funny, she hadn't even realised that she was crying. God, she felt her stomach churn with the worry of it all. She would feel such a fool if she had to admit this to Maya. It was only days since she'd told her sister she was sure that Eddie was about to propose to her. She took a deep breath, trying to reassure herself that maybe the world wasn't crashing in on her.

Liv raced into the farmhouse before Maya could see her tear-stained face. She could hide out in her room for a while, until she'd calmed down a little, maybe put on some concealer to cover her reddened eyes and perhaps she could try to fool everyone else, since as each second passed, it was becoming harder to ignore the truth of things for herself.

'Fancy coming down to Flannelly's with me later?' Maya asked as they washed up after dinner.

'Really?' Liv asked, because Maya was the very last person who ever wanted to go near Flannelly's.

'Yes, I have to drop in some sponsorship prizes for their darts tournament.' She shook her head. She was trying to remind people locally that the solicitor's practice on their doorstep was invested in the village.

'All right, so,' Liv heard herself saying, but she knew, she just wanted to see if Eddie had said anything to any of his mates about when he'd be back in Ballycove. She knew how pathetic that was, even as she thought it, but she couldn't help it. She'd gone back over that last day with him in her mind a thousand times. They'd rowed or they'd had words; it was as close to having an argument as Eddie got. He was, she realised now, far too passive-aggressive to actually have a good old clearing-of-the-air barney with anyone. He'd stomped off and why? All because of Anya. And that just made Liv feel even more miserable.

There was only one thing for it. That evening, she plastered on a tonne of make-up before they headed off to Flannelly's.

'Maybe we should ring Pete and ask him to join us?' Maya said as they were driving towards the village.

'No. I don't think that would be a great idea at the moment.'

'Still not over Anya?' Maya didn't sound convinced.

'Not that, so much – we had a bit of a bicker at each other today.'

'You and Pete?' Maya glanced across at her. 'But you two never argue.'

'Nearly never, it turns out. I just snapped at him over nothing and he took the hump. I'm sure we'll be pals again before you know it, but I'm really not in the mood for him tonight.' She was glad to be getting out of the car and so avoiding any more scrutiny from Maya. It was just too much to think about the state of her friendship with Pete on top of the worry of things with Eddie.

'Fine so, I get you all to myself.' Then Maya put her hand on the door to push it in. 'Just the one?'

'Absolutely.' It was more than enough time to waste in this place.

The pub was emptier than it had been the last evening she'd been in here. Yet somehow, all the regulars seemed to be here, still sitting on the same stools, as if they'd never left, just grown older and wider where they sat. Behind the bar, Nick Flannelly was wiping glasses; his eyebrow raised just a fraction when he spotted the Latimer sisters arriving in the door for a drink. Maya dropped the prizes on the bar and Liv wondered for a moment if she hadn't had to pull Nick Flannelly out of a scrape or two already with the law.

'Well, ladies, what can I get you?' Nick was the owner's son, the sort of kid who served up drink and false welcome with ease and then fault-finding fast remarks on each customer after they'd left the pub. Liv had never liked him and she was certain the feeling was mutual.

She and Maya ordered their drinks and took a table near the front door, but the pub was too small not to be part of whatever conversation was going on at the bar.

'No Eddie tonight?' one of the regulars called to Liv.

'Ah no, he'll be back soon. He's just gone to Dublin with...'

'Oh, we know right enough who he's gone with.' Nick sneered.

'What's all that about?' Maya whispered.

'I'm not sure,' Liv said but her heart felt as if it had plummeted to the depths of her stomach, because, even though she didn't want to, she could make a pretty accurate guess. So much for interrogating them, she could hardly look at them after seeing the mocking look in Nick's eyes.

They stayed just long enough to finish off their drinks and then they left their glasses back on the bar counter and said goodnight to the drinkers stationed there.

The night had grown biting cold, as if someone had dropped a blanket of arctic air about the village, and Liv pulled her jacket closer around her as they made their way to the jeep.

She felt Maya's hand reach out to her, just as she was about to turn over the engine.

'Look,' her sister breathed, although no-one could hear them. Liv squinted to see out the windshield as a light tracing of snow was beginning to fall, but she didn't have to squint for long before she saw Eddie's familiar figure swagger along the footpath. He looked as if he might be a little drunk, but that wasn't what Maya was pointing at. 'Isn't that Anya?' she said, hardly loud enough to be heard on the still air in the jeep. And it was, Anya and Eddie walking down the main street, arms wrapped about each other, like love's young dream. There was no mistaking the relationship between them. This had nothing to do with keeping balance on a slippery path and everything to do with brazenly telling anyone who cared to see them that they were together – a couple. Such a pity that he hadn't told Liv first.

Panic.

Sickening, breath-plundering, vomit-inducing panic. Liv felt as if she was shivering and turned to stone all in one go. It was not sorrow or heartbreak or even betrayal, which she knew she had every right to feel. She heard a groan come from somewhere that had little to do with actually trying to speak and everything to do with some feral emotion that she wouldn't trust in a kitten, never mind a full-grown woman who should know better.

'I'll kill him…' She started to get out of the jeep, but even then, in her blind panic, she wasn't sure if she wanted to murder Eddie or Anya most.

'No you won't.' Maya pulled her down in the jeep, holding her head on the bench seat and folding her own body down on top of her. 'You bloody won't, not here. You're not giving them the satisfaction of seeing you upset, especially not outside Flannelly's pub – you'd have Nick Flannelly out taking photographs before you knew it,' she whispered vehemently. Outside, somewhere beyond the jeep, above their two folded bodies, Liv could hear Eddie and Maya pass by. They were talking, oblivious to everything else around them. She imagined Anya laughing at some joke that Liv never would have found funny.

'Oh, God,' Liv said when Maya finally released her. 'What am I going to do now?'

'You're going to sit there, while I drive us back home and then, we'll have two very strong drinks before we set about putting the world to rights. Tomorrow, when you have a banging hangover, you can think about confronting him, okay?' Maya put her arms around Liv and pulled her close, hugging her so tightly it felt as if she'd never let her go. 'They are welcome to each other, Liv. I know you don't see that now, but really, you could do so much better than that awful Eddie Quirke.'

* * *

She was distracted; that was all. It had been a long shift. She tried the door key once more. No, it hadn't finally broken, had it? Damn it, not now, this door lock had been dodgy for as long as she could remember. Why oh why did it have to go now, when all she wanted to do was curl up on the couch for half an hour?

She looked at the lock more closely. It was much shinier than usual, and she realised, someone had changed it. She was locked out of her own flat. What on earth was she going to do now? Surely Eddie hadn't come back here and changed the locks while she was at work – he wouldn't do something like that, would he? He needed somewhere to live and he certainly couldn't move in with Anya or Pete. Eddie hadn't paid rent in Dublin in years; it was going to come as a huge shock to him. Prices had gone through the roof over the last couple of years and that was if he was lucky enough to find a place available that wasn't fit to be condemned. Would he even have enough money for a deposit? Although, then Liv thought about Barbara Quirke. No doubt, his mother would give him the cash for starting out. She'd probably complain and whine about it, but ultimately, it'd be another chance to fawn over him before he returned to work in the New Year.

God, even the thoughts of Barbara sent a shiver through her. Liv knew with certainty, she'd had a very lucky escape – Barbara would always have made life difficult for her; she was just that sort of woman.

She wanted to slide down to the floor and sit there crying rather than sort this out. Then a text message pinged on her phone. She hadn't checked it since this morning before she'd gone on shift. She pulled it out of her bag. Three missed calls from Pete and a message. She clicked into the message first.

Hi Liv, I tried ringing, you must be very busy ☺ (Oh no, so now he thought she was avoiding him?) *I dropped over to the flat earlier and changed that dodgy lock on your door. I left the new keys where Rachel used to leave the spare. Talk soon, hopefully.*

Liv felt overwhelmed. There was so much in just those few lines. She'd all but forgotten those days when Rachel used the spare key as often as her own. She walked across to the top of the stairs, felt about beneath the carpet runner and slipped two brand-new keys out. Pete. He was still like a friendly guardian angel who was happy to do the practical things to keep her on track. Once she was inside, she inspected the new lock. Pete was right: the old one had been dodgy for too long. Actually, when she and Rachel had moved in first, changing it had been one of those things they had agreed they'd get around to one of these days.

She called Pete to thank him.

'I sometimes ask myself what I've done to deserve you,' she said inadequately and she wondered if he felt this new unfamiliar awkwardness between them. Now that she was actually speaking to him, it felt as if she'd just imagined that kiss, but then, maybe there was a lot more to it in her imagination than there was in reality. She'd spent far too long worrying about it.

'There was every need,' Pete said. 'It's what friends do for each other – help each other out. Anyway, I figured it was killing two birds with one stone.'

'Well, you didn't need to worry about Eddie forcing his way back in. I'm not sure he's bothered enough.'

'Well, it goes to show, he's a bigger fool than I thought if that's the case.'

'Oh.' For a moment the silence that resonated between their connection seemed to resound with so much more than explanations or apologies. 'Well, thank you. I suppose this means I owe you another dinner.' She could have bitten her tongue off after she said it. After all, wasn't it chicken curry and beer that had led to that moment that hung in the air between them now?

'Don't worry; I won't be holding you to it,' he said evenly, but there was no missing the fact that his voice sounded as if he'd stepped not just physically from the phone, but also emotionally further away from her than she could ever remember.

'Right, well, you know where I am if…' Oh, God, could she dig the hole any deeper – it sounded as if she was yelling at him: Come get me; I'm truly desperate.

'Thanks, Liv,' he said before hanging up.

'Yes, thanks,' she said to the dead phone in her hand and, in some strange way, Liv thought she hadn't felt this completely bereft in a very long time.

But it was madness, she kept telling herself as she tried to settle down for the night. She and Pete – it was ridiculous. He'd been Rachel's best friend. And now he was her best friend, apart from Maya, and you can't count sisters, because they don't get a choice in being your friend, do they? She took down the framed photograph of the three of them, smiling, happy faces on a group holiday to Corfu, so many years ago, before they'd even really grown up. She'd found it a few days earlier, buried under a pile of Eddie's clothes.

A thought occurred to her then. It struck her like a tsunami of realisation. If Rachel had lived, wouldn't she have eventually married Pete? The thought quickly took root and somewhere in the very back of her mind, even if she didn't want to acknowledge it, she knew, it was forming into something far more substantial than just a possibility. Perhaps when Pete lost Rachel he lost his soul mate?

It was only as she fell asleep that night that another thought settled on her. What if she had gotten it all wrong? What if she had been in love with Pete all along, but Pete had always been Rachel's? That was how it was meant to be, wasn't it?

14

There had been no sleep. In fact, Liv felt as if she hadn't slept in months and she might never sleep soundly again. Instead, she'd lain in bed and was sure she'd counted out each second before she figured that light might be cracking open on the horizon. She imagined it, a thin streak at first, breaking open a new day.

A terrible day.

There was only one thing she had to do today and that was go down to the village and talk to Eddie. *Confront him,* Maya corrected her. But really, all Liv wanted was the truth, wasn't it? She wasn't so sure. Ideally, she'd have liked a palatable version of the truth.

The longer she lay in the dark, the more she realised the reality of it. By hanging on to Eddie, she was stopping *him* from having the real thing. Maybe, that's what he'd have with Anya. And that just made her wail all the more loudly.

'Huh,' Maya had snorted as she'd poured them two large brandies when they got back to the farmhouse the previous evening. 'Medicinal purposes,' she'd told their father. Soon, she'd managed to put into words what Liv was still struggling to absorb.

'I always said he wasn't good enough for you,' her father had muttered. 'Couldn't count the times I said that to your mother. He's a cheat and a liar and if right was right, he's getting exactly what suits him in Anya Hegarty.'

'That's neither here nor there.' Her mother had put her arms around Liv who was even more inconsolable at the idea of Eddie and Anya being perfectly suited; it didn't matter that her father meant it in a bad way, it just felt as if Liv was even further on the outside than before. 'It's all right, love, you'll see. All of this will turn out for the best in the end, even if it's hard to see it now.'

'How can you say that, Mum?' Because Liv felt that on every level her heart was breaking and she'd never survive this enormous blow.

'Because I know, there's someone else who's meant for you and Eddie Quirke has only been standing in the way.'

'Yes, but what if the only someone else for me has already passed me by?' She'd thought about that gorgeous ring in Eddie's workshop then. 'I thought Eddie was going to propose this Christmas,' Liv had managed between gulping sobs.

'Saints preserve us. Well thank goodness he didn't; that's all I can say.' Her father had nodded to Maya; there was no point in him having an empty glass.

So they'd sat around the table while it all tumbled out of Liv. The beautiful engagement ring and the rest. The more she spoke, the more even she could hear the truth of her relationship with Eddie. It had been all take on Eddie's side and not even a little give. He'd lapped up a free place to stay, home-cooked meals, laundry sorted and free help in the workshop on her days off. She'd been a chauffeur when he was too drunk to drive and a telephone receptionist when his mother called. Actually, the more she'd talked, the more it became apparent that she'd been lavishing him with enough attention for both of them and there had been nothing in return apart from that misguided belief that he loved her, even if he never said it, and the vague hope that one day he would marry her.

Is that all she wanted? For him to somehow become a version (albeit, in hindsight, not a great version) of the husband and future she'd always dreamed of? She could see now, through her tears and her sobbing words, it would never have happened. All right, so she might have eventually pushed him and dragged him towards the altar, but he'd only have been there because he thought there was nothing better anywhere else. That was the truth of it – she could see it now.

By the time breakfast was over – not that she'd been able to eat anything – she knew it was time to go and get herself tidied up and ready for battle. And that was what it felt like. Maya offered to drive her down to Barbara Quirke's bright and early, well before Eddie was likely to have surfaced, or Barbara would have boiled his two soft eggs and made soldiers.

Sure enough, the Quirke house looked as if it hadn't yet woken up when Liv rang the front doorbell. The sitting room curtains were pulled tight and a wad of junk mail hung from the letter box. Liv didn't doubt that Barbara would have snapped that through the door as she'd passed it on the way to the kitchen from her bedroom when she got up for the day. She rang the bell again, knowing only too well that Eddie could bury himself under the quilt all day long and ignore the outside world. She had a feeling that Barbara wouldn't be quite so resilient; her curiosity would bring her to the door, if nothing else. And then sure enough, she heard the shrill voice from within, 'I'm coming, for goodness' sake; keep your hair on, I'm coming.' Barbara was making her way down the stairs and not sounding exactly pleased at having her beauty sleep interrupted.

'Oh, it's you.'

'Yes,' Liv said, but this time, Barbara's severe stare didn't make her flinch. 'I'm here to see Eddie.'

'Eddie? My Eddie? But he isn't...' Barbara put a hand to pat down her hair and suddenly, Liv knew, she'd been lying all along. She'd known that Eddie had been up to no good behind Liv's back. Even if she didn't know about Anya Hegarty, she'd been complicit in covering his tracks. Had she known when Liv had spent an hour getting her shopping from the supermarket? Or when she'd gotten from her bed just to close a shed door that useless Eddie had probably left open? Liv couldn't think about that now; it would make her much too mad and she needed a clear head to deal with Eddie.

'Actually, he is and I want to speak to him now, or else I'll wait and have it out with him in Flannelly's bar later where we both know everything that's said will be round the village jungle drums in no time.'

'I don't see why I'd have anything to worry about... It's

not as if my Eddie has ever done anything to have people talking about us,' Barbara said, but all the same, she peered around the doorframe, up and down the street to make sure that none of the neighbours were catching this exchange.

'No. Are you quite sure about that…?'

'Oh, you might as well come in and don't be making such a huge drama on the doorstep.'

'He's in his room?' But Liv was only confirming it as she took the narrow stairs two steps at a time. For the first time, she noticed just how shabby everything was here. There was an air of neglect about the flaking paint, the thin carpet and the faded drapes all overseen by a picture of the Sacred Heart, whose red-light bulb had long gone out. She pushed open the door to Eddie's room. She'd only been in here a handful of times, never for anything more than collecting or dropping off his belongings, and now it seemed that her final drop-off would be the man himself.

As she looked about Eddie's room there was that same sense that time had stopped here – she guessed around the time his father died.

'What the… Liv, what are you doing here at this hour of the day?' Eddie scrambled up in the bed. At least he was alone. Liv actually felt a small wave of relief pass over her at this thought – God, how pathetic was she? She wrinkled her nose. The smell in the room was sickly and depressingly familiar. She knew it too well: a combination of stale drink, fags and body odour and, today, she could admit to herself just how much it disgusted her. It took a genuine effort not to walk to the window and throw it wide open. 'I meant to ring you. Sorry, it was late when I got back. Is something wrong?'

He was pulling the quilt up around him, as if protecting himself from what was to come.

'You tell me what might be wrong, Eddie.' She walked about the room, not that there was much space. The floor was strewn with discarded clothes and bags and it was difficult to tell what was for laundry and what she would, so recently, have automatically begun to hang up in his wardrobe. God, she'd been such a sap.

'Wrong? I don't know that anything is wrong; it's just you, you look...' He stopped, clearly not yet being wakened enough to put the right word on how Liv looked. He settled on: 'Different.'

'Different? Is that how I look now?' she asked, moving closer to him, not taking her eyes off him. He seemed smaller, almost inconsequential, this little man who had been such a huge part of her life for so long. It turned out, he was nothing to her and she was even less than that to him. 'Funny, but there are so many better words to cover how I might be looking today,' she said smiling at him, but the expression held no joy, apart from the momentary satisfaction of having caught him on the back foot. 'How does betrayed sound? Or maybe foolish? Two-timed, perhaps? Or is that just a term for when you're a kid – surely at this stage in our lives, what you've been doing with Anya Hegarty is having an affair, so what does that make me, Eddie? Apart from stupid?'

'I... what, no, no, you have it all wrong, Liv. It's not what you think it is. I wouldn't...'

'Oh, Eddie, but you would and you did. I saw you both, with my own eyes and everybody knows about it, the whole village, but you already know that probably.'

'But we're... living together, the flat and... everything.' He didn't even try to deny it. If she'd hoped he'd beg for another chance, it had not come. Silence filled the air between them. At her back, Liv heard Barbara linger almost soundlessly beyond the flimsy partition wall.

'No, Eddie, we're not living together anymore. You came to stay in my flat for a night or two and I should have thrown you out ages ago,' she said with far greater confidence than she felt.

'Come on, Liv, we can be grown-up about this, surely. You and I... we never actually... I mean, there were no promises, no real rules about what we were...' He was scrambling, stopping because maybe, for once, he was faced with exactly what she thought they were.

'That's funny, because I thought, you know, when you lived together, when you shared everything you had with another person, it meant more than just – nothing?' She turned away from him, determined not to cry. She would not give him or Anya the satisfaction of going over this later and laughing at her. She took a deep breath. 'You know what? Maybe you're right,' she said, fixing her stare at a poster of some obscure heavy metal band that she assumed had been pinned to Eddie's wall twenty years earlier and had, like herself, become part of his life that he didn't notice anymore. 'Maybe we can be grown-up about this.' The hardness in her voice sounded alien to her and she felt as much as heard Eddie catch his breath behind her back. 'I want you out of my flat by the end of the week. I want my keys back and as far as I'm concerned, we'll leave it at that.'

She knew Maya would have wanted her to press him

for an astronomical amount of rent back-paid, just to put the wind up him, but Liv's anger didn't stretch far enough beyond devastation to play that sort of game.

'You're angry; you have things all confused. I'm not... It didn't mean anything; it was just a fling. Surely we can...' And then he stopped, catching something of her determination on the air, the truth of his situation finally hitting him. 'You can't just ask me to leave.'

'I'm not asking you to leave, Eddie, I'm telling you; find somewhere else because you're not living in my flat anymore.'

'Now, listen here, Liv Latimer' – Barbara was behind her, her expression livid, her voice finally revealing the dislike that Liv had always pretended not to recognise – 'you can't just swan in here and tell my son he's homeless. He has rights, as a tenant, as a... common law husband.' Eddie for his part had shrunk further down beneath his quilt at the mention of the word *husband*, common law or otherwise.

'Actually, Barbara, I can, because it's my flat and he's been seeing Anya Hegarty for weeks, probably months behind my back, and so his place is with Anya, not sleeping each night in my bed.'

'But Anya has nowhere to live either and...' Eddie sounded pathetic now.

'That's right, Eddie, because ye're as bad as each other, and you thought you'd just move her into my flat, so you could have the best of both worlds. God, you really are hilarious. What do you think I am, a complete doormat? Anya's not welcome in my flat and I very much doubt that Pete will want to see either of you within a ten-mile radius of his place either. It's time to grow up, Eddie. You and Anya are more than welcome to each other.' She turned on her heels, pushing past the open-mouthed Barbara, and made her way down the stairs and out the front door, banging it loudly behind her.

She was shaking by the time she got into the jeep again.

'Okay?' Maya said, although they both knew, she was nowhere near okay.

'Fantastic.' Liv tried to smile through her tears. It was a wobbly, noisy attempt, but it felt better than disintegrating into a wretched mess.

'Well, did he deny it?'

'No. Yes. I don't know, sort of, but not really.' She was glad to be sitting in the car next to Maya speeding away from the narrow street. 'I think he was in shock that I turned up at the foot of his bed at this hour, more than anything else.'

'So, you just had it out with him?'

Maya flicked on her indicator. Soon they'd be driving past the pier and on the road out to open fields and the soothing countryside. Liv craved the sight of fields, stone walls and endless blue-grey sky.

'Not really. I just told him he wasn't living at the flat anymore.' She looked out the window at the sea opposite. 'Oh God, can I do that, after he's been living there for so long?'

'Squatter's rights?' Maya laughed. 'No, don't worry, that would have taken him a little longer to establish. You've managed to get him out, just in time.' They both started to laugh at that, even if it wasn't funny, and Liv wasn't sure what she felt at this stage – she knew it wasn't happy, but at least it felt good to be here with Maya.

* * *

Liv's phone rang just as she sat on the bus for work. She was doing split shifts all over the place, and there was no point hanging about the hospital, but still, she'd only had four hours away from the place and she was returning for another four; today it felt as if they were desperately trying to plug holes in the *Titanic*. She was just lucky not to be redeployed to a different ward.

She pulled the phone out of her bag and answered it. She didn't recognise the number, but presumed it was probably the hospital. The switchboard there often came up as a private number depending on which extension was calling.

'Liv, hi, it's me, glad I caught you.' Eddie's voice sounded really far away and for a moment, Liv almost forgot that things had changed so completely between them.

'Eddie, what can I do for you this evening?'

'Oh, nothing really, I just fancied a chat, you know,' he wheedled and she held the phone from her ear for a minute and then took a deep breath. She wanted to say, Well then why don't you go and ring up Anya? but she knew that Eddie never called without some purpose, not really.

'Oh, right well, fire ahead so.' She pursed her lips. Let him make a stab at having a conversation with someone who had no intention of making an effort; God knows, she'd done it often enough over the years.

'Well I…' It was almost painful to listen to him.

'Okay, so what is it you really wanted to talk to me about?' she said, taking him out of his misery.

'It's just that I need to get back to work and this whole thing with the flat, it all seems a bit pointless. I mean, come on, Liv, we're mates, aren't we?'

'Are we? Really though, Eddie, are we? Because I thought we were so much more?'

'Well, yeah, I mean that too, but like, what's the point in me finding somewhere else, when we get on so well together, in the flat?'

'So, you could come back and share my flat with me and we could just get on with it?' He was unbelievable. She wanted to ask if he expected her to throw in hot meals and the occasional shag also, rent-free, but she didn't because she was too aware of the fact that the woman opposite her was staring at her with growing interest and obviously craning to hear every single word. Oh, my God, how had she become one of those people who have these huge conversations on public transport? Eddie Quirke really had brought her to a new low. 'And what about Anya?'

'Well, I didn't like to ask, but yeah, she said she'd be happy with the sofa.'

'Excuse me?' She couldn't believe what she was hearing. Did he really expect to waltz back into her flat with his new girlfriend in tow and think everything would be fine?

'Isn't that what you meant?'

'Not exactly.' Liv wanted to explode, but the woman opposite had leant forward now and was actually smiling. The irony of the conversation was not lost on her, even if it went over Eddie's head completely. She cleared her throat before going on. 'Actually, Eddie, it's not a good time to talk. I'm on the bus to work, so…'

'Okay, cool, I can call you later. What time do you finish? I'm hoping to get back to Dublin by the weekend so…'

'Please, don't bother. The answer is no, Eddie. There is no way that you and Anya can stay at my flat and please, don't ring me again.'

'But…'

'And, I nearly forgot, but don't bother coming round to the flat either. The locks have been changed, so you'll find it's just a wasted journey. I'm pretty sure I've left all your stuff at the workshop, but if I come across anything else, I'll drop it off there.' She still had his keys, but he didn't seem to register that. It didn't matter. She'd leave it a week or two and if nothing else turned up when she pulled the place apart for painting, she could always pop them through his letter box.

When she hung up the phone she was shaking. What on earth was wrong with her? This was Eddie Quirke. She was better off without him, a thousand times better off without him, but still it hurt. He had betrayed her; maybe if it didn't hurt, there would be more to worry about. Her phone rang again as she tried to shove it into her bag. Pete.

'Hey?' he sounded breezy.

'Hey, yourself. What's up?' She took a deep breath to steady her nerves after the conversation with Eddie.

'Not a lot, I just wanted to give you a heads up. I've had a call from Anya. I think reality has finally bitten; she's looking for somewhere to stay. I wouldn't be at all surprised if Eddie gives you a call too.'

'Too late.' Liv sighed. She hadn't meant to, but even thinking about Eddie wore her out at this point. 'I've just spoken to him.'

'Oh, Liv…'

'Don't worry, I'm not quite so stupid as to let him back into the flat.' God, she felt as if she might be the most naïve person in the world.

'You sound as if you could do with some cheering up.' It sounded like Pete was smiling at the other end of the phone. 'What about that guy, in the hospital, the one you sacrificed your Christmas for…'

'I didn't sacrifice anything,' but as usual, Pete had managed to bring a smile to her lips.

'If you say so, but… why don't you offer to make him dinner, or something when he gets out of hospital?'

'Actually, he's already invited me out for dinner.'

'A date? That was quick. You are a dark horse.' He was making fun of her again.

'Don't be silly, not a date… just a thank you.' Outside, big fat snowflakes were falling to the footpaths and Liv pulled her coat up around her, even though it wasn't cold on the bus. 'It's definitely not a date!' There were too many reasons not to get hung up on Finn, not least of all, the fact that she could absolutely fall head over heels for him and the last thing she needed was to have her heart broken again.

'You are impossible, sometimes, you know that?'

'I certainly am not!'

'Liv…' And she knew what he was saying, even if he never put it into words. Rachel would want her to move on with her life, to grab every opportunity that came her way and now, Pete wanted it too.

The good news was that Finn O'Connell had been sent home today, so at least he had a clean bill of health, although she was going to miss popping up to him and she had really enjoyed going for coffee and chatting with him on her lunch breaks. She'd agreed to dinner with him, even though probably, she was in no fit state to be out socialising with devastatingly handsome men – after all, hadn't she just made a complete fool of herself over Eddie? It was Pete who really convinced her she had to go out with him in the end – it hadn't taken a lot of convincing to be fair.

* * *

She spotted the jeep in her parking space from the top of the road. Not that it mattered much now that Eddie wouldn't be parking his van there. She should probably think about letting one of the neighbours use it occasionally. It was only as she drew nearer to it that she spotted Maya's registration and her sister's familiar silhouette in the driver's seat.

'Oh, it's so lovely to see you,' Liv said, opening the door to greet her sister.

'Well, I wanted it to be a surprise. I have a few days off and I figured, if you couldn't come down at least one of us could come up. Obviously, there was no dragging Dad away from the maternity ward!' They both laughed at that, but Liv wouldn't want him to leave the farm at this time for all the world. Lambing season was the busiest and best time of the year. 'Mind you, I've been sitting here for half an hour wondering if it was a stupid idea. I forgot about your new lock on the front door.' She got out of the jeep and threw her arms around Liv. Honestly, in that moment, it felt to Liv as if she was actually home, safe and sound; the world as she knew it had not been torpedoed from under her.

'Oh well, I'm here now and I have a spare key, so you can surprise me any time.' Liv grabbed her sister's bag from the back seat and led the way to the front door. She couldn't wait to get inside. Was it bad that she wanted all the gossip from Ballycove? Well, maybe not all the gossip, but certainly, she wanted to hear if the word was out yet about Eddie and Anya.

'Old news,' Maya said as they settled down to tea and toast on the sofa. 'No, the big news doing the rounds in the village now is that Lucy Nolan just got engaged. You remember Lucy – she was a year or two ahead of you at school.'

'The doctor, yes of course, she was seeing that guy… the one who wrote the book?'

Maya nodded between mouthfuls, so Liv couldn't be sure, but no doubt her mother would fill her in when she eventually got home. 'And of course, everyone is looking forward to the New Year's Ball this year.'

'Oh, no, I forgot all about that. I had tickets for both of us too,' Liv said but it seemed like the New Year's Ball was happening in another lifetime. Everything had changed so much since she'd bought those tickets. 'It doesn't matter now anyway – I volunteered to work. Francine owes me so many hours, I'll hardly have to cover a shift until the end of January,' she said.

'You will come home, if you're off for a few weeks? Dad would love to have you helping out on the farm – all that midwifery experience, he couldn't have a better helper.' She fell against Liv now, both of them laughing, but the truth was, by then, the season would be almost at an end and there wouldn't be a lot to do apart from look after any weaker lambs that needed a little extra care.

'We'll see. I'm having this place painted, so…'

'That's exciting. Have you picked colours yet?'

'No, I haven't even thought about it, but I'll probably go for something neutral, nothing that I can go off too quickly.' That was the story of her life though, wasn't it: playing safe?

'I think you should go mad – hot pink and fuchsia, lime green and zesty yellow, give the place a complete facelift. It would do you good – feng shui the crap out of it!' Maya said nabbing the last slice of toast.

'You know what, maybe I will.' Liv looked about her now. She was beginning to see the flat in a way that she hadn't properly noticed it in years. Maya was right: she needed to break out a bit, forget about keeping everything the way it was and shake things up.

'So, what about this guy who fell for you on your way to work?' This was Maya's idea of a joke.

'You are terrible, you know that. His name is Finn and he was knocked down on a very busy road. He's lucky to get away with just a concussion and a few cuts and bruises.'

'It's a bit extreme, if you ask me, throwing yourself into oncoming traffic just for a cup of coffee. Are you sure he isn't some sort of stalker?' She was making fun of Liv now, but it felt so good not to have to take life too seriously after the last few days.

'Stop it.' Liv was laughing so much, she had to put her cup down on the table. 'And it was two cups of coffee, so there…'

'Ooh, it's serious so. When's the big day?' Maya started to hum the 'Wedding March'.

'No, seriously, he's really nice, but…'

'He's asked you out to dinner, yes?'

'Yes.'

'And you're single now, right?' She didn't wait for an answer. 'And he sounds as if he's at the very least already got a place to live, with an income, and if you're to be believed, he's not exactly Shrek to look at?'

'Spot on – you're right on all counts.'

'Then it's a good job I'm here to push you out the door on that date.' Maya shoved her sister playfully but Liv had already made up her mind; she actually wanted to go out and enjoy herself for a night.

15

'I'm perfectly entitled to mope if I want to,' Liv said obstinately as Maya dragged the quilt off her.

'Yes, but not for this long. And anyway, you're due to go back to Dublin soon. How on earth do you think Mum and Dad are going to feel if they think you're completely miserable? It won't do either of them any good.'

'Oh, God, you're right, of course, you're right.' Liv groaned. It was enough to know their dad had to go and have an angiogram in the New Year; the last thing he needed was any added stress thanks to Eddie bloody Quirke, and Liv knew, she'd never forgive herself if she felt that she was the cause of it.

'So, for today, just a long walk on the beach, then, it's the village New Year's Ball,' Maya said, pulling out jeans and boots and dropping them on the bed for Liv.

'Oh, no, there's no way I can go to that, not with Eddie there, probably hanging out with Anya Hegarty.' Even the thought of it made her heart sink. There was no way she could face the village; not yet, it was much too soon.

'He won't be there,' Maya said flopping down on the bed while Liv pulled on her jeans and sweatshirt.

'You sound very sure of yourself.' Liv looked at her sister's reflection in the dressing table behind her.

'I'm certain of it; the tickets are all sold out. When I picked up your pair, I was lucky to get them.'

'My tickets?' Liv had completely forgotten and then she smiled; it was a blessing in a way that only an Irish blessing could arrive. 'Sorry, no can do. I'm going back to Dublin. Francine could do with the extra pair of hands and really, I want to get back to sort things out.'

'You can't miss out, Liv, you just can't.'

''Fraid so. Anyway, I wouldn't have gone, Maya, I'm just not ready to face the whole village yet. You know how people talk. I don't think I could take the pity, apart from anything else.'

'Okay, okay, I can't make you and you're probably right – it's enough to get over it on your own time. You have nothing to prove here,' Maya said with a shrug. She'd never felt the need to explain herself to anyone. 'But, you know, there's someone you need to put things right with too.' She got up and pulled the quilt and pillows off the bed, refitted the under sheet and stretched it out as if it was ironed on, before plumping the pillows and throwing the quilt back on the bed again. 'There,' she said with satisfaction.

'Thanks, sis.' Liv threw her arms around her sister. She couldn't begin to say how lovely it was to have someone do something small just for her, because they loved her. She really had been deprived of even the tiniest acts of thoughtfulness living with Eddie these last few years.

'Don't thank me yet…'

'Okay, what is it you want me to do?'

'You're going to have to ring Pete and say something about overreacting when he was only looking out for you.'

'Oh, Pete will be all right. He knows what I'm like.'

'Will he? He hasn't texted you since yesterday. Come on, Liv, you know that's not like him.'

'Yes, well, he'll come round.' Although, in hindsight, Liv knew it was a terrible slap in the face that she had chosen to believe the better of someone like Eddie who'd treated her badly at every turn over Pete – who had never been anything but a solid friend to her. And if she was honest, she missed hearing from him. 'Oh God, what have I done?'

'Nothing that can't be undone, I'm sure.' Maya handed her the phone. 'Go on, eat that frog.'

'Ugh, what a horrible thought,' Liv said, swiping her phone to her call list. He was the last person to ring her, but she knew she needed a moment before she hit dial. 'What will I say?'

'Oh please, Liv, seriously, when have you ever had to think about what to say to Pete? Just ring him and say you're sorry. Say you overreacted and don't be afraid to say, on this occasion, he was right and…' she lowered her voice to a loud joking whisper '… you were wrong.'

'Okay, well, the least you could do is make me a cup of tea and give a girl a bit of privacy.' Liv sat down at the dressing table, stared at her reflection in the mirror. She looked a complete wreck. The hairdressing appointment that she'd squeezed in a few days before Christmas might as well have never happened; her skin looked as dry as toast; and her eyes – oh, dear, she looked forty, if she looked a day, too much crying and not enough beauty sleep. Eddie Quirke was not worth that, she decided, and as of today, she wasn't wasting another hour of sleep over him.

'Hi.' Pete sounded as if he was distracted when he answered after the third ring.

'Hey, just ringing because…'

'I know, it's all right. The word seems to be out around the village now; apparently, they spent last night too drunk to realise they were wrapped around each other in Flannelly's.'

'I'm so sorry, Pete, I just…'

'It's okay, you didn't want it to be true and to be fair, it did come out of the blue. I probably could have broken it a bit more gently.'

'I'm not sure there is a gentle way to break news like that.'

'Well, it is what it is now, I suppose.' He was matter-of-fact, no joking about this time, and Liv felt as if perhaps, even though he was being very nice, he wasn't his usual self, far more distant and well behaved.

'So, what are you up to for the rest of the holidays?' she asked.

'Oh, not a lot. Visiting Gran again before I go back, but apart from that, just counting down the days to get back to some kind of normality.'

'I feel the same.' She did, didn't she? Well, she wasn't sure exactly, but she certainly didn't want to spend any time in the village while the great romance between Eddie and Anya was being played out so publicly and even though she loved her family dearly, there were things to sort out in the flat. Did she really want Eddie coming back in and spending hours there sorting out his stuff? Did she want to have the same conversations with him over and over? 'Actually, I'm going to ring the hospital next and offer to go in and do any shifts that need filling between now and New Year's.'

'So, you're going back early?'

'Yep, this time of year, there's always a plug to be filled in some department.' Actually, she'd be tempted to go back even if they didn't; now she thought about the flat. The last thing she needed was to leave it too long. It would be too depressing to think of going back to full shifts and still having to sort everything out in her free time. She could imagine the coldness of the place; no, far better to go back in her own time and get her life back into some kind of new order that was of her own fashioning. Then she could start the New Year with a clean slate.

'You're thinking about the flat and Eddie and the mess of having to get this all sorted out as painlessly as possible,' Pete cut into her thoughts.

'Honestly, it's like you can read my mind.' He always could, she knew; it came from both of them sitting beside Rachel, having the same thoughts and fears and never being able to give them voice.

'Maybe I can.' He laughed. 'Look, if you're going back, I can give you a lift, help you clear things out and change the locks, if you'd like.'

'Oh, I don't know about that. It seems very—'

'Sensible, if you ask me. You know, Eddie's lost that front door key more times than he can count?'

'To be fair, he's never been very good at maths.' She managed to knock a laugh out of Pete with that one.

'You know what I mean. Let me do this for you. It's only such a small thing, but it'd mean…' He let the words run off, because she knew what it would mean. It would mean keeping his word to Rachel. It would mean he was still looking out for her, keeping her safe, keeping that connection alive for a little longer. 'And anyway, have you thought about maybe moving all his stuff over to the workshop? You don't own a car, remember?'

'Okay, so, you've talked me into it.'

* * *

Finn rang the doorbell at exactly seven-thirty. Bang on time, and Liv couldn't help but compare that to Eddie's constant tardiness.

'Wish me luck?' she said to Maya before heading for the door.

'Hang on,' Maya said pushing her into the bedroom. 'I'll get this; you go reapply some lipstick or something.'

From the bedroom, Liv listened while Maya introduced herself and let Finn in. When Liv walked into the sitting room, they were standing opposite each other, Finn chatting happily while Maya took the measure of him, and Liv loved her sister all the more for her concerned attitude. No-one was going to do to Liv again what Eddie had done, not if Maya could help it.

'So, you've met Maya?' Liv asked as she put on her coat.

'Yes, she's exactly how you described her, the hotshot lawyer…' He was smiling. It was meant to be a compliment while making fun.

'Hardly.' Maya laughed. 'More like a country bumpkin solicitor

– I'm afraid it's not very exciting. Most of our practice is dealing with tort law and old wills.'

'Still, you're living in one of the most scenic corners of Ireland and working in a job you love,' Liv reminded her.

'True,' Maya said. 'Now, enough about me, what about this one?' She nodded towards Finn in a friendly way.

'Oh, I'm very boring. I write fantasy novels and spend most of my time locked up in a room surrounded by weird little character faces and the rest of it, trying to get away from them.'

'Must be nice,' Liv said, 'having your commute to work no further than from bedroom to kitchen.' She was ready to go now, all buttoned up, with gloves and hat on too.

'Well, have a lovely time, you two,' Maya said opening the door for them. When Liv turned to give her a kiss, she whispered, 'Ooh, la la, exactly what you need to get over Eddie Quirke.'

And Liv couldn't help but think she might be right. Finn O'Connell was everything Eddie was not. He was tall and classically handsome, clean-cut and he dressed well, as if he'd made an effort for seeing her tonight, which was more than Eddie had ever managed, or Liv suspected, ever would, even for Anya.

They walked towards town for a while, making small talk. He told her about getting out of hospital, home to his little house. He'd left the heating on and it felt like walking into the Sahara. 'I had to open all the windows for an hour; I thought I'd actually suffocate.' He laughed. They stopped outside La Redoute. Liv passed the restaurant often on her way to town, but she'd never eaten here. She'd heard that they had a waiting list of up to three months for a table; it was definitely a place to be seen if you were one of Dublin's glitterati.

'Well, this is very fancy; you should have warned me,' she said looking around the restaurant. It was all white, with heavy oak tables and obscene teal-themed artworks on the walls, obviously all by the same artist. They were a collision of subjects, clearly grouped together mainly for their dominant colour. Liv felt completely underdressed. 'If I'd known we were coming to…' She trailed off, wondering how on earth he had managed to get a reservation. She silenced a niggling voice that perhaps he'd meant to bring someone else and they'd bailed on him – that was, she knew, measuring him by Eddie's standards and that simply wasn't fair.

'You look beautiful. I'm just glad to have you here; would you still have come if I'd made a song and dance about where we were going?'

'Of course.' But she wasn't so sure. After all, she had work first thing in the morning. She'd worn her jeans, for heaven's sake; at least they were her best ones, but still. And this place, well, she'd never been anywhere quite so fancy before. She could rhyme off half a dozen celebrity weddings that had been held here in the last couple of years and they were only the ones that couldn't be kept out of the papers. 'But I'd probably have suggested somewhere a bit lower key.' She laughed, because for all its exclusivity it had enough breeding not to make her feel out of place, even if she was the only woman here not wearing a cocktail dress. 'How did you get a table?'

'Ah, that's meant to be a secret, but…' He tapped the side of his nose. She didn't doubt he would know everyone worth knowing on the showbiz scene, what with his previous marriage to Mena Swan. Actually, the more she thought about it, this place was more than likely a second home to him. 'Since you're going to find out anyway, so, I might as well tell you. My brother is a chef here; he's great for emergency dinner reservations. I know, it's a bit starry, but the food is excellent.'

'Phew,' she said, 'for a minute there, I thought I'd walked into an off-stage scene from *I'm A Celebrity* or something like that.'

'Hardly. I'm as un-showbiz as you're likely to get. I'll introduce you to my brother Callum later; he won't be long dispelling any mystery about me.'

'Well, either way, thank you for inviting me. I'll certainly remember this Christmas celebration.' The menu was as thick as an old phone book and there was a real danger that if she fell into the coat rack on the way in, she might have never been found again among the designer coats that were lined up in the tight space allocated. Her eBay purchased Donegal tweed looked a little tragic amongst them all.

The food was, as Finn had promised, out of this world. Not that the portions were huge, but there was a delicacy to everything that left her thoughtful after each mouthful and the presentation – well, if she was an Instagrammer, it would have probably been just heaven.

Their conversation was easy and skated around everything from their work to their families and then he asked her about Eddie, and Liv found herself talking about Rachel too and before she realised it, they were ordering dessert.

'So, what about you and Mena Swan?' The question was out before she even realised she'd asked it. God, she could feel her cheeks flush with embarrassment. All she could do was hope he didn't notice.

'Old news. Nothing much to tell, really.' He stuck his spoon into his home-made ice-cream and held it out to her for the first taste. 'We've known each other since we were kids, grew up on the same street. We were very young when we married; I can't even remember when we started seeing each other...' He shook his head. 'But these things, well, when you've known someone forever, it sounds mad, but it's as if we outgrew each other. Mena was meeting lots of new people at work and, I suppose, I was too. We outgrew each other and we just sort of drifted apart...' He let his words trail off.

'I can only imagine.' Liv couldn't help but think he made it all sound so glamorous; it was all a far cry from being a nurse in A&E. What on earth was she doing here?

'It was messy and emotional and the last thing either of us wanted, I think, really in the end.' He looked at her now, and she could finally put a name to what it was that made him so attractive. It was his vulnerability. He'd had his heart broken; maybe it was still broken. Some men, she knew, never fully get over their first loves. She knew Pete was one of those. Perhaps Finn was too? Mena Swan would be a very hard woman to replace.

'I'm so sorry.' Suddenly, her own dessert – a medley of fruit with a chocolate sauce dripping about it – looked as appetising as a plate of snails. She hadn't put her foot in it exactly, but it was obvious she'd certainly touched a raw nerve.

'It is what it is.' He shook his head. 'We've both moved on, as much as we can for now.'

And, with that, it was as if someone had taken a pin to the bubble of excitement about the evening and Liv couldn't help but feel sorry that they'd even mentioned their exes. Who on earth had brought that up as a polite topic over dinner? By the time the coffee arrived, Liv had decided that she for one was going to be cheerful; after all, there was plenty to be happy about – wasn't she lucky to be sitting here, having a lovely meal when she could just as easily be sitting at home on her own? And somehow, they did manage to resurrect the evening from that one awkward moment. They were actually laughing about some A&E story she remembered by the time they were leaving the restaurant.

'It was a lovely evening, thank you,' she said as they stood outside her flat in the freezing night air. She pulled her coat up closer around her, glad now of its insulating warmth.

'It was,' Finn agreed. 'Maybe we'll do it again?'

'I…' she began. She should say no. Just say no. Because it was all too obvious that Finn O'Connell was still in love with his ex-wife. Wasn't that what the awkwardness was all about? Wasn't that who the expensive present was for? M for Mena. God, she'd been such a fool. She'd almost fallen for him; actually, maybe she had fallen for him, just a bit. 'I think I need a bit of time.'

'Right?' He stepped back from her and he looked as if those were the last words he'd expected. 'But we had a good time, didn't we? I mean, I thought we really connected. I thought that there was something special here…'

'Maybe, but…' How could she put it into words without recreating that awkwardness between them again?

'Well then…' He smiled, as if some penny had finally dropped. 'Ah, I see, you're still not over Eddie. Is that it? You're still in love with him. It's okay, I get it.' His voice was so tender, but she couldn't miss what sounded like genuine sadness there.

'No, God, no, far from it.' She threw her head back and laughed. It sounded almost hysterical; perhaps she was nervous. 'No, I only wish I had ended things with him sooner. No, how is it they put it? It's not me it's you?'

'Isn't that the wrong way round?' In spite of the gravity of things, they both started to laugh.

'Not in this case.' She took a deep breath; might as well plunge in with complete honesty. 'It's just I think you're still in love with your ex-wife.'

'With Mena?' He looked incredulous. 'Seriously, you think Mena and I...' He shook his head. 'Oh no, there's no way. We're friends now, just friends. That's all we'll ever be.'

'But?' She thought about the woman she knew only from the screen. She was drop-dead gorgeous. How could anyone not be in love with her? How could anyone, particularly someone like Liv, ever compete with that sort of high-octane glamour?

'Look, when you were fifteen, I bet there was one boy in school you were mad about?'

'Well, yeah, but...' She rolled her eyes, but he was waiting for her to say something. 'Okay, Derek Evans. He's a forensic accountant with the tax office now.' She shivered even remembering that one kiss at a youth disco. It turned out, he had horrible breath and sweaty hands.

'Same with me and Mena, only we were stupid enough to run away and get married before we had any sense. Seriously, it's as over as it can be...'

'But back there you said...'

'It broke my heart, it broke both our hearts, but there was no future in it. We loved each other, but there was no magic there, not the sort that's going to last a lifetime.' He reached out, pulled her into his arms and she found herself helpless to resist him. Being this close to him made her feel dizzy with longing for him. When he cupped her face in his hands, she thought she'd faint with desire. His kiss was long and lingering, the sort of kiss that made her want to drag him back up to the flat and throw away any doubts she might have. God, imagine making love to him. And with that, she felt her knees almost buckle beneath her. He pulled away from her, held her for a moment at arm's length. 'Look, just meet me for coffee or a walk in the park the next day you're off work. What do you say?'

'I… I just can't do this…' She was powerless to say anything; instead, she pulled away from him. She had to get back to the safety of the flat before she did something really stupid like fall completely in love with him. 'I think we should just call it a night, end it here, before…' She stumbled towards the front door, stabbed her key at the lock a few times before managing to let herself in. She wasn't sure what she was doing, but when she closed the door on him, she had a feeling that perhaps it was too late to worry about falling in love with him. If she was honest, that had happened the first time she'd set eyes on him. When she closed the front door behind her, she was trembling. She felt as if she'd just stepped off a cloud from heaven and into a great big black hole. What on earth had she done?

16

Francine was delighted to hear that Liv could come back early.

'You've no idea what it's been like here. All agency staff and they haven't a notion – well, to be fair to them, I haven't had the time to give any of them a proper introduction to the place. It's just been in at the deep end and hope for the best.' In the background, Liv could hear a buzzer, someone needing assistance; she could imagine Francine, trying to keep everything going. 'So, if I put you down to fill in from two o'clock tomorrow?'

'That's perfect, Francine.' It would be good to draw a line under the holidays. It was time for a new start, a New Year.

'I won't promise what time you'll be finished up, mind, but hopefully, it'll be the normal shift.' She was only half joking.

'I really don't mind, Francine. That's why I'm offering.'

'You might be the only nurse in Ireland to be in a hurry to get back on shift after the holidays.' Francine laughed, but Liv could hear the impatience in her voice. She needed to get back to that buzzer. If the hospital was as busy as it sounded in the background, Liv had a feeling she wouldn't have much time for moping about the place after all.

Her dad wasn't keen on her going back so suddenly. 'Just like that?' he said when he came in for a cup of tea with the good news that he thought the ewe he'd been waiting for seemed to be showing the first signs of labour.

'Well, they need help and that is why I became a nurse after all – to help and look after people.'

'It'd be more in your line to look after yourself from here on in,' Maya snorted under her breath.

'Should Maya drive you back? You can't go bringing everything on the train and then lugging it across the city to the flat before going on shift.' Her mother couldn't hide the concern in her voice.

'And what about Eddie Quirke? Who's going to sort him out when he comes knocking on your door looking for his dinner?' Her father sounded as if he'd like to sort him out personally.

'No, it's okay. Pete said he'd drive me. Actually, going back a little earlier will give me a chance to sort through some stuff. I can have Eddie sorted and out of the flat before he even thinks about returning to Dublin,' Liv said with a finality that was starting to sink in, even for her. The truth was, she knew Eddie would probably sit about and moan about the fact that he had nowhere to live, rather than getting off his backside and doing something about it before he was due back to reopen the workshop. That was Eddie all over; he'd wait it out and probably hope that someone else would solve the problem for him. She was proud of herself for sounding far more confident than she actually felt.

'Well, that's good,' her mother said filling the kettle again. She'd always liked Pete. At one point – it seemed a long time ago now – she'd hoped that perhaps he and Maya might end up together but Maya didn't take long to put her straight on that front.

'So that's settled; you're back in Dublin for the New Year and we'll see you the following weekend?' Maya said. She wasn't asking. Liv knew that if she didn't come back home, there was a good chance that Maya would arrive on her doorstep to make sure she was all right.

'Yes, that's settled and maybe we can plan something nice to do when I get back to celebrate the New Year and new beginnings?' Liv said cheerfully. They'd have to do something, a meal out together or perhaps a family day out, around her father's hospital appointment, but no-one was going to mention that now.

*

After all that, there wasn't much to pack for going back to work. Liv decided she'd leave most of her clothes in Ballycove, since she'd be down again in a week or two and anyway, she'd have enough to sort out when she got back to the flat with trying to clear out Eddie's belongings. In the end, her bag had little more than books, make-up, a huge chunk of Christmas cake and a few jars of home-made jam and chutney from her mother's store cupboard.

Liv decided on a walk later that afternoon and with the three dogs racing ahead of her, she felt a lot more relaxed than she really expected to. The sun was heavy and unusually bright in the cloudless sky, which she knew boded well in terms of seeing the snow off, but she wasn't sure that it wouldn't mean a hard frost later if the weather forecast was to be believed. There was nowhere quite like Ballycove and Liv knew she was lucky to be able to come back here and lick her wounds. Even though Eddie lived here, they'd never run into each other, quite simply because they were such completely different people. Eddie would never come for a walk along the beach, unless there was something in it for him. His natural habitat was the pub or his mother's house and Barbara Quirke's house was a place that Liv knew she'd never go anywhere near again. And that was a relief, because now, with even this tiny distance from the pair of them, she could admit she'd never really liked the woman, no matter how hard she'd tried to convince herself otherwise.

It was funny, but out here, with the wind gathering up the waves into a white foam in the distance, she wondered if she even liked Eddie all that much – not now, obviously, but when they were together. Hadn't she spent much of their time together covering over the cracks of things that irritated her about him? She had made excuses, not just to Maya and her parents, but even to herself. She'd been so focused on filling the gaping hole in her life that Rachel had left after she died; she hadn't stopped to look at what she was replacing her twin sister with.

Liv stood now, the sun creasing up her eyes into a cold watery squint. It was an epiphany, but she realised, she could *never* replace Rachel and she had to stop trying. She felt a small tear race down her cheek. It came from nowhere and at the same time, she knew it came from a deep well of emotion that sat somewhere in the very core of her. She could never replace Rachel and now, standing here with the gathering breeze about her, she knew, she was going to stop trying. In that moment, she closed her eyes, surrendering herself to what lay ahead – she would just accept it. She was a nurse. She wanted to help people. Wasn't that what she'd told her father? Well, from now on, that was what she was going to do and let everything else take care of itself.

Somewhere in the distance she heard a loud bang. Light was beginning to fade when she opened her eyes and spotted a trail of early fireworks lighting up the indigo sky over the pier. They were a trail of green stars feathering out and falling down to the ground below. Like her ring. The ring Eddie had made for some wealthy client – Liv corrected herself immediately. And then she smiled, because for the first time, she could see that ring was little more than a sad imitation of something that was exquisite once, but that moment had passed. Without warning, another single golden firework shot up into the air and Liv felt a tiny glimmer of hope that everything was going to turn out exactly as it was meant to.

* * *

Liv couldn't say why exactly, but when she woke the following morning, it was as if her night's sleep had drained her rather than revived her. She'd drifted off, her thoughts filled with the evening spent with Finn O'Connell. It had been magical. And then, at the end, somehow she'd managed to completely mess it up. Maya told her she was crazy – the guy deserved a second chance. The two sisters had talked until the early hours of the morning, and by the time she went to bed, it was confirmed that she'd made a complete pig's ear of everything.

This morning, Maya had dug out the old teapot that had once sat on their grandmother's table in her little cottage on the side of the hill. She'd made real tea, with leaves and a strainer sitting on the side.

'This is a treat,' Liv said kissing her sister as she placed two mugs on the table for them. 'But you should have stayed in bed for a while longer. There was no need; I'll be off out the door in ten minutes to make it in time for my shift.'

'There was every need.' Maya sat down opposite her, putting two slices of toast before her and digging into her own already half-eaten slice. 'I'm afraid I have to go back to Ballycove today. Emergency sitting of the district court and, apparently, the accused has asked for me specially.'

'That's great; well, maybe not for whoever is in the dock, but you know what I mean...' Her sister had a funny old job.

'Yeah, I know, it's an ill wind. Still, it looks like I'm getting a good reputation and that's only going to be good for the business.' Maya smiled. 'But the thing is, I'm going to drive back this morning so I thought I'd drop you into work and then go straight from there.'

'Yay! Which gives me an extra twenty minutes.'

'I wanted to talk to you, before I go.' Maya stopped, dropped the slice of toast and rubbed her hands together to take any crumbs from her fingers.

'Oh, oh, this doesn't sound good.'

'It's... Finn O'Connell.' Maya passed over her phone. 'When you went to bed last night, I couldn't help it. I...' She pulled the gift that Liv had been supposed to be holding in safe keeping for him from behind her back. 'Sorry, I had to see for myself.'

'Oh, Maya, how could you?' The paper had been ripped off

and presumably she'd already looked inside. She should have handed this back to Finn last night, but Liv had forgotten all about it until now.

'The thing is, Liv, once you stop being mad at me, you might actually thank me.' She took a deep breath. 'Or maybe not.' She bit her lip in that way she always did when she knew she was walking on eggshells, but being Maya, there was no way she wasn't going to see her footsteps through. 'The thing is.' She flipped open the case and Liv gasped.

'It's my ring.' Liv was too shocked to cry, but she knew that the ball of emotion that had lodged in her throat would have its way whether she wanted to cry or not. 'I don't understand.' All this time, she'd been carrying around the ring, she'd believed Eddie had made for her.

'It's not for Mena.' Maya placed it into Liv's shaking hands.

'It's not?' She was confused; of course it was for Mena. It said M on the ticket.

'It's not.' Maya leant forward, pulled out the ring and held it up before them both. 'See, there's an inscription.'

'Oh, God.' Liv didn't know whether to laugh or cry, but hysteria probably tipped the balance towards a sound that startled them both. 'It's bloody tiny. You can't make out what it even says.' She dropped the ring; suddenly, it might as well have been on fire.

'I'll show you what it says, shall I?' She handed Liv the magnifying glass, one of the few remnants of Eddie yet to be dropped off at the workshop.

'Aww.' Liv covered her mouth with her hand before she whispered the words. *Happy Birthday, Mum.* She leant back against the chair, feeling a fizzing mixture of giddy and weak all at once.

'Exactly. Happy Birthday, Mum.' Maya stretched out on the chair. 'So now, who was right?'

'I can't believe it. I've been such a complete fool.'

'At every single turn.' Maya shook her head, but her smile lit up her whole face and it felt as if somehow the whole world had spun half a circle on its axis and they'd landed quite close to where Liv had always hoped she'd be. 'You should call him.'

'I should. Although, I have no idea what I'm going to say to him.'

'Ask him out for a drink; tell him you have something for him.' She raised her eyebrows as if to insinuate there was more on offer than just the return of his mother's Christmas gift.

'You are in so much trouble for opening that box.' Liv laughed, but how could she be cross with Maya?

Liv decided that a text was best. The truth was, she wasn't sure she could trust herself to talk to him and not say something stupid. *Hi Finn. I just remembered this morning that I still have that gift for M. Would you fancy meeting up? Liv.* And that was that – now all she could do was hope she hadn't completely messed things up.

17

The flat was colder than Liv ever remembered it when she got back to Dublin. It wasn't the temperature; rather, it was the fact that somehow it seemed to have become unfamiliar. In reality, the place was sweltering. Obviously, Eddie had left the heat on full and now it was stuffy and airless. It was a mess too. Whatever tidying she'd hastily done before she went home for the holidays had been undone when Eddie and Anya had come back here. There were bags and giant boxes everywhere. Anya's belongings filled every available space; it seemed she and Eddie had just cleared everything from Pete's and dumped it here.

Liv stood for a moment, surveying the mess her flat had become. To anyone else, she knew, it would look as if the place had been trashed, but beneath the hair crimpers and killer heels and what she estimated to be about a hundred pairs of skinny-leg jeans, she could see all her own familiar belongings. She picked her way through the chaos, towards the kitchen, checking the fridge and switching on the kettle absent-mindedly. Here too, every available surface was covered in the debris of Eddie and Anya's recent stay. They had obviously had takeaway – Indian and pizza –and the stale remaining food added to the cloying intimidation of them both still hanging in the air.

She filled the sink with hot water and wash-up liquid, dropped in cups and cutlery from the draining board; if she only had this small space cleared off it would be a start. Liv didn't expect there to be milk in the fridge for a cup of tea; instead, she took down the only clean cup from the cupboard and dropped a camomile teabag into it. She wanted to cry, but somehow the tears just wouldn't come. Instead, she walked about her little flat that somehow seemed to have been stolen from under her nose, in a complete daze. Her mobile phone ringing out pulled her from the edge of what felt like a huge precipice of wretchedness.

'Liv,' Pete said. 'You okay?'

'Sure,' she said, although she knew her voice had come from somewhere outside herself. Maybe, it was a coping mechanism. After all, taking in the fact that her boyfriend and the woman he'd been carrying on with behind her back thought that it was acceptable to come into her flat and dump all their belongings there as if they had the God-given right to move in on top of her, took a bit of getting used to.

'I just thought I'd let you know Anya seems to have emptied everything from my apartment.' He sounded relieved and she could imagine it was a major headache sorted; it cut out any need to let her back into his life.

'I know.'

'What?'

'I know. She's taken all her stuff from your apartment

because she and Eddie have just moved them into my flat.'
Now she heard the betraying wobble in her own voice.

'Oh, come on, seriously? How low can those two be?'
He sounded completely different to the Pete she'd known
for so many years. Angry – it wasn't a word she'd ever have
associated with him. 'Don't worry, I'll come back straight
away, help you sort it all out,' he said and she could imagine
him, turning on his heels and dropping whatever plans he'd
had for his afternoon to help her.

'No, don't, please, there's no point. I'm due in to work in
an hour and really, it's the sort of thing I probably need to
do on my own; after all, it's my mess.'

'Look, this is a lot of things, but it's absolutely not *your*
mess, Liv. You haven't done anything wrong.'

'No? I've let myself be a complete doormat to Eddie
Quirke, obviously. When I told him that moving Anya in
here wasn't okay, he just completely ignored me and now
look at where I'm left. They're parading around Ballycove
like Romeo and Juliet and they still think that somehow I'll
just roll over and let them both move into my flat.'

'Please, don't talk like that. If I know Anya, she'll have
convinced Eddie that it will be all right, and as for Eddie,
well, we all know that he might be a lot of things, but
emotional intelligence isn't one of his strong points.'

'I can't think about it now, Pete. Honestly, I just have to
get to work and when I come back here later, I'll start sorting
through all this stuff,' she said wearily, even though she
hadn't even started yet. She hung up the phone. It was time
to get to work. Some unreasonable voice inside her knew
she'd have to get this sorted before New Year and that didn't

give her very long, but for now, she needed to turn up at the hospital and do her job.

* * *

Even though Liv was absolutely famished and in need of a long hot shower and a good night's sleep, she had this strange longing to see Pete, so she stayed on the bus home from the hospital, bypassing her usual stop and heading on towards the city. Pete had bought a swanky docklands apartment a few years earlier. It had views of the river and, on a clear day, he could see right out to the Dublin Mountains and across the bay from the balcony window. Funny, but it had never really suited him, Liv thought now. He'd had some interior designer come in and do the place over. He wouldn't tell her how much the whole thing had cost, but she knew Smeg fridges that were the size of army tanks and showers that came at you from every conceivable angle did not come cheap. It was all very lads' pad, New York loft living and although, in theory, Liv knew she should love it, she'd never actually been able to relax there. It was why, if they were having a night in, he always came to her flat. She assumed he liked being surrounded by their shared memories. In many ways, he'd been as much a part of putting the place together with her as Rachel had been.

She got off the bus as it rounded past some of the older parts of the city. Everything here was being redeveloped; if it didn't have a destruction order on it, it usually had a blue plaque. This was old Dublin, home to the great revolutionaries, the playwrights and perhaps less likely to be celebrated but also some of Dublin's more notorious criminals. It was still a bit of a walk to the block, but the rain had stopped and it was pleasant here, with the smell of fresh coffee filling the air from the many couture coffee shops, the sound of the river lapping gently nearby and the city slowing down in the distance. It was actually quite soothing to be taking a walk after work. She turned left into Pete's building, stabbed in his security code – they both used the same one on everything as a default: Rachel's lucky number. She punched in fourteen three times and smiled. They'd often joked that if they wanted to rob each other, it would be too easy – in so many ways, there were no secrets between them.

She rode up the elevator. Pete's apartment was top of the house. He had direct access to the roof garden and she remembered now, they'd planned on having some summer evenings there, although they'd never quite happened. It seemed that getting together a foursome was always just too difficult to manage. She wondered now how much of their lives had been engineered around Anya and Eddie keeping their affair going on without them being any the wiser.

Out of courtesy, more than necessity, she rang his front doorbell. Again, the code was easy, fourteen – fourteen. Inside she heard high heels tap their way along the parquet flooring to the door. Liv stood back for a moment. She hadn't expected Pete to have company, and she felt a little foolish. Why on earth wouldn't he? Hadn't she gone out to dinner with Finn O'Connell? What was to stop Pete asking someone out on a date? Had she expected Anya to open the door?

'Oh, it's you,' Anya said, momentarily as thrown by Liv's appearance as Liv was by hers.

'Yes, I'm looking for Pete.'

'Well, obviously. I didn't think you were here to cosy up to me.' Then she stood back, taking in everything about Liv, assessing with the eyes of someone who could see far more than Liv wanted her to.

'Anyway, hasn't he told you?'

'Told me what?' Liv said. She didn't like standing here like an uninvited – or perhaps unwanted – guest.

'No, well, we've been busy.' Anya smiled coyly and twirled her hair suggestively. Liv had a feeling that she knew exactly what Anya was hinting at. 'And well, the phone was the very last thing on his mind; actually, I'd say the only thing he's had on his mind all afternoon, is me…' She threw her head back and laughed.

'Are you moving back in?' Liv thought the words would choke her.

'Yes. That's right; we've kissed and made up. Actually, Pete's just gone out to buy the most expensive bottle of champagne he can find.' She licked her lips suggestively. 'And if it's good enough, I might just distract him some more.'

'I see.' Liv backed away from the door. She felt sick. It was not just the sort of sick that she felt if she'd forgotten to eat, this was a whole new sensation.

'You know…' Anya leant against the door. 'You should think about patching things up with Eddie. Ask him to come back to the flat. At least if he's staying for a while, you might have some chance of getting him back again.'

'You must be joking,' Liv said turning away from her and heading for the lift. She pressed the button to call it up to the top floor. 'You and Pete might have patched things up, but I'd rather be on my own than have Eddie Quirke anywhere near me again.' She looked up at the lift display; the bloody thing seemed to be stalled on the second floor.

'I'm not saying he'd actually take you back, but at least you'd have the company. It'd be better than nothing. After all, Liv, you're not getting any younger, are you, and it's not as if you're a girl who's had to beat the men away from your front door at any stage.'

'Well, you know what they say, Anya, better on your own than in bad company.' Damn it, she thought, looking at the lift, which was showing no signs of arriving soon. She turned on her heels, headed for the stairs and as she raced down the steps, she was sure she heard Pete's voice come out of the lift. She couldn't face him now, couldn't think what they'd have to say to each other now he'd decided to take Anya back.

At the bottom of the stairs Liv sat for a moment. She cried like she hadn't cried for years. Pete and Anya back together; she hadn't seen that coming. But then again, they looked good together, perhaps it would work out in the end for them, maybe. Anya would have learned her lesson. She was probably a lot brighter than Liv gave her credit for; she'd certainly seen through Eddie Quirke a lot faster than Liv had. Liv wasn't sure how long she stayed here, sitting on that step, going over the last five minutes in her head, the last ten years, if she was honest. It was all such a total mess and now she wasn't even sure what was real and what wasn't anymore. She'd thought she and Pete were friends, the best of friends, but now, the way she felt – had she made a complete mess of that also?

There was nothing for it but to drag herself back to the flat.

She texted Maya to let her know she was home safe and sound then switched off her phone for the night. Whatever thoughts she had about making something for her supper had completely evaporated. She just dragged herself into the bedroom and crawled beneath the duvet. She didn't even set her alarm clock for the morning; she was much too emptied out to think that far ahead. For now, all she could think about was nothing.

18

Liv supposed that at this point, if she was trying to cheer herself up, then being grateful for the Tesco Express that stayed open twenty-four-seven was as good a place to start as any. She stocked up on milk, bread, eggs and cheese on her way back from work that night. She knew there was no need to buy bleach or washing-up liquid or any sort of polish – Eddie and Anya wouldn't even know where to find the supplies of those things when they'd used up everything else in her cupboards. That thought annoyed her more than any other, the idea that they'd just emptied her fridge of the bottle of wine, the cheese and butter. It was the selfishness of it and it was so typical of how Eddie had been for as long as she'd known him.

It was strange to think that while she'd been trying to contact him, thinking he was helping Anya move into someone else's flat, she knew now he was actually sleeping with her in Liv's bed. Somehow, that idea didn't rattle her half as much as coming back to a flat with no basic supplies left for her. Perhaps it was because she'd already faced up to the reality that Eddie was a cheat, but it was the state of the kitchen that confirmed the fact that she'd been a complete mug. Either way, it completely incensed her, so she knew there was absolutely no way she'd be able to switch off enough to sleep. If she wasn't going to bed, at least she could set about putting the mess her flat had been turned into back to some order. Maybe she could get a head start on moving every single item that belonged to the pair of them over to Eddie's workshop between her shifts over the next few days. She was counting on Pete to help her with the transport end of things, although she wouldn't organise that until everything was packed up and ready to go. She figured there was no point in both of them losing a night's sleep.

When she finally got home, the first thing she spotted was that Pete had already been there while she was at work. He'd parcelled up half a dozen black refuse bags, which she presumed contained some of Anya's belongings, and Liv wondered if Pete hadn't packed these for Anya at his own apartment before he finally got her to leave. There was an appearance of organisation and care taken about them that resonated more with what she knew of Pete than what she supposed of Anya. A new lock for the front door sat on her kitchen table; Pete would have left it there with the intention of replacing the old one, the next time he dropped over to visit her. The old lock was as finicky as a witch at Christmas; one of these days, she knew it was going to seize up. Changing it was not just about keeping Eddie out. When she went to put her groceries in the fridge, she saw Pete had already stocked it up for her with the basic necessities she'd need for breakfast and a bottle of white wine with a Post-it note attached – *Thought you might enjoy a glass after your first day back.*

He was absolutely right. Liv poured a small amount of wine into the bottom of one of the glasses she'd left washed on the draining board. It was lovely, cool and crisp and she felt the alcohol immediately kick into her muscles, relaxing her even though she hadn't realised that she was quite so wound up after the day.

She walked from room to room, wondering where on earth she should start on packaging up Eddie's belongings and removing every trace of him from her flat and her life. It was hard to know where to begin exactly. She spotted the roll of black refuse bags that Pete had left in the hall. She'd tackle the bedroom first. She flung open the window and pulled the sheets off the bed, loaded them into the washing machine and made it up with fresh linen that she'd picked up a few years earlier on a trip to Belfast with Maya. She smiled as she ran her hand along the soft material; somehow, even if she'd never have admitted it before, these pristine bed linens had always seemed too good to use when Eddie slept here.

Then she turned her attention to the wardrobe and began to empty out every stitch of clothing that hung there belonging to Eddie. She folded each item before placing it in a refuse bag. Old habits die hard, obviously, and there was no point creasing things if she could help it. His collection of trainers took up three huge bags and the room felt as if it was somehow lighter just knowing that she had freed up all that space under her bed without them there.

She was about to run the vacuum under the bed when

she spotted something just beneath the head board. Her first thought was, please let it not be mouse droppings. She wouldn't be hugely surprised, since Eddie had a habit of lying in bed on his days off, glued to his iPad while mindlessly eating breakfast, lunch and dinner if he had the chance. She squinted now, trying to make out the hardly distinguishable shape. It was hard to know what it was, probably a huge ball of dust. She didn't want to think about how long it was since she'd actually been able to give it a good cleaning under here. She grabbed her phone and shone the torch before reaching in and pulling out what looked like an old chain.

Rachel's locket. Liv held it in her hands for a moment, hardly believing that she'd actually found it after all this time. She dropped back onto her knees, picking pieces of woolly dust from the chain and the clasp, rubbing off the tarnished silver with her sleeve. She traced her thumb along the intricate inlaid design.

It had belonged, once, to their grandmother. It must be, she reckoned, well over a hundred years old and it had the worn and smooth feel of having been touched often and treasured for many of those years. Liv remembered exactly when it had gone missing.

It was that first night, with Eddie. They'd both been drunk; fell into bed together, making love in a weary, automatic sort of stupor. She'd woken in the morning, not sure of anything anymore. She'd never been the sort of person to get drunk and fall into bed with someone. It left her with an odd mixture of emotions. Looking back, she wasn't sure that any of them were good. At the time, she'd pulled herself out of the tangled array of sheets and into the bathroom, taking her clothes with her and quickly shrugging into them. She'd wanted to shower, but in her fragile state was afraid that the rattling of the old pipes would wake the whole building and not just Eddie. Instead, she'd sat at her small kitchen table and drank tea for over two hours while Eddie snored oblivious to the mounting stress that she was feeling.

And now she looked back on it, she could see so clearly what she'd worked so hard to hide from herself that morning – it was never right between her and Eddie. None of it was ever going to fit. They were just too different – oil and water, sugar and vinegar. She would never have picked out Eddie Quirke as someone she'd want to spend five minutes with, never mind truly consider agreeing to marry him one day. Actually, hoping and wishing for him to propose to her – God, what on earth had happened to her?

She wondered this briefly as she opened up the locket in her hands.

Was it grief, desperation or loneliness? Yes, she could admit, a little of all three probably propelled her into a relationship that she knew wasn't right from the start. Looking back, she probably knew that Eddie had never bargained on anything more than a convenient shag and a free roof over his head. That was all it had been for him, an open pass and she'd been the one who'd made it into something it was never meant to be.

This was, all of it, in many ways, a disaster of her own making. She looked down at the photograph in the locket. It was a copy of one that they'd had taken years ago, she and Rachel – identical twins looking out at her as if surveying her from another world. If Rachel had been alive, there would have been no room for Eddie. If Rachel were alive... How often had she wished for that?

And now, it seemed as if finding this locket, she'd somehow come full circle. As if Rachel was still clearing the way for her. She examined it carefully. It seemed almost strange holding it in her hand, as if it had been shot through time, an arrow hitting its bull's-eye; making reality stand still and yet, so much had changed since Rachel had given it to her before she died.

She remembered it so clearly. It was Christmas and she really only had days to live. It had been the sweetest and saddest Christmas of her whole life. Liv felt the familiar tears build up behind her eyes. She wiped them away, a little angrily, snapping closed the locket. It wasn't fair. Surely, it was time to think about these things with feelings of happiness and gratitude instead of this eternal overwhelming feeling of sadness and loss.

She turned the locket over then as another memory tried hard to push itself up into her brain. The clasp was new. Pete had taken it to the jeweller's and had it mended one afternoon while she slept across Rachel's hospital bed. The original clasp had been weak, worn out with time and wear. Liv smiled; she'd forgotten that. She held the locket up towards the light, inspecting it with fresh eyes. Pete. He'd managed to find a jeweller who made the new clasp perfectly to sit into the locket; you'd never guess that it had been replaced.

And the chain. Another little voice was nudging past her tears, as if trying to unsettle her ability to wallow for too long. Yes. Pete had replaced the chain. It had snapped when they were at a gig – she'd never know how he managed to spot it. But he picked up the locket from the floor where it had fallen from her neck. This was a good six months after Rachel had passed away. They'd gotten tickets that neither of them wanted to use, but in the end, he'd convinced her. It was Rachel's favourite band. They'd spent the following day trailing around Dublin jewellers to find the perfect replacement chain. Pete had insisted on buying it for her. Liv found herself smiling.

This might have been Rachel's locket, her sister's gift to her, but there was no doubt that Pete had been the one to hold it together. She drew her breath in sharply, feeling for a moment as if Rachel herself had whispered something in her ear, but she was much too far away for her to hear her words distinctly.

It was almost two o'clock in the morning by the time she'd emptied everything from the bedroom and hoovered and scrubbed all trace of Eddie from this space.

Even if the rest of the flat still felt like a collision of the past and an uncertain future, at least, Liv thought, she could fall into bed and feel as if the world was somehow tipping over into its rightful place again.

As she drifted off to sleep that night, Liv found herself smiling. She'd put the locket on; double-checking the chain was securely fastened. Even now, as she wrapped her fingers around the cold silver, she could remember all too clearly how bereft she'd been all those years ago when she thought she'd lost it forever. Now she had it back, she couldn't dampen this feeling that somehow, her past and present were once more in alignment. Tomorrow she would ring Pete. She would tell him about finding the locket and he would help her to get the flat sorted out. Tomorrow, she would ring Pete and they would start again.

The optimism that had surrounded Liv as she'd fallen asleep the previous night seemed to have evaporated when she woke the following morning. Her alarm not going off wasn't the best start she could hope for to the day. And then, a missed bus, the wrong shoes and the avenue coated with a thick veneer of ice had all culminated in her landing on her bottom as she'd tried to race to work so she wasn't too late for her shift.

* * *

By five o'clock the following morning, Liv knew, it was time to give up the pretence of trying to sleep. She'd lain awake for hours, going over the previous night at Pete's apartment. Anya standing there, as if she somehow belonged more in Pete's world than Liv did. Which, as the sleepless hours wore on, Liv knew with growing certainty was quite ridiculous.

Anya would not make Pete happy. In fact, Anya would do quite the opposite. But then, maybe she and Pete were not as ill-suited to each other as Eddie had been to Liv. Perhaps they found the same things funny or just enjoyed each other's company? Maybe. But there was no way that they could ever have the same deep connection that Pete had shared with Rachel.

This was the lightning realisation that had shot Liv's eyes wide open in the all too early hours of the morning. How on earth had she not seen this before? How could Pete not have seen it? She tossed and turned for as long as she could force herself to stay in bed, one overriding, unacknowledged truth passing through her. Rachel knew.

Rachel had always known. Hadn't she as good as said it before she passed away?

Finding Rachel's locket that morning was like a bolt from beyond. It had literally floored her. She had been reaching beneath the bed, as far as she could stretch, to pull out the matching high-heeled shoes Maya had given her the previous summer when the tip of her finger ran against the slim metal of the chain.

She knew exactly what it was before she'd even pulled it out. But seeing it, in her hand, made her gasp. She pushed herself back against the wall, her legs folded into her, as if averting an oncoming heart attack. And that was what it felt like – a full-frontal, brutal attack on her heart.

Once more, it seemed Rachel had the power to reach beyond time and mortality to touch her in a way that made the pathetic mess she'd made of things seem insignificant and it was as if everything was suddenly clear. It was all perfectly fixable.

This locket – so old, so precious – stood for everything between them. Not just her and Rachel, but all three of them – Pete as well. Wasn't it Pete who'd fixed the delicate clasp? Wasn't it Pete who'd rescued it from the floor of a heaving nightclub? Wasn't it Pete who'd bought her the new secure chain on which it now hung? Wasn't it Pete who'd held the delicate locket together? It was. The truth was, it was Pete who'd held everything together after Rachel died. In fact, it was Pete who'd held them all together when Rachel was alive too and he'd been doing it ever since. He'd been buoying Liv up with thoughtful texts, dropping off little gifts when she needed her spirits lifted, always being there if she was stuck. Even when she didn't realise she needed help, he supplied it, quietly, seamlessly, without any expectation of thanks or compensation.

A wave of something between nausea, migraine and yes, grief, washed over Liv. It was her turn to save Pete. Anya was in his apartment. They were getting back together. Hadn't Anya said so? Hadn't that been the insinuation when she'd looked at her with those catty green eyes? She couldn't let that happen. Anya didn't love Pete, not the way he deserved to be loved. That was a sobering thought.

She had to try for Rachel. Rachel had adored him; they'd just never had the time, soul mates pulled apart cruelly. Liv loved him far too much to sit back and see him ending up with Anya. Even if he never spoke to her again, she couldn't see him set up for a lifetime of being used. He deserved so much more. He deserved to know what it was like to be loved, really loved, and not just because he was generous and thoughtful, or because he was good-looking – yes, he really was very attractive. She wanted to cry with frustration, but she knew she'd done enough crying. It was time to put aside the mistakes of the past and figure out a plan for the future.

At five o'clock in the morning, sitting on the floor of her bedroom, that was exactly what Liv began to do. She began to make a plan, one that meant neither she nor Pete would ever settle for less again.

She stepped into the shower with a new determination. No matter how things worked out for her, she was going to do the right thing. She was going to live a life more authentic, one that Rachel would be proud of and, yes, one that Pete would admire too. She would live a life big enough and generous enough for two – she would make it up to Rachel, for being the one who got a chance to live, by making sure she did the best job of it she could from here on in.

After she ate breakfast, she decided the first thing she'd do was make a list. She was going to fill up her life with things that meant something, not just work, but she had been thinking about that homeless shelter that Rachel used to volunteer at years ago. She would contact them; ask if she could help out. She would make it her mission to travel home more regularly, to help out with the farm, to be there if her father needed support with whatever the angiogram told them. She would be a friend, a true friend to Pete and, she decided, sticking her chin out with more determination than she realised she still had, she would start today.

She dialled Pete's number as she was picking her way up the avenue to work. The snow of the last few days had built up in the grounds and although the maintenance men had no doubt spent hours and energy trying to clear the pathways, they had frozen over once again and now, the slight upward slope was more like a devilishly gradated ice rink than the entrance into one of Dublin's busiest hospitals. She was so glad she'd worn her hiking boots. But it was beautiful, she decided, as she reached the relative safety of the front entrance, here at least, the constant application of salt and grit seemed to have given some steadiness to the surface.

'Hey, you're up and about early?' Pete answered on the third ring. He sounded tired and groggy, as if she had just woken him.

'No rest for the wicked. I'm due on shift in twenty minutes. I'm just at the hospital now.'

'God, you make me feel guilty. I should probably go in to

work and clear off my desk to start the New Year on an efficient note.'

'Whatever else you need to feel, Pete, guilt over not working hard enough isn't it!' She was laughing at him, it was true. He'd made partner in his firm a decade before any of his colleagues. Sometimes, it had seemed to Liv that was all he did – work and take care of everyone else.

'So, what can I do you for? Need a lift after work tonight?'

'I…' It wasn't why she'd rung, but then, what was she going to do? Blurt out on the phone that she didn't want him to see Anya anymore. That Anya Hegarty would never be good enough for him, in Liv's opinion. That she wasn't The One.

'What time are you finishing?'

'Meant to be eight o'clock, but I've offered to work until later if they need me. You know how it can be over the holidays. The team are only staggering back in and New Year's can be busy in a way no other night of the year is.'

'Right, I'll pick you up at eight?'

'Not at all, I'm sure you have better things to be doing than driving out to pick me up,' she said.

'I'm always happy to go collect you.' He sounded a bit let down and she wondered if he and Anya had made a plan to ring in the New Year together.

'What are you up to?'

'I have no plans. It's basically the same as any other night of the year, apart from the view from my window. Remember last year?' he said and she could hear him smiling. She did remember. They'd spent it together. She'd come back to work in Dublin before Eddie, who'd probably gotten drunk in Flannelly's and not even heard the midnight bells. She and Pete had stood at his enormous picture windows, a glass of brandy each in their hands, watching the fireworks light up the night sky over the bay beyond.

'I really enjoyed it.'

'Well, if you and your friend fancy dropping by later, maybe we can do the same again this year,' he said. There was no agenda, nothing beyond two friends chilling out and watching the fireworks.

'I'd like that, but what about…' She wanted to ask about Anya, but what was the point? She remembered standing at his apartment the night before, Anya in the doorway, as territorial as a lioness. Suddenly, she felt a chill run over her; Liv didn't want to mention her name, not if Anya was lying next to Pete right at this moment. And, she realised, she didn't particularly want to ring in the New Year with them either. 'No, do you know what? I think I'll just head into town and then go straight home. I could get a call to be in at work first thing yet, you never know,' she said softly. She could meet him for lunch one day next week. They could go somewhere near his office, just the two of them and she could tell him then. What exactly? That Anya wasn't good enough for him, that he could do so much better, that he deserved so much better – he deserved someone who would never cheat behind his back. He deserved someone who would adore him. Someone like Rachel would have wanted; or, at least, a variation on that anyway.

'Seriously, Liv, you'll never get a taxi tonight and the last place you want to be is on a bus with New Year revellers.' He didn't add that it would be too depressing for words; he didn't have to.

'No, I'll be fine, really. For all I know, it could be tomorrow afternoon before I get to leave here.' She laughed now.

'So, why did you…'

'Ring you?' God, did she only ever ring him because she wanted something? She'd park that nugget to unpack later when she could face it. 'I just rang to wish you a happy New Year, of course.' She mustered up as much enthusiasm as she could, and actually this morning maybe it felt as if she really was full of good cheer.

'Right, well, a happy New Year to you too,' he said uneasily.

'See you next year.' She rang off, knowing there was so much more she needed to say to him, but not being quite sure where to start.

19

S he struggled out of her coat and changed into her uniform with a nagging pain along her right hip and down into her leg. Reaching into her locker she pulled out two painkillers; otherwise, she knew that within a few hours she'd be hobbling around the A&E like an unsteady pensioner.

'I'm afraid it's all hands on deck again today,' Francine said wearily. 'We're rushed off our feet and there's no sign of things getting any quieter.'

'Never mind, we'll just get on with it, shall we?' Liv asked, although she knew that the chance of getting out of here before midnight was now slim or nil. Any feelings of either guilt or being somehow hard done by were quickly forgotten. The A&E was as busy as she'd ever seen it and there was hardly time to catch her breath between coming on shift and having a late lunch break that afternoon. The good news was that Francine had managed to secure six agency staff to come on for the night shift, so even if the worst came to the worst, there would at least be enough nurses to help out.

When Liv sat down to eat her lunch, the pain in her hip

had travelled, not just down her leg as she'd suspected, but right up and into her back. She took two more painkillers with her coffee and determined that she would not be a complete ninny and complain, but rather, she would just get on with it and hope it would run its course before the end of the day. She imagined there would be a fair bit of bruising, but hey – it wasn't as if anyone was going to be seeing her in her underwear any time soon, right?

She pulled out her phone to call Pete just before she was due back on shift. She imagined he'd either be shooting the breeze in his apartment or maybe at work, tidying up any loose ends before the year was over.

'Hi.' The voice on the other end purred when it was answered. Anya.

Without thinking, Liv put the phone down immediately, crashing it against the table as if it had burned her badly. What on earth was Anya doing answering Pete's phone?

What indeed? Of course, Liv wasn't entirely stupid. Pete might have come over to her flat yesterday while she was at work and filled her fridge and left a new lock for the front door but he'd been gathering up all Anya's belongings too. How stupid was she? She'd assumed he was tidying them up so they could put both Eddie and Anya out of their lives, pack them up in black plastic bags and haul them to the workshop and they could all live happily ever after – isn't that what she really thought? But she had been completely wrong. Stupid, stupid Liv. She cursed her own stupidity now. Of course Pete had come over to take all of Anya's stuff back to his own apartment. That was why he'd folded everything up so meticulously. He wasn't packing her stuff up so he could dump it somewhere else; he was packing her up because she was moving back in with him. God, how had she managed to worm her way back in with him?

Then another thought occurred to Liv. What about Eddie and Anya? What had changed? Had the gloss gone off their relationship once the cold reality of having to find somewhere to live had set in? Eddie would have surely laid it all out for Anya. They couldn't stay together in Liv's flat, so her only option was to move back in with Pete. Had she gone round there while Liv was at work and wheedled and cajoled him into taking her back?

Suddenly, here in the glaring light of the staff kitchen with the hum and clatter of the ward behind her, Liv felt a dark cloud descend on her like she'd never known before. It was the last day of the year, a day when she should have been making a plan for a much better year ahead, and she felt nothing but completely distraught.

She wanted only to curl up into a small foetal ball and... what? Die? 'God forgive me,' she said. She'd seen what too many families had to go through when someone came into A&E and had decided that the only way out was the finality of death. She couldn't do that to the people she loved and anyway, she knew, deep down, this would pass. This had to pass. Even if it felt as if things would never be right with her again, as if she'd somehow missed taking a vital step in some badly signposted direction to her future happiness, she had to keep on going.

But, oh God. She closed her eyes, scrunched them down as tightly as they could go and tried hard to imagine what her sister would say to her. She would tell her everything would be fine, she just had to hang in there. And somehow it felt as if Rachel was very near.

She shook herself out; of course that was utter nonsense. She was completely alone here in this busy, crowded city and maybe more than she'd ever been before, because it felt as if even Pete had left her side.

She checked her watch, rubbed the tears from her eyes. The pain down her right side didn't seem to make any difference to her anymore. It was time to get back on shift. She needed to wash away this feeling of misery that had engulfed her. She picked up her phone, switched it off for now. No-one would be ringing her and that just added another layer to her misery that she didn't need reminding about every time someone else's phone pinged with a message of New Year wishes. At midnight she'd ring her parents and Maya, wish them a happy New Near and try her best to convince them that she was fine.

She managed to get through the remainder of her shift on automatic pilot. She tended to her patients, talked to her colleagues and followed the instructions of the doctors on call, but inside, she knew, in some strange unfathomable way, something was changing. She was empty, like a walking urn, just going through the motions to get to the end of her shift. She could feel herself, as if from afar, plugging in the hours, minutes; every second, hollowing out its echo in her misery.

Finally, Francine sent her home. It was still New Year's Eve. She hoped she might just about make the last bus. But of course, making a bus or walking the four miles home made little difference to Liv at that point. She'd wearily put back on her warm clothes for the journey, make her way back out of the hospital, hardly noticing colleagues who wished her a happy New Year. It was all just background noise. The world had become a blur that didn't penetrate enough on her blunted spirit to make any impact whatsoever.

* * *

A&E was completely mental for most of the day. They were, as Liv had predicted, short-staffed, but at least, when it came to the end of her shift, it seemed they had a full house for the night duty.

'Go on, with you,' Francine had said and even she was leaving bang on time. They walked together out through the main hospital foyer. 'We won't be sorry to see the end of that year,' she said as they made their way out into the crisp night.

'Ah, it wasn't all bad,' Liv surprised herself by saying. After all, she'd managed to lose a terrible boyfriend, and maybe she was falling in love with the man who'd saved her life – quite a tally since the first day of Christmas. She couldn't help but feel optimistic, as if something really special was just around the corner, like taking a deep breath before life slipped into where it was always meant to be.

'It's good to see you smiling again, anyway,' Francine said and leant in to embrace Liv before they set off in opposite directions. 'Next year can only get better, eh?'

'Absolutely,' Liv agreed and she felt that surge of hopefulness rise up even more potently in her.

'Hey, Liv.' She turned around to see Pete padding along the grass verge. 'I decided to collect you anyway.' He smiled at her and she thought her heart would burst with happiness. For a moment, she stood, not sure if any words would come. How strange, to feel this relief, just knowing that he wasn't ringing in the New Year with Anya. She wanted to ask him where Anya was. What had happened and of course, why was he here, but she was just too happy to see him to let any of those questions dull this perfect moment.

'Hey, you,' she said grabbing him before he toppled over as he hopped onto the icy path in front of her. 'I thought you'd be far too busy making things up with Anya tonight?'

'Why on earth would you think that? I've only just managed to get her out of the apartment. Actually, I think that's all sorted. I've loaned her a down payment on a new flat. She'll be renting over the café and she's going to talk to the bank about taking over the lease on the business.' He looked relieved.

'How did you manage all that?' And she could almost imagine him, sitting there, hammering things out and cajoling Anya, keeping everything upbeat, while beneath she knew he was a man who'd always known what he wanted and he'd negotiated deals with much higher stakes than just the cost of a deposit on a flat for two.

'Oh, I knew Anya always liked up-front money and since she and Eddie hadn't anywhere to stay, my offer was probably the only one they were going to get.' He smiled then.

'What?'

'Well, I think the gloss might be wearing off for both of them already. He's been getting on her nerves and she rolls her eyes every time he mentions his mother. He's completely unaware, of course.'

'You know what they say, love goes out the door when poverty comes in the window.' Anya and Eddie would both feel the pinch of having to stand on their own two feet financially from here on in. Funny, she should have taken some pleasure in knowing that they were stuck with each other now, but instead, she just felt mad at Anya for tricking her into believing that Pete had taken her back. It had made her completely miserable every time she thought about it during the day.

'Well, maybe it'll work out for them. God knows they deserve each other.' He was holding on to her arm now and Liv wasn't sure if it was to keep her safe or keep himself upright. 'Come on, I managed to get parking quite close.' He flicked the fob on his keys and she spotted his car lit up just a couple of metres away.

'Wow, it looks like the universe is certainly looking after you with the best parking spots tonight.' She was making fun of him, but it was true: he deserved all the luck in the world, just for being the sort of guy he was.

'No, actually, I've been here a while. I didn't want to miss you,' he said opening the door for her gallantly. 'If you hadn't come out soon, I planned to text you, just to let you know I would be here waiting for you.' He sat into the driver's seat.

'That's so nice of you, Pete, really,' she said.

'Not at all. It's the least I can do. I hated thinking of you taking a bus at this hour, sober and tired when everyone else had been partying. That would be too sad for words and who wants to start the New Year off feeling utterly wretched?'

'Are you up for getting something to eat?' she asked, fastening her seat belt. Although, at this hour on New Year's Eve, everywhere would be booked solid. 'We could get fish and chips and watch the fireworks in the city!' New Year was a time to be with the people you loved.

'That sounds like a good plan to me.' He was pulling out now, slowly and carefully because even if the road here had been cleared, the tarmac sparkled with dangerous ice. With that, Liv's phone rang in her bag and she dug about to find it before she missed the call.

'Hey, Liv.' It was Finn. 'I know you're at work but I just wanted to wish you a happy New Year before the bells rang on the old one.'

'Aww, that's lovely, Finn, but actually, I managed to get a reprieve for good behaviour. I finished on time.'

'That's great. I don't suppose you'd like to ring in the New Year with me?' He sounded unsure, as if he was almost too shy to ask, and Liv closed her eyes for a moment, trying to reconcile the handsome guy she knew him to be with this even nicer version she was getting to know.

'I'd love to. We're going to get fish and chips. Fancy coming along?'

'Why not?' He stopped. 'Er, who's we?'

'My friend Pete and I – you'll like him, I promise.' She was laughing. She'd have to ward off Pete's smart comments. Already he was making faces at her, as if his ego was inflating to the size of an elephant.

'Are you sure I won't be in the way?' Finn asked.

'Not at all, mate, the more the merrier!' Pete said and they agreed to meet along the canal and watch the fireworks together.

'So, that's your knight in shining armour.' Maya had obviously told him about Finn and how they'd met. He started to hum 'Holding Out for a Hero' – badly.

'Very funny.' She laughed because he really couldn't sing to save his life.

'He sounds like a good egg, but I'll be checking him out; make sure you don't end up with another glugger.'

'I'm not going to end up with anything. It's just fish and chips – for three!' They were drawing closer to the city now. The paths were more worn here, where late-night walkers had slushed up the freshly fallen snow before it had a chance to carpet softly underfoot. It felt as if they were gliding quickly towards not just the end of another year, but the end of an era.

'Still, it would be nice if he turned out to be The One, all the same,' he said.

'Come on, Pete, the truth is, you'll always be my knight in shining armour – you know that!' She was making fun of him. The streets were empty, but the freezing temperatures had coated everything with a dusting of glittering ice to remind them that they needed to move with caution.

Liv sank back into the passenger seat, relaxing in the warmth and comfort. It was, she had to concede, much nicer than taking the bus. Pete managed to get a parking space along the Grand Canal just a five-minute walk from her favourite Italian chipper in the city. The aroma of frying fat and cooking chips and fish made Liv instantly ravenous. She texted Finn to let him know where they were and they leant against the bridge while they waited for him. She listened as Pete explained exactly how things had ended between himself and Anya. He was definitely over her.

'Tinder?' She held out her phone, making fun of him again.

'Not likely.' He laughed. 'No, I think I might as well face the fact that there was only one girl for me.'

'Don't say that; Rachel wouldn't want you to give up.'

'I'm not giving up, but the fact is, I just don't want to settle for anything less. I'm happy, knowing that I've already known the great love of my life and who knows…' He smiled as if he knew something no-one else would ever understand.

'What?'

'Well… who knows what the future holds; perhaps one day, Rachel and I…' He sniffed loudly, working hard to keep his tears at bay, but he was still smiling, impossibly optimistic, in spite of himself. Liv put her arm around him, pulled him close to her. She loved him so much, almost as much as she'd loved Rachel, and she knew Rachel would want him to move on.

'She'd want you to be happy here, in the real world, not looking forward to hooking up again on some existential plane that only exists for soul mates.' Liv shook her head. Honestly, she was going to make it her resolution to fix him up with a decent girl, someone who would let him put Rachel to rest, finally.

'Hey.' Finn kissed her cheek lightly, slicing through the maudlin direction of both their thoughts.

'This is Pete. He was my sister's… well, he's my best friend and he gave me a lift.'

'Good to meet you, mate,' Finn said warmly. They sauntered to the chip shop, which was mercifully quiet, and ordered large portions of fish and chips smothered in salt and vinegar with cans of Coke to wash it all down. 'My treat,' she said as she reached into her pocket to pay. It was the least she could do since she was the common denominator here. It was just lovely to be spending the New Year with them both.

They managed to find an empty bench on the bridge and chatted happily while they ate their takeaways, waiting for the New Year to be rung in with an explosion of fireworks filling up the sky over the city centre. It felt good, relaxed and comfortable, as if they'd all been friends forever.

Liv almost jumped when she heard the first firework going off over their heads. Once they'd finished eating, they walked to the bridge to get a better view. Again this year, it felt as if they had the whole show to themselves, until Liv looked down and saw a woman, oddly familiar, on the towpath beneath them.

With Finn's arm around her and Pete at her side, she'd felt a warm glow of belonging trace around the edges of these steadily deepening bonds between them. Watching each burst of colour fill the air, until the penultimate blast, two golden rockets, flying up, high, up and up so by the time they exploded into their full glory, she and Finn were standing with their heads almost trained backwards, their mouths open, awestruck. The rockets had stayed together, most of the way, and she had thought at first, they were just like her and Pete, and she had grabbed for his hand to let him know that he was not alone. But he was not there; instead, he had bent over the side of the bridge, his eyes trained on the woman who stood on the towpath below.

The rockets stayed side by side all this time, but then one seemed to go off course. It took what looked like an early nosedive and ended up the less spectacular finale, while its sister rode higher in the sky, its trail seemingly endless until at last it exploded, filling the entire sky with golden lights. It was, she realised, her and Rachel. She was that final rocket; she needed to light up the world for two. From here on, she would light up the world for two.

Then another, the final firework. She knew it, somewhere deep in her bones; this was the finale. It was a long green array of explosions, shooting up first and then across the sky – a trail of shooting stars.

Somewhere below the bridge along the towpath, she heard a scuffle, a murmur and a splash that hit her conscience much too loudly not to be in part imagined. She had to drag her eyes from the spectacular show of green above. Pete was running towards the path, already making his way over the damp paving, pulling off his jacket, spinning wildly on the ice as he scrabbled along the path. When she looked down, the woman had gone, but in her wake, Liv spotted the unmistakable footprint near the water – she'd fallen. Or had she jumped? It didn't matter either way.

'The woman,' she shouted, tearing herself out of Finn's arms, but Pete was already there clambering over the wall and hanging until he dropped onto the towpath. 'I'm coming,' she screamed and then she was racing off down beneath the bridge, Finn left standing behind her, with no idea of what was going on. As she ran, she imagined Finn, looking around, wondering if it was some sort of prank and then, maybe following her. Yes, Finn was chasing behind them now, but he would be too late.

The woman was already out of sight. Liv couldn't figure where she had gone in exactly, but Pete was swimming across towards the centre of the canal, diving in as if by some divine understanding he knew exactly where to look for her. And then, she saw it, the most amazing sight. She knew what it was, of course she knew it was just a reflection, but still it felt as if it was hypnotising her in some strange way. She was looking at a trail of shooting emerald stars in the water, like a path she knew she had to follow to help Pete rescue that woman and bring her back to safety.

And as she dived into the icy water, she felt that there was something about that woman that was so familiar. She'd known it when she spotted her from the bridge, but she hadn't fully recognised it, so consumed was she in her new-found happiness.

20

L iv *had* missed her bus. That was the trouble with New Year's: everything in this city seemed to run on a different time schedule, as if the normal world operated outside itself for a few crazy hours just this one night a year. She was hardly aware of how many bells Immaculate Heart church rang out as she walked along the towpath next to the canal. It was twelve, if she'd been interested, but the fireworks that spun out into the black sky overhead were enough to make her stop and she realised that she had managed to put one foot in front of the other and walk into a New Year.

Would every New Year be like this from now on? It didn't bear thinking about and yet, she couldn't imagine it any other way. The swamp of sadness that she'd slipped into so suddenly on realising that Pete was being pulled away from her by Anya seemed to be one that was so deep and cloying it felt as if she'd never properly make her way back onto firm ground again, even if she wanted to.

Liv dropped down onto the bank. The ground, cold and wet, seeping through her jeans, didn't even register properly beyond the discomfort of her hip as she smashed her knees against the cobbled bank. It hit her now, Rachel's hip had always given her pain. She'd been born with a congenital hip, a legacy of two babies squashed together, for what ended up being forty-two weeks and then breech births, which had landed them both in intensive care for a few days afterwards. She knelt there, watching the fireworks – green, red, purple, gold and silver – illuminate the night. On the bridge above her, she noticed some people lingering. There was something familiar about them, the woman in particular. It almost made Liv catch her breath. She turned away then. It was too painful to watch such contentment at this late hour.

A huge golden rocket took off and exploded so high that Liv had to lean her head back, her mouth slightly open, gaping at the spectacle. And another, not as set on its path, deviated and seemed to burn out before its time, while the first just kept on going. That was like her and Rachel. Twins. They'd been a matching pair. Identical. The one life ended before it had much of a chance to start; the other, well, Liv didn't have far to look to see what an empty sham she'd allowed hers to become.

Too often, when the chips were down, she'd wondered what would Rachel have done. What kind of life would she be living now if their paths had been switched? Probably, she'd have married Pete, had a swarm of kids and a great big golden retriever. Overhead, the rocket seemed to have played itself out and in the smoky darkness it left behind Liv felt an overwhelming sense of loss crush her once again. She hadn't felt desolation overwhelm her on this level, not since Rachel died.

Then she noticed it. There was something in the water.

A trail of green, probably some sort of underwater weeds, but the more Liv stared at it, the more it seemed to glow in the reflection of the city above. It was hypnotic. It looked like the northern lights, revealing life in the water beneath her. She leant over further, craning her neck as far as she could to get a proper look. Suddenly, she began to slide towards the water's edge, the damp ground beneath her providing no grip, and then her hip gave way from under her, propelling her forward so she fell further and further down the embankment. It felt like slow motion, as if the trail of green below were pulling her in. Liv heard herself laugh. A strange tinkling sound, as if she were a child, tickled at some funny story, or maybe playing a game that held her tight so her nerves made her react with a sound that was neither happiness nor excitement, but instead fear coiling up inside her as if it might snap at any moment. It was obscure but not unwelcome.

She thought she heard the woman from the bridge laugh. It was just a sound in the darkness, but it echoed within her, as if perhaps it had come from her own lips. Liv looked up. She had an odd feeling that it was like looking in a mirror. There was something about the woman, something that made her stop and stare for a moment, but it was no good; she couldn't make out anything properly from down here.

Overhead another shot. A long trail of green lights flooded up higher and higher, arching far above the city, before setting off on a trail, from north to south. Liv felt herself moving, her head craned, back as far as she could manage it. They were almost over her, directly above her. She forgot about holding on, forgot about the icy patches that could be treacherous on the path, never mind down here at the water's edge.

All she could see was a long trail of green lights – like the ring she'd believed was hers. Like shooting stars, flooding across the night sky. They filled up everything with green, even the canal. Her eyes were drawn now to what had just been an inky ribbon before. From here, on the bank, it seemed she could see within the water's depths, strangely lit by shooting stars. The reflection of the fireworks above worked themselves into a mesmerising display in the water. They were like emeralds trailing down to its very deepest parts.

It was beautiful. The most fantastical sight she'd ever seen. She had a crazy notion that she wanted to follow them. Somehow, she felt a growing surge of peace rise up within her. It radiated from her heart and warmed every bone in her body. The pain in her hip melted and she felt happy. She looked up again, watching as the fireworks trailed away, burning out so they were vanishing into the night sky, leaving behind just a soft puff of smoke. She sighed, deeply.

And then, she felt the oddest thing. As if someone had breathed something in her ear. It startled her, unsettled her, so her fragile grasp on terra firma was lost and all of a sudden she was slipping away, towards the water below.

Somehow as she neared its edge, she could still see the trail of emerald stars, just wavering beneath the smooth surface of the water. *Splash*. She thought she screamed as she lost her footing, hitting the water with only the slightest splash. She felt oddly calm, despite the cold, despite the fact that she was quickly out of her depth on one of the coldest nights of the year. Perhaps someone would hear her. *Help. Help.* Only Liv could hear her own panic; the sound was strangled in her throat. The people on the bridge were too wrapped up in each other to have anything to do with her. The fireworks were over. It was time for everyone to go home.

When the black water finally dragged her under, Liv welcomed it. Somehow, rather than making her cold, it actually felt as if it was wrapping her with a welcome of home, so she didn't even struggle. Instead, she found herself gliding along the trail of green glinting stars. All around her, she thought she could hear whispers, calling her home. Even if she could clamber back onto the towpath now, part of her knew she didn't want to.

This time, there would be no losing Rachel, because really how can you lose yourself?

* * *

The iciness of the water was a shock that she should have been expecting. Liv dived in without thinking of anything beyond the fading circles of where that woman had just disappeared into the darkness. The truth was she hadn't imagined she'd ever jump into icy canal water in the dead of night, but she hadn't had the time to think, much less the time to have any expectations, of freezing water, darkness or fear. Pete was in here too, somewhere, and the icy feeling about her heart had as much to do with the fact that he had disappeared from sight as completely as if he'd never been there to begin with.

She swam across, trying hard to find the reflection she'd seen from the towpath. Scrambling about in the water, they had both vanished. The woman had gone; she knew for certain the woman had not surfaced again, not after she went in, but that couldn't be right, could it? Surely, even if she intended to jump into the water, human instinct would propel her up again? Liv swam round in what felt like an ever-widening circle, dipping her head beneath the water, trying to see in the darkness, hoping each time she came up for air that Pete would be by her side.

It was no good. She was almost out of breath, her hip aching from an injury she couldn't remember ever having, her breath gasping because her lungs felt as if they'd been stabbed directly through her cumbersome clothes by the canal's freezing fingers. And then, although she couldn't see anything but the shimmer of the lights overhead – the last array of emerald stars dropping slowly towards the ground – something pushed against her. It was big, too big to be anything but another person. It rubbed along her back, spinning her about in the water. Twisting her around so she didn't know which way she was faced anymore in the blackness of it all. She dived further down, the water clogging up around her clothes, so she had to work harder to move. Down here, she kept her eyes peeled for some hint as to where the woman was, where Pete was, but the darkness was impenetrable; the only way was to swim through it.

And then, as if someone whispered in her ear, she found herself turning about in the water, a gentle tugging at her, not against her clothes, but something vibrating within her, drawing her deeper into the canal, compelling her forward. Her eyes adjusted to the murk and darkness of the stinging water until she saw the reflection once again.

A small, winking trail of green, probably the reflection of the fireworks above, but it was the only guiding light she had. She heaved her body up once more and gasped for breath, then dived in the direction she was certain those lights had been just moments earlier.

On and on she swam, a tightening panic that she might be moving in useless circles while the water's cold cloyed further into her bones. It wasn't far, but already she was out of breath. Her oxygen levels were making her heart beat too fast, her pulse race in her veins, exhausting her, so even if she made it to the point of where the first light had been, she would be fit for little more than to float off up to the surface.

She dived down, deeper and deeper. She had to save the woman in the water. She had to find Pete. This was no time to give up, because now, with all that had happened since the first day of Christmas, she realised she had too much to live for – her family, Pete and now Finn, her job, her life – she was going to live enough for both her and Rachel. Wasn't that what she'd promised herself only hours earlier?

And then, just as she felt she could swim no more, about to give up and head for the surface, she saw them. Standing on the water's edge. But they couldn't be, because they were deeper than she'd imagined the canal bed could possibly lie. It was Rachel. Rachel and Pete together, as if standing in some magical snow globe. And she was watching them from outside. Oh, they looked so happy, Liv felt as if she might burst with the overwhelming feeling of happiness and sadness that welled up in her heart to see them both together again.

She started to walk towards them, half afraid that by moving she might spoil this moment of perfection, even though some part of her knew that this was not right.

They were calling her. *Liv.* Liv knew, she had to go to them. *Rachel.* She whispered her sister's name, felt it dry up on her lips.

It was so sweet just to feel she could say that name and know that Rachel might be here.

Yes. It's okay, Liv. It's me. Everything is going to work out perfectly, for both of us. She imagined her saying the words. It was in her imagination, wasn't it? But then Rachel looked at her, a sudden deadening panic in her eyes. She couldn't catch her breath. Was she drowning, here in the darkness, just when it seemed she had so much to live for?

She felt herself spin around, trying to figure out what was what. Everything was completely confused, as if she'd fallen into a maze and she couldn't figure out what to do next. They were identical. It was like looking in a mirror, but where she just felt so happy to be here with Rachel, she could see the panic rising in her sister's eyes. *Go back, go back; it's time for you to go back to your life,* Rachel was saying, but Liv couldn't leave her, not yet. She swam towards her now, the gut-wrenching exhaustion, a mixture of freezing cold and an emotional shock beyond any she'd ever imagined, began to tug against her chest. She was swimming hard and still getting nowhere. There was no way forward and she watched as her sister's eyes filled with the sort of fear that Liv had only ever felt when she'd watched Rachel pass slowly away from her. She had to get to her. She pushed harder, harder and harder until it felt as if her whole body might explode with the effort and then she knew, she was moving forward. She was making her way slowly towards Rachel and Pete.

But they were screaming at her now. *You have to go back. You can't follow us. It's not your time yet.*

Liv wouldn't go back; she just wouldn't leave them here. She had to concentrate. She couldn't for one moment take her eyes off Rachel. It seemed as if she'd been swimming forever, but somehow, here she knew that time had frozen over as surely as the ice had begun to patch itself along the water's edge.

When she stood opposite them, it took a moment to gather her wits. She had to save them both. And then she realised she couldn't save Rachel. She couldn't help it, she threw her arms around her sister, grasped her to her as if she'd never let her go. *I love you*, she mouthed to Rachel, *Don't forget me.*

And then, she felt herself being pulled away from them. Dragged up, held firmly with strong arms around her. She was out of breath. She hadn't noticed before, but now, it felt as if her lungs might explode. The pain was excruciating. It was just a short distance, but the effort was mammoth. Liv thought that she'd never experienced anything like it. This is what it must feel like to push back a tsunami from the edge of the world. The water wolfed more fiercely against her skin. It dug in malevolent daggers all around her body. Just as she felt her body giving up, a tiny crack of light appeared above. Green emeralds shooting off across the water. She looked back at Rachel who was smiling at her. It was their sign. Shooting stars. Somehow, Rachel was still standing next to Pete and Liv cried out. It was too late.

She felt her body, as if it was something separate to her, being dragged to the top of the water. Finn O'Connell. He'd swum out to save her. She must be dreaming. He was pulling her back to the bank now, wading along with her in his arms, murmuring into her wet hair. *Oh thank God. I thought I lost you. I couldn't bear to lose you, Liv.* It was all too much. Liv closed her eyes. Pete and Rachel. They were both gone now.

'Oh, thank God. Thank God, Liv. You're safe now, you're going to be fine. I have you now.' He was leaning over her, on the towpath. Liv could hear him, but she couldn't speak. Was it too late? Had it all been for nothing? She heard Rachel's voice, pleading with her from beneath the water, urging her to live. *Please, you can make it this time. Wake up, please, just wake up.*

'What the…' She was spluttering, now her body was taken over with a paroxysm of coughing, doubling up and expelling the filthy canal water.

'Oh, Liv, never do that to me again, do you hear?' Finn O'Connell was crying, but he sounded more relieved than anything else. 'I don't think I could have coped with losing you now,' he breathed into her wet hair.

'That's the second time you've saved my life,' she murmured, but she was trying hard to make out the shapes beneath the water. Finn was completely unaware that he was being watched from halfway across the canal. In the darkness, Liv lying on the bank strained to see what she could only imagine was there. And then, a pang of loneliness swept through her. 'Pete?' She was crying, because she already knew the answer.

'I'm sorry, I'm so sorry. I couldn't see him anywhere.' Finn wrapped her in his arms and pulled her close to him. Somewhere in the distance she heard the sound of a siren, pealing through the busy Dublin streets towards them.

'Oh, no, not Pete…' A shot of pain ripped up through Liv and she shivered with the ferocity of engulfing sadness that seemed to shroud her so instantly that everything went completely black.

21

They had swapped places. That was Liv's first thought when she woke up in her hospital bed the following morning. Finn O'Connell sitting forward on the hard chair, holding her hand, waiting for her to come round.

'Oh, thank goodness. I have to call someone to tell them you're awake.' He started to get up.

'No. That can wait. Tell me first, was it a dream? Did that really happen?' she asked, but maybe she already knew, because the aches she felt in her body were nothing compared to the gaping hollow that had opened up in her heart.

'A dream?' He looked around the room a little awkwardly, as if he wasn't fully sure what to say. 'I'm so sorry. Your friend – he seemed nice, Pete?'

'Ah, yes, Pete.' Liv smiled thinking of him and for a moment she wondered where he was, but then, as if someone had picked a tuning string at her heart, she knew instantly what had happened. 'He's gone, isn't he?'

'I'm so sorry. They still haven't found him. It's as if he just...'

'Disappeared.' She felt a fresh surge of anguish rush up in her, catching her breath so ferociously that for a moment it felt as if she was drowning all over again. It was like a wave that when it crested, she knew would wash her out with the most consuming grief. But then, she remembered what had happened underneath those emerald stars. As images of Pete and Rachel came back to her. It was tempered with something else too, something she'd probably never be able to explain, but she knew, wherever Pete was now, he was finally happy. 'He's with Rachel now. That's what he wanted; he told me so just before the fireworks started.' She found herself smiling, despite her tears. Finn slipped his arm beneath her shoulders, pulled her up towards him.

'Oh God, Liv, I'm so sorry I couldn't save him too.' She could feel his regret slipping with every word from him.

'No.' She held him a little away from her. 'You don't understand. He's with Rachel now. They're both happy. I *know* they are. They were always meant to be together and now they are, forever.'

'Oh, my darling, darling Liv.' He kept saying over and over again. He was holding her so closely; she had a feeling he would never let her go.

'What happened?' she asked, rather stupidly. 'I don't remember anything after you pulled me from the water?'

'I'm not sure I remember half of it myself. Someone called an ambulance and then the fire brigade arrived too. They brought us here and...'

'I just remember the fireworks. Gold and green.' She remembered it so intensely, the two golden rockets, each on their own trajectory, two sisters with their own paths ahead of them – Liv and Rachel. And then the array of green lights, a volley of shooting stars that had reminded her of Rachel. She'd looked towards the water then; it was all so vivid.

'That's right. Two gold cannons.'

'One went off track,' she said softly, thinking of Rachel and that very idea sent a wave through her that resonated like a tuning fork, sending its vibrations much further about her than she expected.

'Did it? I don't know if these things ever have a track.' He was smiling at her now. 'Come on; let's get some of those doctors in here to take a look at you and see when they're going to let me take you home.'

'Home?' Liv asked because her flat and the life she'd had for the last few years seemed like a million light years away after all that had happened in the last few hours.

'Home with me, for now, if you'll let me take you home; at least until you get on your feet.' He shook his head, but there was no missing the concern in his eyes or catching on his words.

'Home.' She liked the sound of that. Her lip wobbled as she smiled at him through her tears. He lifted her towards him again and she clung on, hard and helpless. Who knew how long she cried for, but it didn't matter; it wouldn't bring Pete and Rachel back. And Finn rocked her over and back, as if she was a child who needed comforting, cradled in his arms. At the end, she hiccupped loudly and he held her away from him a little distance. His shirt and her hair were both tear-soaked.

'It's okay,' he said gently. 'It's going to be okay.' She wanted to believe him, but she couldn't help wishing that Pete and Rachel had been given the same chance and then, she began to cry again and was glad to feel the encircling strength of Finn's arms around her once more.

22

Eight Months Later

Liv tucked the light rug in around the top of the basket.
She knew it was probably a futile attempt to keep the
bottle of pinot grigio cool, but still, it would stop the rattle
of glasses against the side of the bottle.

They'd made a picnic, nothing fancy, just cheese and rolls
and a little fruit, but it was Saturday and it looked like a long
deliciously warm day would stretch ahead, with nothing
more to do than potter about. They'd decided to wander
about the Phoenix Park for a few hours and maybe lie in
the grass dozing the afternoon away while the clouds above
their heads made wispy patterns in the sky. Finn had picked
up the wine the evening before, but they'd tumbled into bed
together before they'd had a chance to open it. Well, it was
a celebration of sorts. Eight months since New Year's night.

'I'll take that,' he said grabbing the basket from her arms.
That was Finn all over: he wouldn't let her lift a finger if he
could do things for her and Liv loved every moment of it. It
had taken a little time to get used to being spoiled instead
of doing all the running, but they'd managed to settle into

something a bit more even-handed as the months had rolled from winter to spring and finally into summer. Actually, they had settled into life together with an ease that felt as if they'd always been together.

The city had that summer morning feeling, as if it was taking a long deep breath before the day began, but even as they drove along the streets, the aroma of strong coffee and freshly baked bread wafted in the air, waiting for the city to swing into morning action.

'A walk around the Glen pond first?' Finn asked once they drove through the gates of the Phoenix Park.

'That would be perfect.' Liv smiled at him. She loved when they drove somewhere together, just that opportunity to take surreptitious glances across at him, watch as his hands moved along the steering wheel. It turned out she was madly in love with him. For the first time in her life, she knew what it was to fall hopelessly, crazy in love. Now, as she so often did, she luxuriated in reminding herself that this was her happy ever after and it was real, it was actually happening for her, just as she'd always dreamed it would. They parked the car in the shade and set off down the Furry Glen, the walk around the Glen pond and along one of the grassy tracks off it, took up the morning. They'd ambled slowly and stopped often to admire the geese, the foliage and the beauty of their surroundings.

By the time they dropped down on the grass beneath the shade of a huge oak, they were both ready to eat and then close their eyes against the midday sun.

It was almost two o'clock when Liv woke with a start. Finn next to her was snoring gently in the shade. The temperature had risen, so in the distance it seemed as if everything was set on shimmer. She reached into the basket and pulled out the large bottle of water they'd brought along to share. It had lost its icy coolness, but it was still pleasant, waking her a little more. All around them, the park had filled up with families and couples, relaxing in the sunshine. In the distance she could see a game of football had begun, but she knew, even from here, it wouldn't last long. The players were already wilting in the summer sun.

Beside her, Finn stirred and sighed deeply as if he'd just stepped into a deeper level of sleep and she reached out and picked a stray blade of grass from his T-shirt. She was examining it in that way you do when you have absolutely, lusciously, nothing else to do with yourself when she heard a familiar voice. She looked across, half expecting to see Maya or perhaps her mother, the voice was so familiar. But there was no sign of anyone close enough for their words to reach her. On the faintest breeze, she caught the tinkling sound of contented laughter and it sent a shiver of something she could only describe as pleasure through her.

There, in the distance, was a couple, wandering far across beneath some darkened oaks. There was something oddly familiar about them. Liv stretched forward to try and make them out, but it was no good; they were in the shade and there was the bright sunlight to negotiate between them first. She lifted her sunglasses high onto her forehead, watched as they weaved along together hand in hand. They reminded her of earlier, herself and Finn, wandering along, so wrapped up in each other that they hardly noticed anyone else.

And then the woman stopped and the suddenness of the

movement made Liv catch her breath. They were staring at each other and for all the world, it felt as if they might be no more than six inches apart, such was the intensity of the connection. It was like looking in a mirror and Liv felt as if her heart had missed a monumental beat.

It was Rachel. Liv knew it instinctively. It was Rachel and Pete – they'd come back to let her know that everything was perfect. They'd come back to put her mind at rest on this the most lovely day they could have chosen. Then, she pulled her eyes from her sister and her gaze fell upon Pete. Her lovely, perfect, best friend Pete. Some days she missed him so much it ached, but she knew, he'd always been meant for Rachel, just as she'd been meant for Finn.

In that moment, Liv knew she was letting him go. She was letting them both go. She'd never told Finn what had happened that night under the water in the canal. Perhaps she feared that he wouldn't believe her. Now, she tugged on his arm, felt him, rather than heard him mumble, but he rose blearily from his sleep. Wordlessly, she pointed across at the couple and she knew he knew.

The silence that stretched tight and reverential in that moment felt as if it extended far beyond the little patch they sat on beneath the shady oak. It resonated across the path, across the city, perhaps across the entire universe, as if God's law was holding its breath for just one sacred second to let them know that everything was exactly as it was meant to be.

And then, as she watched, Liv saw Rachel raise her hand. It was hello. It was goodbye. It was thank you and yes, she knew, it was I love you. 'I love you too,' Liv whispered, because maybe wrapped up in all the other emotions and worries of the last few years, it was the one thing she'd missed saying. 'I love you, Rachel.' And then, as the couple turned towards a copse of trees, disappearing out of sight, Liv felt a small tear race down her cheek. She knew this time, it really was goodbye.

Later, when they'd both tried to digest what they had seen, Finn turned to Liv and asked, 'Did I dream that?'

'No, I don't think you did. I don't think we could both have dreamed exactly the same thing, do you?'

'No.' He shook his head, because Finn was at heart much too practical to ever really believe in anything that wasn't a fact he could prove or work to disprove. 'They looked happy,' he said a little wistfully.

'*We* look happy.' Liv leant towards him, kissed him gently on his lips. 'And I think that's the whole point, don't you?' She smiled, because now, everything really did feel as if it had slipped into place. Just as it was always meant to; quite perfectly.

Author's Note

Like every Christmas, there just weren't enough days in the holidays to squeeze this story into. So, because I'm in charge of everything in Ballycove, for once, I'm extending the Christmas holidays and if you are the sort of reader to meticulously go through each day, you will be right in thinking that there are a few extra days thrown in for good measure. Two, to be exact. Really, it just means that Ballycove is an even nicer place to live than it was before!

With that in mind, I do hope you'll come back next year to stay in The Guest House...

Acknowledgements

Every book comes from somewhere – or at least that's what I always thought. But it turns out, as I continue on this writing journey, that I've been so lucky to get to share with you, that not all books are born the same way.

This book came from nowhere and I'm not sure that as I sit here tonight, trying to think of who to thank that I'll even get close to figuring out where to start, much less finish.

So, first off, thank you to the Aria Girls – my lovely editor Rachel Faulkner-Willcocks who has helped me knock this book into much better shape and Bianca, Helena, Nikky, Jessie, Jade, Victoria, Ayo and Amy who all worked tirelessly behind the scenes to make sure this book fell into your hands. Thank you to Laura Palmer for her enthusiasm for a Christmas book that is a little different to my other books.

Thanks to Simon Hess, Declan and Helen.

It is lovely to have an opportunity to work with you all.

Thank you to Miriam Kett at Newbridge Silverware for the gorgeous sun, moon and stars locket from their fantastic collection.

I'm lucky to have a brilliant agent, Judith Murdoch, who

continues to be equal parts sage, master planner, the voice of reason and good fun too.

Thanks always to my family – Cristín, Tomás, Roisín and Seán – the best gang. To James for more than I can begin to list – I hope you're not keeping count! To Bernadine, David and Christine Cafferkey – for ongoing support and advice on too many fronts to mention. I count myself as very, very lucky to have you all.

The book world, as I know it, is a wonderful place – there are so many bloggers, reviewers and booklovers who spread the love for books, just for the joy of sharing something that will delight others. I am indebted to your generosity for the kind things you've said about my books to date, for the reviews, the blog tours and the recommendations. You have helped to make this journey even more joyous than I could have ever imagined.

Finally, I've said it a million times probably, already, but I have the very best readers. Once more, I do hope you've enjoyed this book. It is slightly different to my other books, but it's written with love and the hope that even if you do shed a tear, you will end up with a warm-hearted glow by the end. In other words – I hope you enjoy it every bit as much as I loved writing it!

Faith xx

About the Author

FAITH HOGAN lives in the west of Ireland with her husband, four children and two very fussy cats. She has an Hons Degree in English Literature and Psychology, has worked as a fashion model and in the intellectual disability and mental health sector.

Return to Ballycove for a stay at
The Guest House by the Sea...

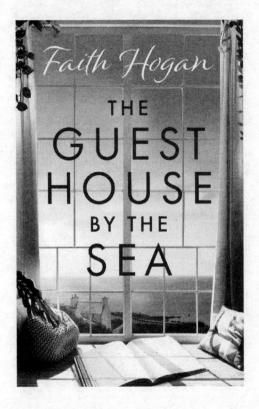

People come to the guest house for fresh air
and views across the Atlantic. But if they're lucky,
they might just leave with the second chance
they didn't know they needed...

**The latest gorgeous and uplifting novel from
Faith Hogan, number one bestselling author of
The Ladies' Midnight Swimming Club.**